SWAY

SWAY

KAT SPEARS

ST. MARTIN'S GRIFFIN ✿ NEW YORK

This is a work of fiction. All of the characters, organizations, and events portrayed in this novel are either products of the author's imagination or are used fictitiously.

www.stmartins.com

Designed by Anna Gorovoy

The Library of Congress has cataloged the hardcover edition as follows:

Spears, Katarina M.
    Sway / Kat Spears. — First edition.
        p. cm.
    ISBN 978-1-250-05143-1 (hardcover)
    ISBN 978-1-4668-5219-8 (e-book)
    1. High school students—Juvenile fiction. 2. Interpersonal relations—Juvenile fiction. 3. High school students—Fiction. 4. Interpersonal relations—Fiction.
    PZ7.S7395 Sw 2014
    [Fic]

                                                              2014430044

ISBN 978-1-250-05142-4 (trade paperback)

St. Martin's Griffin books may be purchased for educational, business, or promotional use. For information on bulk purchases, please contact the Macmillan Corporate and Premium Sales Department at 1-800-221-7945, extension 5442, or write to specialmarkets@macmillan.com.

First St. Martin's Griffin Trade Paperback Edition: September 2015

10 9 8 7 6 5 4 3

For Jack, Josie, and Ingrid. Love each other well, and always give the impossible a chance.

Sway helps you make money and money helps make you sway. But sway is not money.

—*25TH HOUR*, DIRECTED BY SPIKE LEE

SWAY

PROLOGUE

NOTHING IS GOOD OR BAD, ONLY THINKING
makes it so. Shakespeare was the one who said that. It's
the only interesting thing I've learned after three years of
high school. And now here was my senior year looming
ahead of me, just waiting to suck.

High school is a lot like prison—terrible food, group
showers, somebody on a power trip always telling you when
to do things. They tell us when to eat, when to use the bathroom, when to talk, when to be quiet. They're also big on
telling us everything that we're not supposed to have.

The more you tell people they can't have something, the more they want it. It's one of the laws of the universe. Real power, in prison and in high school, doesn't come from telling people when to do what. Real power is the ability to get the inmates what they want—things they aren't supposed to have—which happens to be a particular talent of mine.

When Ken cornered me I was leaving school, on my way to my car. I hadn't anticipated the attack but, all the same, wasn't surprised by it. I was the only person who knew his secret, knew that his transformation from vicious bully to Christlike saint was all an act.

And maybe I had it coming. Hell, I knew I had it coming, but the threat of getting my ass kicked had done nothing to change my behavior.

Love for a girl like Bridget makes guys do crazy, stupid shit. It's the only explanation I had for the things I had done. I suppose with the way I'd been playing it, the attack from Ken could have come weeks earlier. After all, he was in love with Bridget too, and he was already stupid and half crazy to begin with, so it followed that he would lose it sooner rather than later. I told myself that I loved Bridget better than he did, in a way he never could. I knew her faults and loved her anyway. Ken didn't know her at all.

He appeared suddenly from behind a parked car and drove his shoulder into my flank in a technically perfect football tackle. Coach Andrews would have been proud of him. There was a crunch as my shoulder hit the car window but the crunch was from my collarbone, not the glass. My breath gusted out with a comical *oomph* as I hit the car door and slid toward the gravel.

Ken recovered quickly and landed a punch on my jaw. Since I was already heading for the ground, the blow wasn't as devastating as it otherwise might have been. Still, my head was ringing and blood was dripping from my lower lip as I swayed on my hands and knees. I stubbornly refused to collapse though my body wanted me to.

"You think I'm some kind of idiot?" Ken asked through gritted teeth. His short black hair was still perfectly gelled in place despite his violence. "I know you're after Bridget, trying to get at her through her kid brother."

"Ow," I said as I shifted to a sitting position and rested my back against the car tire.

"There's more where that came from," he said, and kicked savagely at my ribs. Now both sides of my chest hummed with pain. "You stay the hell away from Bridget. And you won't be around Saturday night for Pete's birthday dinner. You got that?"

Ignoring him, I spit a mouthful of bloody saliva onto the gravel and touched my jaw to see if it was swollen. My eyes were shut so I wasn't expecting it when he grabbed me by the front of my shirt and dragged me to a standing position. "Answer me," he said.

"What was the question?" I asked.

He hesitated stupidly as he searched his memory for the question, then said, "I asked you if you got it."

"Got what?"

"You want some more?" he asked, giving me a shake.

I grinned but I think it came across as a grimace because he seemed pleased with his handiwork and shoved me back down to the ground.

My grip on the car door handle slipped twice before I pulled myself to a standing position. Now my teeth were chattering, as the cold had seeped through my clothes from the ground and it made my jaw hurt worse. Ken was long gone by the time I crawled into my car and rested my head on the steering wheel while I waited for the heat to kick in.

My tongue probed the inside of my lip, testing the gash cut by my teeth. It wasn't too bad. My ribs and shoulder ached and I thought about going to Digger's, sinking into the couch after a bong hit and losing myself in an episode of *Sons of Anarchy*, his new favorite, now streaming on Netflix. I had to admit, it was a pretty good show.

I knew I would make an appearance for Pete's birthday dinner despite Ken's threats, but I had to question my own motives. The smart thing to do was to back down, forget about Bridget and her dopey kid brother, and get back to business. Joey was right about that, and Joey is almost never right about anything.

"Nothing is good or bad," I muttered to myself as I backed out the car. "Stop thinking."

I drove for a while, ended up on the narrow suspension bridge that spanned the river—wishing for something to numb the pain in my head but not wanting to go home for some ibuprofen. And in some way, the pain in my head was punishment for the way I had treated Bridget. I deserved to suffer.

No one used the bridge much anymore, since the bypass provided a quicker way to reach the downtown and the campus. It was a scenic spot where people came for a view of the town cradled in its lush valley. It was as picturesque as a Hudson River School landscape, but a place where evil preyed on mere mortals.

The bridge spanned a narrow gorge where the river ran swift, the riverbed full of jagged boulders. As loud as the rapids were, they still couldn't drown out all thought, just created a pounding insistency in your brain as the white water boiled beneath your feet and occasionally sent up a spray of mist that tickled your throat and dampened your hair. The drop from the foot of the bridge to the river was only about forty feet, but it was enough. There was very little chance anyone could survive the fall.

I thought about calling Joey. She would get my head straightened out—tell me to stop risking everything because of some Disney princess with impossibly soft skin and doe eyes.

And that was exactly the problem. I had let emotion and personal feelings cloud my judgment. There was a solution to all of it—a happily-ever-after ending wasn't out of the question. Once the pounding in my head stopped I'd be able to think it through, figure out a way to make it all work. Get the girl, kill the bad guy, slay the dragon, find the treasure—I could make it happen.

Then again, it would be an easy thing, one leg up on the rail of the old bridge, one leg over, and I'd be four stories below, my head broken open like a cantaloupe on the jagged rocks. Give the people on the six o'clock news something to talk about. We'd see how sway everyone thought that was.

ONE

THE FIRST TIME I EVER HEARD BRIDGET SMAL-
ley's name, it was a day like any other. There was no reason for me to think everything was about to change. That's
the way life happens, why you have to be able to see all the
angles every time you make a choice. What's true today
might not be true tomorrow.

When the last bell of the day rang, my butt was already
halfway out of my seat and I took the stairs two at a time to
the first floor. A group of chattering girls banged through
the stairwell door and I stepped back to let them go by me.

As they passed, I was enveloped in a cloud of bubble gum and fruity body spray. Nauseating.

The hallway quickly filled to capacity with students leaving their classrooms while I tried to slip through unnoticed. A blond girl in heavy makeup squealed when she saw me and held out an arm as if to put it around my neck in a hug. She looked vaguely familiar. In fact, I might have taken her on a date once, but I ducked her arm and then slid along the wall for a few steps to avoid a herd of freshmen as they spilled out of the gym.

Two varsity basketball players were terrorizing a wimpy kid by playing keep-away with his backpack and blocking the corridor. The kid was obviously not destined to last long in the high school ecosystem, but there was no way I was going to engage in any misguided acts of heroism to help him out.

Instead of trying to get past the basketball players, I cut through the teachers' lounge to emerge in the math and science wing just as David Cohen was passing by, talking with a short kid whose name I didn't know.

"Hey, David," I said as I fell into step beside him and gestured for the short kid to get lost. "How's it going?" I asked.

"It's going," he said, eyeing me suspiciously. The short kid moved away and was instantly lost in the throng of students hurrying to leave the building.

David was a full head shorter than I, probably barely five-five, made to look even shorter because his shoulders were permanently slumped under the weight of his overstuffed backpack. His Jewfro was much frizzier than mine, though we had the same coloring—brown eyes, brown hair.

I glanced casually at my six to make sure no one was

paying attention to our conversation before saying, "Listen, I've got another job for you."

"Another one?" he asked with a grimace.

"I need two term papers for Bartlett's class."

"Oh, come on, Jesse, I barely have time to get my own work done," David whined. "You've already got me doing labs for half the football team. How am I supposed to get two term papers done too?"

"I understand it's a lot of work on short notice, David," I said, my voice automatically shifting to smooth and soothing to divert his tantrum, "which is why I'm going to pay you fifty dollars for each paper."

"It's not about the money," David said with a shake of his head. "My dad is the president of the university, Jesse. Believe it or not, he makes more money than you do."

"Yeah, well, for now he does," I said, though David was so busy wallowing in self-pity, he wasn't really listening.

"I'm under a lot of pressure to get good grades," David continued, operating under the incorrect assumption that I gave a shit. "I've got Model UN, student government—a lot of responsibility." He crammed a hand in the pocket of his gray slacks and pushed his glasses up his nose with the index finger of his other hand. "I've got so much going on, I should be paying *you* to get *my* homework done."

"I know everyone's got high expectations for you," I said as we walked. With David it was all about managing his tantrums and I needed him to be on his game, had a lot of money riding on his abilities. Not that I was so desperate for the money—I had pulled down a salary higher than any teacher at Wakefield High School last year, tax free.

"Maybe there's another way I can help you," I said. "If you don't need the money, what do you need?"

He barely hesitated, which told me this request had been on his mind before our conversation even started. "I want to go out with Heather Black."

"Not a problem," I said, my brain already calculating the costs I would have to offset against this transaction. "Just give me a few days."

"Really?" he asked, his voice rising to a squeak. "But . . . didn't you used to date her? Wasn't she your girlfriend?"

"Sure, yeah, we dated," I said with a nod, "but I wouldn't say she was my girlfriend. Relationships are not my thing. There's too much emotion involved."

"I was . . . I was kind of joking," David said. "I didn't think you could actually . . . How are you going to get Heather Black to go out with me?"

"Don't worry about it." We both stopped at my locker and I spun the combination lock. "You ask her out next week and she'll be willing."

"Will she . . . ? Do you think . . . ?" His cheeks went pink and he pushed his glasses up again. "Do you think she might put out?" he asked as he leaned a shoulder against the locker beside mine, trying to look casual and failing miserably.

"Your dad's rich, remember?" I said. "Which means you barely even have to be charming. But she's not a hooker, David. I can't make those kinds of guarantees. As long as you don't blow it completely, she'll probably let you get to second base."

"Yeah?" he asked, the enthusiasm behind his voice

enough to tell me that this deal was sealed. "What's second base?"

"It depends on the girl," I said with a shrug. "Knowing Heather, it will be farther than you might get with someone else. So, two papers delivered with a week of lead time so they can change a few things, make it look more like their own work."

"Yeah, okay," he said with a weary sigh.

"Alderman!" A shout reverberated down the hallway. The halls were almost empty now, most everyone gone for the day, which meant I was behind schedule.

"Oh, shit," David said under his breath. "It's Burke. I'm out of here, man." And just like that, he was gone.

I spared a brief glance over my shoulder and there was Mr. Burke, principal of Wakefield High School—avid golfer, fly fisherman, father of three—and a major disappointment to his wife, the community, and himself. His high forehead was wrinkled in a frown, but not an angry frown—a worried, disappointed frown. Worry and disappointment defined Burke's life.

His face was long and thin and his hair swept back from his forehead in a high pouf, giving the impression his head was even longer than it really was. I always wondered why his wife didn't tell him to keep his hair shorter, try to create the illusion his head wasn't so long. I suppose his wife didn't care any more about him than did the students at Wakefield High School, which was not at all.

"I've been looking for you," Burke said as he stood behind me, waiting for me to acknowledge him.

"Oh, yeah? The front office doesn't know where to find me during the school day? I'm pretty sure they have my class schedule." I shut my locker and turned to give him my full attention.

"I—I've heard that you're a person who could help solve a problem for me," he said.

I cocked an eyebrow in question. "Who told you that?"

"A few people have mentioned it," he said evasively. "This is a high school. No secrets."

"You're right about that," I said as I lifted my messenger bag onto my shoulder. "What is it you think I can do for you?"

He hesitated for a minute, making up his mind, then rubbed his hands together as if to warm them. "There's a particular student who's causing problems for me."

At first my mind leapt to the idea that he was actually having an affair with a student. There were some girls just freaky enough they would give it up to an authority figure like Burke, even if his head resembled a winter squash.

"What kind of problem? If you want my help, you're going to need to be specific," I said, fighting the urge to check my watch. I was already behind schedule and now I had to think through how I was going to get David laid. The calendar was filling up quickly.

"Travis Marsh," he said.

"I think I know him," I said. I nodded and squinted one eye, as if searching my memory for Travis's face. "Gritty guy, blond hair?"

Of course I knew who Travis was. I sold him at least a quarter ounce of pot a week. It was unclear why Travis persisted in coming to school. He never studied, barely attended class, and was probably reading at about a third-grade level. I could only assume teachers passed him just to remove the threat that they might end up with him in their classroom for another year. Travis was big, over six feet, and muscle-bound. Sometimes he liked to bully the weaker kids, but he had never given me any problem.

"That's the one," Burke said, reeling me back to the present.

"What about him?" I asked.

"He's a threat to my authority," Burke said, his voice tight with strain. "He doesn't care how much trouble he gets in. No matter how many times he gets sent to the office, he just treats it like a joke. The other students, my staff, everyone sees me as ineffective because I can't control him. The other day, he put graffiti on my car."

"How do you know it was him?" I asked.

"He signed his name," Burke said, his voice heavy with defeat.

"Did you call the cops?"

"The police said it wasn't proof enough, that anyone could have done it and signed Travis's name. No fingerprints, no serious crime, so they aren't going to pursue it. But half the students saw it before I covered it up. Travis Marsh is threatening the very fabric of this school's discipline system. He has to be stopped." By the end of this little tirade, beads of sweat had broken out on his brow and flecks of spittle dotted his lower lip.

I gave him a minute to compose himself before speaking again. "What do you think I can do about it?" I asked.

"I want him gone," Burke said, though I could tell it cost him something to admit it.

"Gone? Like dead?" I asked, mostly to amuse myself, but still curious to see what he would say.

Burke looked stricken, his eyes wide. "No!" he cried. "I didn't mean . . . Jesus, you couldn't . . . I mean, you wouldn't, right?"

"You couldn't afford it, even if I was offering that kind of service," I said with a dismissive wave of my hand. "So, what did you have in mind?"

He still looked a little uncertain, one hairy knuckle pressed against his chin like a contemplative chimpanzee. "He's only seventeen. According to the law, he can stay in the public school system for three more years. Things will spiral out of control by winter break if he's still here. I need an excuse to expel him—an incontrovertible reason," Burke said. This last comment was weighted with the full implication of what he was asking.

"It's an interesting problem," I said pensively.

"Does that mean you'll do it?" he asked, then held his breath as he waited for my reply.

"Maybe. You know there's a price involved?"

"I assumed as much," he said as he started to reach for his back pocket.

"Not that kind of price," I said. "You keep your money. Once I've solved your problem, you'll owe me a favor. Give me a week. If I need to communicate with you, it will be through an associate of mine." He opened his mouth to protest but I cut him off. "Don't worry. She's discreet. And we need her so that there can be no connection traced back between you and me."

"Okay, fine," he said, and started to smile, then seemed to remember that wouldn't be appropriate.

I brushed past him on my way to the door. Now I was really behind schedule.

TWO

WHEN I PULLED UP TO THE CURB AT KEN FOS-
ter's house about an hour later, he and his posse were tossing
a football around in the front yard. His house was a massive
brick Georgian-style structure with an ornate cast-iron
gate blocking the gravel drive. The perfectly manicured
lawn might as well have been green carpet, no stray fallen
leaves permitted to clutter the garden beds or blemish the
chemically treated grass.

I had ignored the six texts Ken had sent me since the
end of the school day. It's not like he was paying me to be
his pen pal.

Ken was surrounded by his usual entourage. With their black and gold letter jackets they looked like a swarm of wasps. They were all WASPs, and the corner of my mouth curled up as the thought struck me as funny.

Ken's closely cropped black hair glistened with styling product and he had a permanent five-o'clock shadow darkening his jaw. Ken was considered dreamy by just about every skirt, and some of the helmets, roaming the halls of Wakefield High School. Usually I tried to fly under the radar of guys like Ken. He was too much of a public figure—captain of the football team, leading candidate for homecoming king, and all-around douche.

"Hey, Sway!" Ken called to me as I climbed out of my car. I cringed mentally at his use of my nickname. "Where the hell've you been? I've been texting you all afternoon."

"Hey, Ken," I said, ignoring his question and his posse.

"Did you get it?" he asked, moving closer to peer into the back of my car.

"Of course," I said. "Two kegs of the crappiest beer available."

He laughed, though I hadn't said anything intended to be funny.

Ken and I were not friends. I don't really do close friendships. Attachments to other people are a liability. I orbited his clique, the good-looking, athletically capable kids who hogged all the popularity and the attention, but none of them were my friends.

The posse wrestled the kegs out of the car while Ken and I stood back watching them. It took all four of them to carry the kegs up the driveway and around the house to the backyard, leaving just Ken and me standing by the curb.

"You sticking around?" Ken asked. "My parents are gone all week, so this should be a killer party."

"I might be back later," I said noncommittally. "For now I'm just here long enough to get my money."

"Right," he said as he reached to pull his wallet out of his back pocket. He counted out a stack of twenties and handed them to me. I had turned to go when he called me back.

"Hey, Alderman," Ken said, his voice lowered conspiratorially. "Listen, there's something else I wanted to talk to you about."

"Oh?" I asked with feigned interest.

He took a moment to look around the deserted yard, make sure he was not overheard. "I want you to get me a girl," he said.

"Well, you know, that's not really my line. Not that I object to it on moral or legal grounds," I said, holding up both hands in supplication, "but, strictly speaking, I don't mess with prostitutes or call girls."

"Not that kind of girl," Ken said, sounding a little pissed at the suggestion that he would be desperate enough to pay for it. "Just a regular girl."

"What do you want me to do, abduct her?" I asked.

"Very funny, wiseass," he said, and I noticed his cheeks went a little red. Intriguing. "You're the guy who gets people things, right? And what I want is for you to get me a girl."

"It won't be cheap," I said, making sure we were clear on that point.

"Whatever you're charging, I can afford it."

I suppressed a sigh and gave him my full attention. "I'm listening."

He glanced over each shoulder again to see if we had an audience before saying, "Her name is Bridget Smalley and I want her to go out with me."

"Have you tried just asking her?"

"Of course I asked her," he said with a roll of his eyes. "She said no. Said she didn't think we had anything in common." His brow was wrinkled with confused frustration. I'm sure this was the first time in Ken's life he'd been denied something that looks and money could buy.

Technically, David Cohen had not hired me to get him a date with Heather Black. At least from his perspective he saw it as me doing him a favor, didn't realize that by accepting such a favor, he was putting himself in debt. David was the most socially awkward person on the planet, so getting him a date with anyone would be worth a half dozen term papers. Getting him a date with Heather Black, the most popular girl in school, would give me enough capital to own David for the rest of his high school career.

But Ken hiring me to get him a girl just didn't make any sense and it wasn't exactly a job I wanted. Still, business is business, and I'm not in the habit of turning down money.

"Why do you want to go out with her?" I asked.

"Who gives a shit?" he asked hotly. "You hosting your own talk show or something?"

"And you want me to do what?" I asked.

"I want you to make it happen," he said. "Figure out how to get her to go out with me."

I let my mind wander for a minute. Thinking, for me, is not as straightforward as it is for most people. It takes time to work through all the angles.

"Well?" Ken said expectantly.

"I thought girls were falling all over themselves to go out with you. What's so special about this chick?"

"Well, she's beautiful, for one thing."

"Lots of girls are beautiful," I said dismissively.

"This one's different," Ken said.

"Will she be here tonight?"

He shook his head. "No, I asked her. She said her parents have a pretty strict curfew but I think she was just blowing me off."

"And you just want me to get her to go out with you?"

"Yeah, just get her to go on a date with me. I'm thinking she's the type you've got to take it slow—like three or four dates before you really expect her to put out."

"Sounds expensive," I said. "Maybe a hooker would be cheaper."

"Yeah." Ken chuckled a little at that because he's the kind of asshole who would find that funny. "But this girl . . . Well, anyway, it's worth a little extra effort."

"If you say so," I said. "Give me two weeks and I'll have something for you."

"Two weeks?" he huffed, indignant. "What the hell are you going to do that requires two weeks?"

"Look, I'll get you the girl if that's what I'm hired to do. My method is confidential. Take it or leave it."

"Fine," he said. "But homecoming is only two months from now. I want her to be mine before homecoming."

"You said her name was Bridget Smalley?" I asked as I pulled out my phone and tapped in some notes on my calendar. Between brokering term papers, getting juvenile delinquents kicked out of school, and delivering party favors for keggers like Ken's, I barely had time to think. Not thinking was the ultimate goal.

THREE

IT WAS A PERFECT NEW ENGLAND AUTUMN
evening, the failing sunlight painting the world gold, so I
drove to Digger's house with the top down on my '63 Thunderbird. The town was choked with bright splashes of orange, red, and yellow as the trees tuned up for their annual
show. I wound my way through the historic downtown—
quaint tree-lined streets with antique shops, boutiques,
and restaurants—this time of year filled with tourists who
came from New York and beyond for the fall colors.

Outside of town the majestic historic buildings gave

way to subdivisions of newer prefab homes and then, farther out, trailer parks and wooden Cape Cod–style houses
that were little more than shacks. Here there were only strip
malls filled with Walmarts, dollar stores, and tobacco outlet
shops. Most people never saw this side of the town—few had
any reason to venture out here on the fringe where the
janitors and bus drivers and lunch ladies lived.

Digger greeted me at the door with a grunt and didn't
wait to see if I followed him inside.

"God damnit!" he snapped as he sat down and slapped
his wiry thigh in disgust. "I told her to DVR one god-damn
show for me and the fucking thing is full of shit about fat
chicks trying to lose weight and episodes of *Jersey Shore*."

Digger was complaining about his wife, an inexplicably
appealing woman with overplucked eyebrows and a large collection of tracksuits. He would never talk about her that way
in her presence, was terrified of her, but when she wasn't
around he liked to talk big, like he wore the pants.

The fact that Digger was married is proof that there is
someone out there for everyone. Wiry and gritty, with dirt
caked into his torn cuticles, he appeared ten years older
than his actual age of thirty-four.

Digger was content at the top of his own little empire.
He had risen to the rank of not just a tenant but an owner
of a double-wide trailer, a fact that made him something of
a god among the backwoods people who had reared him.
He probably moved ten pounds of dope a month and the
only reason he had never surfaced on any law enforcement
radar was because there just weren't many people who
could bring themselves to care that he even existed.

He worked full-time as a gravedigger in Mount Comfort cemetery, not far from his trailer park, probably making nine dollars an hour but enjoying the work. His people had scraped a living from the hardscrabble soil of hill country for generations and it was in his DNA to do backbreaking work and never be appreciated for it. The income from his dope dealing kept him well plied in Mountain Dew, Newport Golds, and enough satellite television channels to make NASA green with envy.

At some point in his history he had served six years for armed robbery in a federal penitentiary. Since leaving the joint, he had never been able to return to normal, hardly ever left his house other than to go to work, and was prone to some strange paranoias. A normal paranoia would be a belief that the cops had him under surveillance, but he focused on more creative worries that usually involved global conspiracies—birth control in the water supply, or drug cartels putting additives in marijuana to reduce the productivity of working-class white males in America.

Digger was a punk. A stoner. A hillbilly.

And a survivor. I can respect a survivor.

Not that he was exceptionally bright or entrepreneurial, which in his business is a requirement if you want to get anywhere near the top of the heap. Digger was like a guy who sells dime bags at a Phish concert. That's not enterprising—he's just another loser in a sea of mediocrity. I respect the guy who sells grilled cheese sandwiches in the parking lot after the Phish show. He's innovative, a thinker, the kind of person you want on your side after the apocalypse comes and the survivors are living off cock-roaches and radioactive water.

This afternoon, Digger was hepped up on some kind of goofball. Not the bright green ganj he was pushing, the buds sticky and heavy and virtually free of seeds. He was wired and kept shifting in his La-Z-Boy, his skinny ass making barely a dent in the cushion.

He carefully shredded the weed and loaded a bong hit, which, I knew, would get passed to me. Pot-buying etiquette dictated that the buyer had to take a bong hit in the presence of the dealer. Some long-standing myth was involved, that an undercover narc wouldn't smoke dope for real because then he would be subject to criminal charges himself. All bullshit, of course. Anyone who believed that had less legal knowledge than the average schlemiel who watched *Law & Order*.

Weed is not my drug. It makes you slow and stupid. But etiquette was etiquette and I would take the bong hit.

I don't create waves. I ride them.

"Man, this shit is the kind bud," Digger said with an eager smile as he held the three-foot Graphix bong out to me like a sword. "Shotgun," he said, as if I hadn't taken a hundred bong hits sitting at his four-piece living room suite.

I tried to hold back the cough, knowing it would just make my head dizzier. A surprisingly good buzz, a creeper.

Digger could tell I approved of the pot and it made him happy. He really was kind of like a kid and I wondered how he had ever happened onto a gig as golden as this one. He worked with a few guys like me, one rep each at the three high schools in the area, and counted on us to move his product. It wasn't even real work since the right people knew where to find me, knew the rules, and had the money to pay.

"Weren't you just here like three days ago, man?" Digger asked me as he leaned back in his chair and lit a Newport.

"Yeah, business has been good."

"Apparently. What do you want?"

"Couple of ounces."

He left the room and returned a minute later with a grocery bag. I opened it and pulled out two ziplock bags as Digger started fiddling with his remote again.

"This one's light," I said, tossing one of the bags on the coffee table.

"Aw, shit, man, I bet that god-damn bastard is stealing from me again."

Digger was talking about his wife's son, a twenty-year-old with bad acne and a nasty disposition. Grim was his name; at least that was what everyone called him, even his mom. I knew Grim in another context and made regular work out of avoiding him.

I managed to extricate myself from Digger's den after another thirty minutes of meaningless conversation and a second bong hit.

I called Heather Black on my way home from Digger's place and she sounded surprised yet pleased when I asked her out for the following Friday night.

"Sure," she said. "What's the occasion?"

"No occasion. I just feel like going out for a meal. We'll go to Paolo's," I said, knowing it was her favorite because it was expensive. A girl like Heather, all her taste is in her mouth.

FOUR

WHEN I GOT HOME THAT EVENING, DAD WASN'T there. Not surprising. The sound of Wagner's *Tristan und Isolde* filled the house, which meant that Joey had used the hidden extra key, and she was in a mood. I dropped my messenger bag on the kitchen floor and went into the living room to find Joey stretched out on the couch.

Dressed all in black, hair dyed black, fingernails black with paint, and almond-shaped eyes outlined with goopy black makeup, she looked younger than her seventeen years. If she was pretty, it was impossible to tell under all the trappings of her teenage angst. Her figure had not changed much since eighth grade, which is when we met in the waiting area outside the principal's office. Joey had always had a big mouth and it got her into trouble on a regular. She couldn't stop herself from making wiseass comments about everything, but she could keep a secret better than anyone, and that made her a valuable partner.

Joey was lying perfectly still on the couch, arms crossed over her chest like a corpse.

"What are you doing here?" I asked as I turned off Wagner and put on the XM radio.

"I was listening to that," she said.

"I hate Wagner."

"Not always," she said. "Only since your mom—"

"What's with the getup?" I asked, ignoring her comment.

Her reply was only silence for a long minute as she tried to test my patience. "If by 'getup,' you mean my predilection for the color black," she said as her eyes slid shut again, "I'm protesting the culture of greed and corporate corruption that influences our consumption. I'm denying the fashion of the moment, the media's attempt to dictate what beauty is."

"Uh-huh," I said, distracted as I surfed for the channel I wanted.

"Where have you been?" she asked.

"Busy day."

"Busy with what?" she pressed.

"If I told you, you wouldn't believe it."

"I'm waiting to be astounded. Hold on, let me practice my look of amazement." Her eyes flew open and her mouth gaped as she blinked rapidly. "How was that?"

"Creepy," I said with only a glance in her direction. "Don't you have a home to go to?"

"Speaking of creepy, my mom's boyfriend is staying over tonight. I'm perfectly comfortable right here." Though she would never publicly admit it, Joey was embarrassed by her poverty and her mother, who was too young to have been out of high school when she gave birth to Joey. Her mother worked as a waitress at a local restaurant, wore too-short skirts for a woman her age, and had a tramp stamp at the base of her spine.

"You have something for me?" I asked.

She sighed as she sat up, then reached into her bra and threw something onto the coffee table.

"Do I need to check them?" I asked as I sank into the chair across from her.

"If you want," she said, sounding pissed, with a twitch of her shoulder, "but if you're asking me if they're okay, then the answer is yes."

"I'm just asking. The last time you picked up merchandise for me, you didn't check them and I ended up with almost six hundred dollars' worth of fake IDs I couldn't sell, because the birth year on them made the person only nineteen years old. It's not like Skinhead Rob has a return policy."

"You're never going to let me live that one down, are you?" she asked with a weary roll of her eyes.

"Should I?" I asked, matter-of-fact. "I'm not selling

people IDs so they can register to vote. They expect them to work to buy alcohol."

"Yeah, okay, Sway," she said, using my nickname because she knew it would annoy me, "I get it. I fucked up last time. But it's only because Skinhead Rob freaks me out. I hate going to his place. And that pimply guy Grim always looks at me as if he wants to rape me."

"Well, you're not bad looking," I said, "which almost makes up for your piss-poor attitude. I'm surprised you aren't flattered by the attention."

"Stop trying to piss me off," she said as her eyes narrowed into slits. "I'm not interested in getting sucked into your head games right now."

"You get pissed off at me whether I make the effort or not," I said as I clasped my hands over my gut and tipped my head back. "I'm just being honest." I was hungry, but too tired to get up and fix something.

"Oh, yeah," she said with ironic sincerity. "If nothing else, you're always honest. Anyway, DJ Kiddush is spinning at Plant Nine this Friday. Want to go get your freak on?"

"Can't," I said. "I have a date."

"A date with who?"

"Heather Black."

"You're seeing her again?" she asked, disapproval clear in her tone. "You know, you could do much better."

"You think so?" I asked as I idly swung the chair from side to side.

"Sure. You're a hottie. If I were straight, I'd totally be into you."

"You're just saying that because you're my best friend."

"I'm your only friend," she corrected.

"True. But, no, the thing with Heather, it's just business."

"What kind of business?"

"Nothing worth mentioning, though I did get an interesting request from that douche football player Ken today."

"I hate that guy," Joey said with feeling. "You shouldn't do anything to help him out."

"I'm not doing it out of the goodness of my heart. It's just a job."

"Well, anyway," she said, "I hate him."

"I'm surprised to hear you care anything at all about him."

"He always calls me a dyke," she said with a shudder.

"You *are* a dyke."

"No," she said loudly as she held up a finger to school me. "Dykes wear flannel and Chuck Taylors and hate men. I'm a lesbian. I have never worn flannel in my life."

"If you say so."

"You want to get Chinese food?" she asked suddenly. "I'm starving."

I shook my head with a grimace. "No, not Chinese. It's the only thing my dad ever brings home."

"That's because your dad has a lot of class. With my mom, it's always pizza."

"How about Indian?" I asked. "You fly, I'll buy."

"Why not?" she said as she stood and grabbed my keys from the coffee table.

"You be careful with my car," I said. "I like it more than I like you."

"Yes, dear."

"Hey, Joey?" She was almost out the door when I called her back.

"Yeah?" She backed up a few steps and waited, her eyes narrowed suspiciously.

"I really hate your hair like that."

"Awesome," she said as she wrinkled her nose and stuck out her tongue at me. "Then I'm going to keep it like this forever. Hey, by the way, Gray Dabson assaulted me in the hallway today. Said he wants to talk to you."

"Thanks for the heads-up." I shifted my head to a more comfortable angle against the chair and closed my eyes. "I'll avoid him like the plague."

"Good luck. He seemed pretty determined. He wants your help with something."

"Can he afford it?" I asked.

"I wouldn't be mentioning it to you if he couldn't," Joey said impatiently. "I'm not an idiot. He's had an after-school job since middle school, a bunch of money saved up for college."

I sighed and sank down lower in my seat.

"I know, I know," she said. "It's hard to be the king."

"Jealousy is an ugly emotion, Joey."

She snorted and left without another word.

FIVE

MS. FULLER, THE HEAD GUIDANCE COUNSELOR
at Wakefield, sent a pass to pull me out of class the following day. The school kept a special eye on me—wanted to
make sure I wasn't one of those ticking time bombs who
showed up during lunch one day in a black trench coat with
an assault weapon to take out a few of the popular kids.

It was only a minor inconvenience. I would spend about
twenty minutes talking with her and she, in turn, did her
best to convince my teachers that I needed positive rein-
forcement to preserve my mental health. The net result

was better grades than what I really deserved. After all, no one wanted to be responsible if I traveled the same road as my mother.

At first I resented the required visits with Ms. Fuller in the counseling office, but I had learned to use them to my advantage. Ms. Fuller had a lot of influence with the teachers, especially the male ones. She was the motherly type, no doubt, but the way she carried herself reminded you exactly what a mother did to become a mother in the first place.

She was also a fixer, one of those people who liked to surround herself with damaged people, wanted to feel like she was really helping broken souls. I was like her wet dream of troubled students—no mother, emotionally absent father, and willing to put myself out there and bare my soul in her private office, surrounded by her motivational posters featuring fluffy kittens and rainbows and baby chimpanzees.

Her influence was critical when it came time for progress reports or report cards. I did enough work to keep afloat in my classes, stay off the radar of any of my teachers, but most of the time I was phoning it in. For any major assignments, I had a freshman at the local university named Kwang on the payroll. He wrote most of my papers—easy money for him and he wasn't spending his weekends at keggers so was more reliable than the average nineteen-year-old. No one was going to give me any points for class participation or extra effort. It was the time I spent with Ms. Fuller that could make or break my sway with the teachers.

"How are you, Jesse?" Ms. Fuller asked as she came around her desk to give me a friendly pat on the shoulder.

"Pretty good," I said, taking up my regular post in one of the hard-backed wooden chairs, the kind of chair that was so uncomfortable, its only purpose could be to seat students in a school office.

She rested her bottom on the front of her desk and crossed her arms over her chest. The result was an impressive bulge of cleavage that I spared a brief glance. As she removed her glasses and twisted to place them on the desk, her skirt hiked up and I caught a glimpse of the dark place.

Every Marvin Gaye song ever written about getting it on was about a woman exactly like Ms. Fuller. I wondered if her husband knew it and appreciated the fact that he had access to her lady bits. The shadow of her cleavage, the shift of her hips when she walked, the long graceful neck, all added up to a definite MILF.

"How are things at home?" she asked.

The soundtrack in my head abruptly cut off strains of "Let's Get It On," and I reminded myself to focus on the task at hand. I shrugged—a shrug that expressed courage through feigned indifference. "The same. My dad's not home much."

"I'm sorry you don't have a better support system," she said, sounding genuinely sorry about it. "It's sometimes hard for parents to understand that even though their child is older, can look after himself, he still needs a positive adult influence to guide him."

"Well, I do all right on my own," I said.

"Of course you do," she said. "And I don't want to judge

your father too harshly. I couldn't imagine being in his position."

"Go ahead and judge him," I said. "I do. He's a loser."

Now she could barely conceal a triumphant smile, her eyes lighting up with victory because this is exactly the kind of comment that guidance counselors love. By criticizing my father in front of her, I was acknowledging her as a member of my team, distinguishing her from the L7s, the parents who just didn't understand their kids.

"Maybe a loser," she said, "but I'm sure he loves you. You know, it *is* okay to be angry, especially to be angry with him. It's perfectly natural."

"I don't really feel anything," I said, the last honest statement I would make during our face-to-face.

"How are your classes going?"

A complete fucking waste of time. "Okay, I guess."

"Just okay?"

"I'm keeping up," I said, staring at some invisible point in the distance, nodding my head. "It's hard. I get distracted, frustrated with it all sometimes. It all seems so meaningless." This was tricky. I couldn't give her the impression that I was so distraught that some special intervention was required, but at the same time, she needed to be moved to drop helpful suggestions to my teachers in the teachers' lounge.

"What about girls?" she asked. "You dating anyone?"

"You know you're the only girl for me, Ms. Fuller." I said this with a small smile as I dropped my gaze to my lap.

She gave a nervous chuckle and plucked at the hem of her skirt, stretching the fabric to cover her exposed knees.

As if her knee was the part of her anatomy that could drive me wild with desire.

"Sorry," I said, by all appearances with utmost sincerity. "I guess making jokes is easier than talking about—well, you know."

Moved by sympathy, she leaned over to reach for my hand and squeezed it in hers. Her hands were dry and cool, the skin soft with some scented lotion. I suddenly felt myself responding to her physically and let the sensation take over for a minute. She was in her middle forties and her figure was more rounded than slim, but she was one of those women who knew how to dress to highlight every advantage. I wondered if she knew how many Wakefield boys employed fantasies of her for self-induced orgasms.

"The truth is, I'm glad my dad is never home," I said as I leaned forward and rubbed at the creases in my forehead. "When he is there, he's drunk, and I know I should feel sorry for him, try to understand what he's been through, but really I just don't give a shit."

"But you understand that none of this is your fault? Right?" Her eyes were moist, almost dripping with pity and concern.

"Yeah, sure, I know that," I said.

"Hey," she said as she gave my hand a slight shake. "You hear me? None of this is your fault."

"I know," I said, fixing my gaze on hers so she couldn't look away without creating an abrupt break in our connection. In that moment, I knew she was mine.

She swallowed audibly and her eyes glistened with tears. "I'm here for you, Jesse, and I'm glad you feel like you can talk to me. I want you to know that I would do anything I could to help you."

"I do know that," I said. "I know that I wouldn't have made it through without you. You, uh—" I cleared my throat and dropped my eyes as I had seen people do when they were afraid their feelings were too conspicuous. I had accomplished my mission, was done with the interview, but I needed her to be the one to end it. "—you mean a lot to me," I said, knowing it would move us into awkward territory.

My comment hit its mark and reawakened her sense of what was proper for a teacher–student relationship. As she moved to put some distance between us, I fought to keep my expression neutral. My dick was dismayed by the sudden denial of her attention. Sometimes my dick and I had a difficult time agreeing on things. She was pulling away from me but she was smiling again, her heart touched by the innocent affections of a boy.

"Jesse, I don't want you to worry about anything," she said as I stood to go. I could see she had made up her mind to do whatever it would take to help me. In fact, I was feeling so good about our relationship at that moment, I wouldn't consider honor roll out of the question for my fall semester.

SIX

IT'S EASY TO PUT OFF FOR LATER THE CHORES
that you dread, but I had agreed to set up Ken with the girl
of his dreams. I started by getting Bridget Smalley's class
schedule from my contact in the main office and looking
her up in last year's yearbook in the school library. In the
yearbook picture her chin was down, her eyes looking up
to meet the gaze of the camera. She looked demure and
just slightly uncomfortable with having her picture taken,
her smile almost apologetic—as if she didn't really want to
put too much out there. Definitely pretty, but then, it's not
as if I was expecting her to be ugly.

Bridget's last class of the day was chemistry and I just happened to be passing the door when she emerged from the classroom. I had seen her picture, so I knew what to look for, but was unprepared for how much prettier she was in person, one of those people whose beauty refused to be captured in digital, her expressions and the empathic knowing behind her eyes making up half her appeal. The picture had also failed to capture her coloring, which was like an oil painting under the hand of a Baroque master.

She had hair the color of honey—anyone not paying attention would call her blond. It was a unique shade that denied to be classified as a color, but you could try. I imagined a man could spend days thinking about nothing else. Her eyes were a liquid, chocolate brown, her skin sun-kissed, tanned unevenly in a way that told you she came by it naturally, the highlight of her cheekbones tinged with red.

As I looked at her, I was surprised Ken had even noticed her understated natural beauty—he was a Philistine when it came to women. But his affairs were none of mine. This was purely a reconnaissance mission.

On Tuesday, I followed Bridget after school, no easy feat since she caught a public bus that wound through the narrow streets of downtown. The bus deposited her in the quaint historic district and she walked to the Sunrise Assisted Living building. Old folks' homes seemed to always be named that way—"sunrise," as if to imply the inmates were starting a new chapter instead of just being warehoused to wait for death.

By the time I found a parking space and made my way to the entrance, she had disappeared somewhere inside the building. There was a receptionist dressed in pink hospital scrubs, the kind covered with kittens and balls of yarn, or teddy bears and little hearts, so the outfit looked more like pajamas than a professional uniform. She was young, early twenties maybe, and as I approached, she only smiled. Though I had been formulating an excuse for being there in my mind, I quickly realized she wasn't going to challenge me so I just gave her a nod and kept walking. Most of the time, a confident stride and a purposeful look can get you in just about anyplace without a hassle.

A short hallway led to a large, cheery room with a television at one end and a collection of card tables scattered throughout, where old people sat playing cards and checkers and dominoes. My eyes scanned the room and found Bridget talking to an old woman who sat in a wheelchair.

The area beyond the recreation room was a long corridor lined with walkers and wheelchairs. Private rooms, I assumed as I walked along, taking quick glances into the rooms with open doors. A few were occupied with people watching television or sleeping. I got to the rec room in time to see Bridget pushing the woman's wheelchair through a glass automatic door that led to a courtyard garden.

An old man sat in a wheelchair near the window, head bowed as if asleep. He was alone and sat away from the others. I approached him, wondering if I might get lucky and he was so far gone, he wouldn't notice the difference if I just took him for a spin around the grounds.

"Hey," I said. "You in there?"

"What the—?" He jerked his head up, awake and, apparently, somewhat with it. "Who the hell are you?" he asked as he sat up suddenly in his seat, his hands flat on the arms of his wheelchair as if he were going to spring up and get me in a choke hold.

"Relax. Sorry, I thought you were asleep."

"I was!" he said, sounding pissed.

"Look, I said I was sorry. I was just looking to borrow an old person for a little bit."

"Borrow? An old person?"

"Yeah," I said, looking around to see if there was a better prospect.

"What are you planning to do with the old person? You some kind of pervert?" he asked.

"Gross," I said. "No, I just need an excuse to be here."

"Why?" he asked curiously. "You planning on robbing the place?"

"What?" I asked, because I hadn't really been giving the conversation my full attention. Then it hit me what he had said. "No. Nothing like that. Look, I can't really explain, but I just need to have an excuse to walk around the garden for a few minutes. Want to go for a walk?"

"With you?" he asked, as if the idea was mildly repulsive.

"Maybe you could pretend to be my grandfather for the next ten minutes or so. I can pay you."

"Pay me to be your grandfather," he said as he stroked his chin with a thick, gnarled finger, the nail etched with white lines. "Interesting. And you're not here to rob the place?"

"No."

"Because you know, all these people," he said with an expansive gesture around the room, "they're old and frail— half of them don't even know what decade it is. Someone could walk in here, rip 'em off. It would be easy. They don't even pay attention at the front desk."

"Yeah, I noticed that. You ever think about stealing from the other inmates?" I asked.

"Wouldn't be much point. A lot of what you can get in here is valuables that would need to be fenced—mostly jewels and electronics. Maybe some credit cards but there's a limited value in those. I'd need a partner."

I nodded in understanding. "I can see you've really thought this through."

"Yeah, well. Thinking is all I can do in this place. I can't stand that fat slob who's hosting *The Price Is Right* now. He's lost a lot of weight but he still looks like a fat slob to me. Might as well just be fat, is the way I see it." It was clear that if I didn't interrupt his senseless babble, we'd be standing here all night, talking about game show hosts and low-yield heists in old folks' homes.

"Listen," I said—patient, reasonable, "I just want to walk into the courtyard for a few minutes and talk to someone. You want to come with me, pretend to be my grandfather, and give me an excuse to be here?"

"Grandfather?" he asked. "How old do you think I am?"

"Old enough to be my great-grandfather," I said, cutting off this line of speculative conversation before it could even get started. "Seriously, I'm sort of in a hurry."

"Why should I do that for you?" he asked.

"I can pay you."

"What the hell do I need money for?" he asked, obviously keen on hearing himself talk. "You think I don't have enough hemorrhoid cream or something?"

"*Uch*, okay, just stop. You're going to make me sick. We can negotiate later," I said. "I just need a grandfather for the next ten minutes—think you can do that?"

He crossed his arms over his chest, wiry gray hair in stark relief against the muddy age spots that covered his forearms, as he narrowed one eye and glared at me through the other, filmy with cataract. "What are you up to?"

"Nothing illegal," I said.

"Fine."

I gripped the handles on his wheelchair and propelled him down the hall and out into the relative cool of the late-September afternoon, the interior temperature warm enough to bake someone my age. Bridget and the old woman sat beside a metal fountain that splashed water gaily against a pile of large tumbled stones. The old lady wore a woolly sweater, her shoulders hunched and her head hanging like a bird of prey.

I fixed my face into a friendly smile as we approached the bench where Bridget sat with her grandmother, who resembled Mr. Magoo from the old cartoon. "Hi," I said, feigning a little surprise at seeing Bridget as I parked the old man near the bench where he could watch the fountain.

"Hello," Bridget said, squinting up at me, the sun in her eyes. "You go to Wakefield, don't you?"

"Yes. You too?"

"Yes, I'm a senior," she said. "Bridget Smalley. What's your name?"

"Jesse. Alderman."

"I've heard your name. It's nice to meet you," she said, sounding unreasonably happy about it. "This is my grandmother, Dorothy Cleary."

"You'd best not sit near us," Dorothy said as she glanced furtively over both shoulders. "The CIA is watching me. All the time they're watching." She nodded toward a second-story window in the building and, in an ominous tone, said, "There. They've got cameras on me. They'll be after you if you're not careful."

"Is this your grandfather?" Bridget asked, ignoring Dorothy's rant.

"Hiram Dunkelman," the old man said as he leaned forward and offered her his hand to shake.

"I haven't seen you here before, Jesse," Bridget said kindly. She was acting so nice, it seemed like it had to be a put-on, but I couldn't detect anything other than genuine delight to meet us in her eyes. I'll tell you honestly, it creeped me out a little. I kept trying to figure what her angle was, why she would bother being so nice to some old loser and his grandson who wasn't anybody important enough to have gotten her notice at school in three years.

"I've been living here for just over a year," Mr. Dunkelman said, "but this is the first time he's come to visit me. He's kind of a dumb-ass. Ungrateful kid like his mom."

"Oh," Bridget said. She wanted to take it as a joke but looked from me to Mr. Dunkelman, waiting for one of us to smile. When neither of us did, she just cleared her throat and turned to her grandmother, who looked like she was just about asleep. "You warm enough, Grandmother?" she asked, her voice raised to such a volume it startled the ducks preening themselves on the warm rocks. The woman seemed oblivious of Bridget's ministrations and I wondered if she even knew where she was.

"You're here a lot," Mr. Dunkelman said. "I see you with your grandmother—what?—once a week?"

Bridget nodded. "Yes, I usually come every Thursday, but this week I can't come on my regular day so I thought I would just sneak in a quick visit today."

Mr. Dunkelman turned as far as he could in his seat to fix a scowl on me. "See?" he said. "She comes once a week. What do I get? You don't even come to take me to temple for Rosh Hashanah."

I opened my eyes wide as I tried to cue him to shut the fuck up.

Bridget shot me a sympathetic smile and said, "I don't know how much difference it makes, whether she really knows I'm here or not." She rubbed the old woman's gnarled hands as she spoke.

"The sea air can give you a wicked cold," Dorothy said. "That's why I spend most of my time belowdecks, or in my cabin."

"Sometimes she thinks she's on a ship," Bridget whispered conspiratorially to us out of the side of her mouth.

We all politely ignored Dorothy Cleary's lunacy with a brief silence. It was Mr. Dunkelman who broke the awkward pause.

"I'm sure she appreciates that you come," Mr. Dunkelman said, elbows on the arms of his wheelchair, leaning forward as he spoke. "Just the fact that you touch her, let her get a change of scenery. I'm sure it makes a difference for her." He said this as he shot another accusing look in my direction, as if I really were his ungrateful grandson who never came to see him. I bit my lower lip in an effort to keep from laughing or cussing him, or both.

Bridget's smile brightened and I felt my heart lurch in my chest as it missed a beat. Where the sun touched her hair and the planes of her face, she shone gold, warmth and light radiating from her like she was an angel backlit by the heavens. I looked away as Mr. Dunkelman resumed their conversation. Bridget and Mr. Dunkelman chatted amicably for a few minutes while Dorothy and I sat mutely, both of us captivated by the ducks, now bobbing in the fountain, dipping their beaks periodically. The whole situation was quickly becoming surreal.

Finally Bridget stood and took command of Dorothy's wheelchair again. "Well," she said, "it's been nice talking to you both." Including me, even though I had barely said two words since our introduction. "I have to be somewhere, but I hope to see you next time I'm here for a visit."

Mr. Dunkelman and I both stood as a show of politeness as she left, even though it was clearly a struggle for him. As I wheeled him back into the building, I said, "Thanks. That was perfect."

"She's beautiful," he said. "I can see why you wanted an excuse to talk to her."

"It's not what you think," I said, distracted as I watched for a glimpse of that golden head of hair.

"If you say so," he said. "You got a car?"

"Yes."

"Good. You pick me up here Saturday at eleven."

"Excuse me?"

"My payment," he said impatiently, as if he were talking to a half-wit. "That's my price. I want to go to the football game over at the university."

"That's not what I meant by payment," I said. "I'll give

you cash, I'll even get you tickets to the game if that's what you want, but I've got plans for Saturday."

"Better cancel them," he said. "I'd hate to have to tell Bridget we lied to her, tell her you offered me some desperately needed companionship if I would pretend to be your grandfather. I'd say you'd have no chance with her after that."

"You think this is about the girl, for me? That I'm trying to get laid or something?" I asked.

He shrugged, indifferent. "Doesn't much matter to me. Only thing matters is you don't want her to know you're a liar. That gives me a nice advantage."

"You're a nasty old fart, aren't you?" I asked, but I kind of respected the way he had turned the situation around to suit his own needs.

"Just to show you there's no hard feelings," he said as he took control of the wheelchair and steered himself toward the common room, where the television played at top volume, "I'll pay for drinks and dogs."

"Fine, I'll see you on Saturday," I called to his retreating back, "but then we're even."

SEVEN

BRIDGET AND I ENDED UP LEAVING THE BUILD-
ing at the same time. I held the door and nodded for her to
go in front of me as she dipped her head with that sweet,
apologetic expression that was already familiar to me.

As we walked through the exit together, I asked if she
needed a ride home and she hesitated before answering.
Her reluctance didn't surprise me—a girl as beautiful as
she was would be used to getting more attention than she
probably wanted from guys.

"I'm heading to the Siegel Center," she said. "You sure
it wouldn't be out of your way?"

Again she surprised me, as I got the sense that she was truly worried she might cause an inconvenience. There was no hint that she was using the idea as an excuse to get out of riding with me. I still couldn't see her angle.

"It's not out of my way," I lied.

"Okay, then," she said as she fell into step beside me, her backpack slung over one shoulder. "So, your grandfather seems really mad at you."

"Yeah," I said. "We've got baggage."

"Oh," she said quickly, apologetically. "Right." She seemed to have remembered now why she had heard my name before. My name had been churned through the gossip mill in town for several months the previous year.

Bridget thanked me when I opened and held the passenger door of the car for her. She carefully arranged her skirt around her legs once she was seated, like she wanted to minimize the amount of skin she shared with me. What I could see of her legs, the skin was brown from the sun, with pale lines on the tops of her feet, the mark of shoe straps.

"So," I said as I settled into the car beside her, "your grandmother always say weird shit like that?"

"Yes," Bridget said with a nod. "She has dementia. The CIA is not really out to get her," she added, her head inclined conspiratorially.

"How do you know?" I asked.

She didn't laugh, didn't give me a weird look, just thought about it for a minute, then said, "I guess I don't."

"Maybe she worked as a spy when she was younger," I said.

Now she did look at me. "You have a very good imagination, Jesse."

"You think so?" I asked.

"Yes. Do you use your powers for good or for evil?"

"Define good," I said as I pulled away from the curb and steered into traffic.

"Do you write stories, create beautiful artwork?" she asked. "Or do you make up lies to get what you want?"

A smile was playing at the corners of her mouth as she said this and I realized I had misjudged her. Her good nature was not the result of naïveté or lack of intelligence. Intriguing.

"Nothing is either good or bad," I said, "but thinking makes it so."

"Shakespeare," she said, her tone triumphant. "*Hamlet* is my favorite."

"It must be hard for you," I observed, "always being the smartest and the best looking." I noticed her cheeks redden but she just gave me a drop-dead stare.

We rode in silence for a minute and I thought I had made her angry, but when she turned to speak to me again, there was no evidence of it in her voice.

"So, Jesse, if you could have one superpower for a day, what would it be?" she asked.

"Is this some kind of test?" I asked.

"I suppose," she said as she stared out the window, watching the world going by. Since she wasn't looking at me, I took the opportunity to study her legs again, the golden hairs along her arm, the rise and fall of her perfect breasts as she breathed. "I like to ask people that question," she said, interrupting the path of my thoughts. "I think it's a good way to get to know someone. You know, if someone says they would like to be invisible, that means they would probably steal from you or invade your privacy as long as they knew they wouldn't get caught."

"What about you?" I asked. "What superpower would you want?"

"I change my mind about it," she said, her finger idly twirling a lock of her hair. "But I think I would like to be able to read minds, know what people are really thinking instead of just what they are saying."

"Most people aren't thinking anything any more interesting than what they are saying," I said. "In fact, that would probably be an awfully boring superpower. Besides, I can usually tell what people are thinking."

"Oh yeah?" she asked with one eyebrow cocked at an impish angle. "What am I thinking?"

"That I'm full of shit. That was an easy one."

She just shook her head, her hair a shimmering pool around her shoulders. "Haven't I seen you around school with that girl . . . uh . . . Josephine, right?" Bridget asked.

"Joey," I corrected her. "Only call her Josephine if you want to make her angry."

"Joey, then. She was in my art class last year. She's very . . . creative. Is she your girlfriend?"

"Definitely not," I said, equal emphasis on "definitely" and "not."

"Why definitely not?" she asked, seeming to get some amusement out of her line of questioning.

"Because she's a special kind of crazy," I said. "You can't

sleep with a girl who has issues like that. They go *Fatal Attraction* on you. Next thing you know, there's a small wood-
land creature boiling in a pot on your stove top."

Her laugh startled me. I hadn't been making an attempt
at humor but I felt a warm glow spreading under my skin
all the same as she laughed appreciatively at my comment.

"What about you?" I asked, telling myself it was all part
of the job. "Boyfriend?"

"Why do you want to know?" she asked smartly.

"I'm just making conversation."

"No, I don't have a boyfriend."

"Why not?" I asked. "What's wrong with you?"

"Why does something have to be wrong with me?" she
asked. "Maybe I just don't want a boyfriend. Are you some
kind of chauvinist?"

"Now I feel like you're trying to confuse me on purpose," I said, turning my attention away from the road long
enough to give her an admonishing look.

"I don't have a boyfriend, because I haven't found what
I'm looking for in a guy. That's all."

"And what is it you're looking for, Bridget Smalley?"

"Someone who's kind, smart, and funny," she said.
"Someone who appreciates art and music and likes to talk
about interesting things."

"You forgot the handsome part," I said.

"Oh, I don't really care about the way someone looks,"
she said with a dismissive flutter of her hand.

"Oh, really?" I said, letting my tone convey my disbelief
as I rolled to a stop at an intersection and studied her for a
minute before hanging a left.

"It's true," she said insistently. "If I like a person, if they have a good heart, that's what makes them beautiful."

"Did you read that in a fortune cookie?" I asked.

She swung an impatient look in my direction, one eye narrowed with unspoken criticism. A long pause followed while we played the silent game.

I lost.

"Yeah, okay," I said. "I suppose if a person is . . . nice, it can make them seem better looking."

She smirked in triumph to herself and sat up a little straighter as she returned her gaze to the window.

I pulled into the parking lot of the Siegel Center. Though I had driven by it a thousand times, I had no idea what it was or what went on inside. "What is this place?" I asked.

"They do programs here for people with special needs," she said as she gathered her purse and jacket from her lap. "I volunteer at least one day a week—sometimes two—helping out with the kids. Do you want to come in? Check it out?"

"Why not?" I said, and pulled into a parking space. She was already halfway out of her seat when I got to her side of the car but I held her door until she was clear and shut it behind her.

"Such nice manners," she said, and I got the sense she was teasing me again, but not in a way that was meant to poke fun at my expense, more like a flirtation.

"So, what, are you like Mother Teresa or something?" I asked.

She snorted and I marveled at the fact that even when

she snorted, she made it cute and kind of sexy. "Hardly," she said.

"You visit your grandmother, you volunteer at the Siegel Center. What do you do for fun on the weekends—rescue kittens or work in a soup kitchen?" I asked.

"Now you are making fun of me," she said. I lengthened my stride so I could reach the door before her and hold it open. She thanked me as she walked through.

"I'm not making fun of you," I said. "I'm truly interested. The concept of altruism fascinates me, though I don't really believe in it. You must have a selfish motive for all of your good deeds."

She squinted one eye as she surveyed my expression, then smiled, as if to show that all was forgiven. "You're very perceptive, Jesse, if not a little annoying. I've decided I'm going to like you, even though you don't want me to."

My stomach went hollow and my tongue suddenly dry as she said this and I felt heat in my face. It was a strange sensation and I wondered if I was coming down with something. A minute later, the hollowness of my gut subsided as I followed her silently down the hall. Bridget greeted every person we passed, most of them by name—the receptionist, other volunteers, even the janitor. People lit up when they saw her—their faces split into smiles and their voices were warm with genuine gladness as they greeted her. Walking with Bridget was like walking with Jesus on the road to Galilee.

Once through the building, we walked out onto a lawn with a raised garden and a playground. A group of kids, most of them elementary or middle school age, was outside playing with a few bored-looking adults. There was a sudden roar from the group and I jerked with alarm, but Bridget did not seem fazed by it. A lot of the kids came running, at least the ones who could run, to surround Bridget and began hugging and kissing her with indiscriminate affection.

I'll admit I was a little creeped out by it. These kids were all freak shows—a fat kid with a pie face and teeth that jutted in twenty directions, a girl with glasses as thick as ballistic-proof Plexiglas and an honest-to-God flipper instead of a right arm, a kid on crutches with a right leg that was bent at an impossible angle and drool all over his chin. My first instinct was to run, and I looked to Bridget to gauge how she was reacting to them.

Incredibly, she was all smiles, submitting to bone-crushing hugs and even a kiss on the face from the kid with the drool. I felt my gag reflex rise when I saw the wet patch he left glistening on her cheek and turned my head to look at something—anything—else.

"Hey, guys," Bridget said merrily. "This is my new friend, Jesse. Can you say hi to Jesse?"

Jesus, she was actually encouraging them to interact with me, and for a second I was afraid I was going to have to fight them off like wild animals. But they just smiled and waved at me and said hi. I gave them a halfhearted wave and was rehearsing my excuse to leave in my head when Bridget tugged at my sleeve and said, "Come meet my brother."

I was relieved to see her brother was not some kind of mutant but a normal-looking kid with a lanky frame, glasses, and a sour expression, who was leaning against the wall of the courtyard with earbuds in his ears.

"Pete, come here," Bridget said, waving to him. Pete reluctantly left his position along the wall and walked over to us. He had a limp, which gave him a weird, rolling gait, and when he got closer, I could see he had not been graced with the same good looks of his sister. The resemblance was there, but his face was not as perfectly even and chiseled as a Greek statue. "This is Jesse," Bridget said, gesturing to me. "He goes to Wakefield too."

"I know you," Pete said, almost like an accusation. "We had the same study hall last year."

"Oh, yeah?" I asked with some feigned interest.

"Yeah, I mean, of course I don't expect you to remember. You always sat in the back and I was always down front with the—" He broke off without finishing his thought.

I caught the look of sympathy that clouded Bridget's eyes as she studied her brother and I wondered how much of a social pariah he really was.

"Didn't you used to date Heather Black?" Pete asked.

"We went out," I said noncommittally.

"Heather Black is like the most beautiful girl in school," he said.

"Yeah, well," I said, "she makes up for it by having a really shitty personality."

"Jesse is fashionably indifferent," Bridget said without a hint of irony in her voice. "I've got to go spend some time with the kids. If either of you want to join us in a game of kickball, you're welcome. Pete will protect you," Bridget said with a wink as she walked away.

Pete and I took up a post against the wall and stood silently watching Bridget with her brood. I decided I could use the opportunity to gather some more critical information about Bridget for Ken. "You a martyr too?" I asked Pete, breaking the silence between us so suddenly that he jerked in surprise. "Spend all your time helping those less fortunate than yourself?"

"No," he said forlornly. "There's just one angel in our family."

I nodded in understanding. As an only child, I didn't really get the animosity that existed between siblings. It was hard to comprehend a relationship that could make two people alternately love and hate each other with such passion, sometimes expressing both within the span of only a few minutes' time.

"She volunteers here because the Siegel Center helped my family so much when I was younger," Pete said, as if that were explanation enough for why a beautiful, popular teenage girl would give up her time to play kickball with a bunch of dopey kids.

"Helped your family with what?" I asked.

"I don't know. Adjust to having a kid with special needs, I guess." His voice was bitter as he said this, which got me interested enough to turn and look at him.

"Why?" I asked. "What's wrong with you?"

"I have cerebral palsy," he said.

"What does that mean?"

"Cerebral palsy is a brain disorder."

"And what?" I pressed. "Are you retarded or something?"

"No, I'm not retarded," he shot back as if *I* were the one who was retarded. "Having CP doesn't mean you're necessarily learning disabled, though some people with CP are."

"That's why you walk funny?" I asked. "Because of this CP?"

He stared at me for a long minute, his expression incredulous though not angry—at least not that I could tell.

"Yes," he said with a mirthless laugh. "I walk funny, I wear glasses, and I have a weird face because I have CP."

"I didn't really notice the weird-face thing," I said, studying his, "but now that you mention it—"

"I don't have full control of the muscles in the left side of my face. That's why it looks different."

"Oh. So, Bridget volunteers here every week?"

He rolled his eyes. "Yes, Tuesday after school, and I always have to come."

"Why?" I asked. "I mean, if you don't want to, why do you come?"

"She's only volunteering because of me. If I didn't show up, it would be weird."

"Weird for who?" I asked.

"I don't know," he said, exasperated now. "Me. Her."

"Why don't you just tell her you want to do something else?"

"Like what?" he asked, like suddenly I was the guy with all the answers.

"Well, if you don't have anything else to do, why do you mind coming here so much?"

"What do you do after school?" he asked.

"Work, mostly."

"You have a job?"

"I'm self-employed."

He chortled, which seemed to be all he had to say on the subject, then asked, "So, are you in love with my sister?"

"Why would you think that?" I asked.

"All guys are in love with my sister," he said, sounding a little pissed about it but not, I guessed, out of some sense of being protective. More like he was tired of being the sibling who wasn't so very.

"And why's that?" I asked, as if I didn't know.

"Because she's beautiful," he said, again with a tone that implied I was a half-wit.

"So? It doesn't matter how beautiful a girl is—chances are there's some guy, somewhere, who's sick of her bullshit."

"Not Bridget."

"Oh, yeah? What makes her so special?" I asked.

"It's not an act," he said. "She's genuinely a good person."

"I just met her today," I said, "so no, I'm not in love with her."

"Give it time," he said gloomily, which I was starting to see was his outlook on just about everything.

"Does she date much?" I asked, since we were on the subject.

He just shook his head. "Oh, man, and you said you just met her today? God help you, buddy."

We both fell silent as we watched Bridget coordinate the most ludicrous game of kickball I'd ever witnessed. When she caught me watching her, she just smiled brightly and lifted her hand in a discreet wave. I caught myself returning her smile and shot a glance in Pete's direction to see if he was watching, but he was studying his iPod and not paying attention.

After a while, Bridget got the kids to help her clean up the equipment and it was another round of hugs and kisses before they all waved good-bye and she came to retrieve her brother. The three of us walked to the parking lot, where I offered them a ride home.

Bridget directed me to their neighborhood, which was just outside the center of town—an older neighborhood but not part of the historic downtown.

"So, you do this every Tuesday, huh?" I asked Bridget nonchalantly. "Volunteer with retarded kids at the Siegel Center?"

"The kids that I work with all have some form of physical disability, but only a few of them actually have any kind of learning disability. I do the sports with them because it either helps them to build confidence in their bodies, even if they're differently abled, or helps them to develop coordination."

"That's what they want you to call them?" I asked skeptically. "Differently abled?"

"Well, it's just an accepted way to describe people with disabilities. Kind of like saying that just because they are different doesn't mean they aren't just as capable."

"You think calling them differently abled makes *them* feel better, or makes you feel better?" I asked.

A harsh laugh emanated from the backseat and I glanced into my rearview to see Pete, a smile on his face—though not a happy smile, more like a sneer—as he waited for Bridget's answer. Before that moment, I hadn't even realized he was listening to us since he had been wearing his earbuds.

She bit her lip at the sound of Pete's laughter, and the cloud of sympathy and sadness I had seen in her eyes earlier returned. "I don't know," was Bridget's answer. She said it in a quiet, thoughtful voice as her hand drifted up to nervously twirl a lock of wavy honey hair just behind her ear.

My comment had hurt her somehow, in a way that I couldn't understand. The sudden urge I had to touch her, to cover her hand with mine or rub her knee, surprised me.

When she turned and caught me watching her, she smiled, but it didn't reach her eyes.

Their house was a modest two-story with wood siding and a chain-link fence that was rusted in a few places. They definitely weren't rich, maybe not even comfortable. I put the car in park as she unbuckled her seat belt and gathered her things from the floor of the car. Pete was already out of the car and halfway up the front walk.

"Thanks for the ride, Jesse," Bridget said as she hesitated with one foot out the door, her hand on the door handle. "Maybe I'll see you next time you visit your grandfather. He seems like a nice guy."

"Sure, yeah, like Attila the Hun," I said.

I watched her until she was out of sight before pulling away.

Later that night when I got home, Dad was there and not alone. As I stood silently in the kitchen, I heard laughter coming from the living room, my father's throaty baritone and the high-pitched, breathy laugh of a woman. I heard the pop of wood against wood as he opened the sideboard where he stowed the liquor. I thought about leaving as quietly as I had entered and returning once they were otherwise occupied upstairs, but I was tired and I wanted nothing more than to go to bed. I tossed my keys on the counter to alert them to my presence and walked into the living room.

Dad was standing over the coffee table, pouring two glasses of Maker's Mark over ice with a slightly unsteady hand. He swayed slowly from side to side to keep his balance.

"Hey, Jesse," he said, as if surprised to find me in my own house.

"Hey, Dad," I said.

"Say hi to Angela," he said as he squinted one eye at the glass he held and then tipped the bottle to add to it.

"Hello," I said with a nod at the woman on the couch. She craned her neck to see me, her face lit up with a smile, her eyes wide with surprise and stupidity.

"This is my boy, Jesse," Dad said in a tone that implied we shared something other than DNA.

"He's cute," she said with a squeal. "Must take after his mother." They both broke into laughter again and she threw her head back to reveal a full bosom bursting out of a dress that was designed for a body twenty years younger than her own.

She was cheaply made up, like most of the women Dad brought home, her black roots visible against her dyed blond hair from ten paces.

"Yeah, well, he's a moody little son of a bitch, but I'll tell you what, he takes after his old man when it comes to playing the guitar. Isn't that right, Jesse?"

I didn't answer, just eyed him coolly.

They didn't take any notice of the frigid air between us and I suppressed a sigh as I set my bag down on the floor and took off my jacket.

"Angela came to see the band play at the Inn tonight," Dad said, as if I cared how he had met his latest conquest.

"Your dad was great," she said as she reached for her drink on the coffee table. "Such a good show."

"Yeah, we had a great set," Dad said without any apparent modesty. "But you should hear this boy play. Man, he's got such a good ear, he could tell you the pitch of a belch. Isn't that right?" Dad asked me as Angela let out another belly laugh.

"If you say so," I said.

"Hey, why don't you go get your guitar?" Dad asked me with a snap of his fingers. "Play us a little something."

"I sold it," I said dully. "I don't play anymore."

Dad sobered some at that, his upper lip curling in a snarl. "You what?"

"I sold it," I said.

"That guitar was worth more than that damn car you drive," he said.

"I sold it to pay for groceries," I said, which shut him up long enough for me to make an exit and head for my room.

I docked my iPod and turned up the volume to let Mozart's Piano Concerto no. 21 fill the empty space, then flopped onto my mattress. I reached under the bed to pull out the guitar case and lay it gently on the quilt.

Though I had not played my guitar since my mother's death, I knew I would never be able to get rid of it. At one time, it had been almost a part of me. Now it lay there like an amputated appendage, a traitor to its body.

The rosewood was like satin under my hand as I trailed my finger along the length of the sounding board, the subtle ridges of the strings, and the gentle rise of the frets. After months with no practice, my fingertips had softened, now more sensitive than they had been in years. Though I longed for the physical sensation of the instrument in my arms, the vibration of a perfectly formed note reverberating from the guitar's body into mine, I didn't even so much as let one of the strings squeak under the slide of my skin.

Over the past few months, I had visited with the guitar many times, had felt its yearning for me to hold it and play it. Though an antique and worth more cash than my car, it was an instrument that was meant to be played. Several times I had contemplated throwing it across the room, imagined the splinter of wood, the death groans of the strings against the fret board, like the shuddering respirations that signify dying. The courage to destroy it always subsided quickly. There was not enough emotion to inspire the destruction of my oldest friend.

EIGHT

COMMODITIES PASS THROUGH MY HANDS LIKE
water—term papers, drugs, fake IDs—but they don't hold
value the way information does. Real wealth is measured
in secrets, the secrets of other people, and my own. Secrets
are power. Every time someone paid me cash for something, they also unwittingly paid me with their secret. I
owned them.

It's easy to become drunk on that kind of power. Gath-
ering and keeping information about people is a business,
and an art form. If you exploit secrets too often, people

stop giving them to you. Knowing when to use information is just as important as having it.

Joey and I were in the library over lunch break when Gray Dabson finally sniffed me out. I had successfully avoided him for most of the week but he was determined.

Gray Dabson was a tall, lanky kid—student council president, decent basketball player, straight-A student, and editor of the yearbook. The most remarkable thing about him was his freakishly large Adam's apple. As he helped himself to a seat across from me at the scarred wood table in the back of the library, I wondered if he was sensitive to the fact that people couldn't help but look at his neck instead of his face while speaking to him.

"Jesse," Gray said as he held out a hand in greeting. I eyed his hand for half a second before taking it for a brief shake and wondered what his angle was.

"What can I do for you?" I asked. Joey was listening intently from several seats away though she never took her eyes off the book that lay open on the table in front of her.

"The other council officers and I have decided to hold a car wash this year to fund student activities." He paused after delivering this news, as if waiting for me to commend the originality of their idea.

"I guess the whole bake sale idea is overdone," I said dryly.

"Exactly," Gray said with a nod. "We felt the same way. The senior class fund-raiser made over seven hundred dollars last year and we really need to top that number."

"What did they do last year to raise money?" I asked, though I'm unsure why I asked, because I didn't really care.

"It was a bake sale–car wash combo," he said. "People could shop for baked goods while they got their car washed."

"Ah." Mind-numbing.

"Logistically, it was a nightmare," he continued, obviously immune to my lack of interest, "and there were a lot of expenses. John Williams was president of the council then and his dad ended up underwriting all the expenses so they could keep one hundred percent of the profits, which is a little unfair. We can't possibly hope to net that amount of money if we have to cover our own expenses."

"So, what does any of this have to do with me?" I asked.

"I had the idea that if we had the cheerleaders out washing the cars, we might get more people to show up. I'm not saying I think they should dress suggestively," he added quickly with a glance in Joey's direction. "But the cheerleaders are outgoing, have a lot of school spirit. It could help our cause."

"And?" I pressed.

He cleared his throat and said at a discreet volume, "I approached Heather Black about it since she's the captain of the squad. She told me to go to hell. I thought you might have some influence, some pull with Heather."

My gaze wandered down the table to fix on Joey, who was now watching us curiously. When she caught my gaze, she mouthed a word meant only for me. The movement of her mouth was so exaggerated, it was impossible to tell what she was saying.

"What the hell are you saying?" I asked her.

Gray frowned in confusion and looked back and forth between us, as if watching a tennis match. Joey just shook her head and dropped her gaze back to her book. Gray cleared his throat again and dived back in. "So, do you think you could talk to her about it? Heather, I mean."

"Wasted energy," I said. "Even if I can convince her, she won't be enthusiastic about it and you'll end up owing more than you'll make back."

His face fell and his Adam's apple jumped as he drew in a breath and blew out a dejected sigh. I let the silence tick by for ten beats as I worked things out in my head. Then I let another five seconds of silence pass before saying, "But maybe I can help you in another way."

"Really?" he asked, his voice an unnaturally high pitch. "Like how?"

"In fact," I said, warming up to the idea, "I can guarantee that your event will be popular and you'll make more money than you know what to do with." I paused and let it sink in for a moment.

"How are you going to do that, exactly?" he asked.

"My methods are confidential," I said. "Take it or leave it."

"Fine, okay. As long as I have your guarantee," he said with a nervous smile that faded quickly when I looked him directly in the eye with a disapproving stare. I let him squirm for a minute before shifting my gaze.

"My fee will be twenty percent of the gross income," I said, "and you'll be responsible for any expenses incurred."

"Twenty percent!" he said with a squeak, and his Adam's apple bobbed crazily. "That seems . . . excessive," he said, flashing an apologetic smile. "I mean, you do understand the money is going to support the student council and fund some of the amenities we offer for the whole student body? The prom, homecoming, senior class trip—all of these are partially covered by the funds we raise at the car wash. I was thinking . . . well, I guess I thought . . . maybe you'd like to donate your services?"

"I don't understand the question," I said, ignoring unintelligible mutterings from Joey's end of the table.

"I mean, you could volunteer your time," Gray said.

What a douche. At this point, I was mostly just baffled by the idea that this guy had managed to win any kind of elected position. I could only assume no one else wanted the job.

"Listen, Gray," I said, speaking slowly so I wouldn't have to repeat myself. "That twenty percent, that's my incentive. I do a better job for you, for your event, if I've got a serious financial incentive at stake. That's your insurance policy. I would think that a guy like you, a guy who knows his way around a management position, would understand that."

"Of course, yeah. I can totally see that," he said, sounding more uncertain than ever. "Just as long as I have your guarantee that we'll make the money we need. This event is supposed to cover the expenses for homecoming. You know, decorations, band, all of that."

"What did I just say?" I asked sharply. "You'll make more money than you know what to do with. My percentage isn't going to change that. So, look, twenty percent off the top and you'll owe me a favor." I threw in the favor as a last-minute consideration. No telling when it would come in handy.

"Sure, Jesse," he said, eager as a Labrador now. "What's the favor?"

"I don't know yet," I said. "I'll let you know when I do."

I stood and gathered my things, and Gray took the hint to leave. Joey didn't say good-bye, just gave me a punch on the shoulder as she left for her next class.

Ken was waiting for me when I got to my locker, a throng of goofy freshman girls giggling and batting their eyelashes at him.

"Hey, Sway," Ken said as I approached.

His adoring throng broke up and started to move away as Ken leaned into the locker next to mine to talk to me. "You got anything for me yet?"

I emptied my messenger bag into the top shelf of my locker to stall for time as I thought about what I would tell him. "I talked to her once. She's a total nerd. Seems like she spends most of her time doing volunteer work."

"Yeah?" he asked breathily. "She's not dating anyone, though, right?"

"I don't know. We didn't talk about it. Give me another week and I'll have what you need. Though I'll be honest, I'm not really sure why you're wasting your time on this."

"You wouldn't understand," he said. "She's different from other girls. She wouldn't use a guy for his money or get with another guy just to make you jealous, you know?"

"I guess," I said halfheartedly. "Pretty girls are a lot of work—poor return on investment most of the time."

Ken grinned. "You know it. But this one's worth it. Believe me."

"You're a mess," I said with a shake of my head. "You'd better get your emotions in check or this girl's going to walk all over you." I felt a lump in my throat as I said this, realizing my jaw was clenched tightly, and I wondered what the hell was wrong with me.

NINE

I TOOK HEATHER TO PAOLO'S ON FRIDAY NIGHT
and it was all work. Heather loved going to Paolo's because
(1) it was expensive and the place to be seen in our town on
a weekend night, reservations always hard to get; and (2)
the decor involved a lot of strategically placed mirrors so
Heather could admire her own youth and beauty from
many angles while she carefully avoided eating any of the
food she ordered.

Tonight she wore a black dress littered with rhinestones
and multiple layers of flounces that clashed with my

summer-weight wool jacket and slacks. Her blond hair was streaked with highlights, too artistically blended to be natural.

Anthony, the owner of Paolo's, greeted me with a smile and a handshake as I asked after his son, a shy, queer kid who had been bullied mercilessly his freshman year at Wakefield. I had someone who looked after the kid now, didn't let anybody mess with him. Socially he was still a little off, but at least wasn't taking regular beatings for it.

"He's very good, Jesse, very good," Anthony said with a broad smile. "I thank you for all you've done for him."

"I didn't really do anything, Anthony. Justin's a good kid. He just needed to make friends with the biggest guy in the school."

Anthony laughed and clapped a hand on my shoulder. "This is true, yes."

Anthony showed us to a circular booth and snapped our linen napkins with a flourish before laying them gently on our laps. He gave a slight bow and another smile before leaving us to the care of the waiter.

"I was surprised when you called me," Heather said once the waiter had taken our drink order.

"Why's that?" I asked as I carefully kept my eyes from straying to the line below her jaw where her pancake makeup ended and her real skin tone began.

"Just because," she said, her voice close to a whine. "You haven't called me in a long time. Even when we were seeing each other, you always acted like you didn't care if I was coming or going."

"I've just been busy," I said. "Got a lot on my plate." I

picked up the menu and scanned it intently, though I always ordered the same thing.

"I know you haven't been seeing anyone, haven't been dating. You haven't dated anyone seriously since you broke up with me."

"Is that how you see it? That I broke up with you?" I asked without looking up from the menu.

"What would you call it?" she asked, leaning forward, her bosom resting on her clasped hands. "We went out. I wasn't seeing anyone else. Then you just . . . left."

"Some people are better on their own," I said, wondering where the hell the waiter was with our drinks. Heather reached across the table and put a hand on my forearm, her fingers so cold, it raised goose bumps on my skin.

"I'm glad you called," she said, then trailed her fingers up toward my elbow. "Do you know why girls love guys who play the guitar?" she asked.

"Tell me."

"It's your arms," she said as she parked her chin on the heel of her other hand and smiled suggestively. "Something about the muscles in your arms. They're different from the muscles guys get from lifting weights. It's very sexy."

"I don't play guitar anymore," I said, wanting to pull my arm away from her touch.

"Right. I . . . uh, I forgot," she said with a horribly inappropriate nervous laugh.

The waiter came with our drinks and we ordered dinner. As I knew she would, Heather ordered the most expensive thing on the menu, then ate only a few bites of it.

Tonight was going to cost me, in more ways than one, but it was a long-term investment. Keeping David happy meant less work in the long run. I just had to keep that in mind as the night wore on.

"So," Heather said as she watched me pile the last bite of my food onto the back of my fork. "Does this mean I'm going to start seeing more of you?"

I wiped my mouth with my napkin and set it aside before I answered her. I had to tread carefully here. "You know I've got a lot on my mind, right?" I asked. "I need my friends, that's all."

"Are you saying I'm your friend?" she asked as she twirled a lock of hair over her finger and her eyes got a little misty.

"Sure, of course. But—" I let my eyes wander to the other diners as I said, "I guess it's hard for me to talk to anyone. Maybe anyone other than David."

"David who?" she asked with a puzzled frown.

"David Cohen."

"The nerdy guy with the baggy clothes?"

I smiled sheepishly. "Yeah, you know, he's not all about image and getting wasted. He's a good guy."

"Huh," she said, "I never would have figured you guys for friends."

"Well, we are," I said. "People don't really know him, don't understand him because he's smart, interested in different stuff. And, you know, even though he's super rich, has a huge trust fund and all of that, he keeps it to himself. Doesn't put on airs about having a lot of money or anything."

I could see her brain working overtime, calculating all the things a guy with looks like David's might buy for a girl with the physical charms Heather possessed.

Her eyes were moist and I knew she was hungry for more detail. She wasn't going to get it, but I dropped one last sweetener to ensure her interest. "Anyway," I said with a shrug, "I just wish other people could see his good qualities, maybe appreciate a person for something besides looks for once."

"I wish everyone thought the way you do," she said. "I mean, everyone thinks I have it so easy because I'm beautiful and popular, but it's not as if I don't have problems too." She put on a pout that looked well practiced. If I ever did think about getting it on with Heather again, one of her pouts was enough to put me off. It was fascinating to watch someone who was so completely self-absorbed.

I sat back and tried to coast through the rest of the evening. My work was going as planned, but I still had to figure out how to get her home without putting my mouth on her overglossed lips.

TEN

IT TURNED OUT THAT MR. DUNKELMAN LIKED
to complain. A lot. When I picked him up on Saturday to
go to the football game, he complained about how hard it
was to get in and out of my car because the seats were low
to the ground. He complained about the print on everything being too small to read. He complained that sausage
gave him the runs even though he ate two with onions and
mustard during the game while I silently prayed that his
bowel irritability wouldn't manifest until after I dropped
him off at the old folks' home.

But most of all, he liked to complain about how un-grateful his children and grandchildren were, none of whom, according to him, ever came to see him. It was his intent to run out of money at the moment of his death so his heirs could not profit from his demise. And, appar-ently, he had plenty of money to go around, which he in-tentionally wasted on risky investments and crap he saw on QVC just to piss off his kids.

When I asked him why he didn't leave his money to some charity, he said they were all fronts for anti-Semitic terrorist cells or were run by Oprah Winfrey, whom he hated with the passion of a religious convert. "She's fat, she's thin, she's fat, she's thin—always talking about how she's eating her emo-tions," he said. "I'll tell you what she's eating is a lot of pies."

"You got something against fat people?" I asked, mostly to give him shit, but he took the question at face value. Liter-alism was one of his other personality traits that could be alternately irritating or amusing, depending on my mood.

"I don't have anything against anybody," he said.

"Except anti-Semites and fat people," I amended, "and, by extension, Oprah Winfrey."

"All I'm saying is if you're going to be fat, just embrace it and be fat. Don't go on television and whine about it all the time. You seen these shows they have on TV now? It's a game show—honest to God—where the way to win is to lose the most weight. That's what we've become in this country. A bunch of fat slobs who only lose weight if there's a cash prize in it."

"You're like a font of wisdom," I said. "Now tell me an anecdote about how much you sacrificed during WW Two."

"How old do you think I am?" he asked.

"Definitely old enough to remember World War Two," I said as I drained my last sip of beer.

"I was a kid during World War Two," he said, indignant. "I served in Vietnam, the early years. I was such a dumbass I volunteered for service in '65. Thought I was going to get to see the world, take advantage of the G.I. Bill."

"I was born in 1995," I said.

"Shit," was all he said, then he watched the game for a while in silence.

After that exchange, he didn't complain as much. Except for complaining about his bowels. That was a constant. Everything he ate or drank had some potential negative outcome for his bowels. I began to wonder if by the time you reached the wisdom and experience of old age, it no longer mattered because all you could think about was your shit—color, consistency, frequency. And if it's a bunch of old guys running the country in Washington, D.C., how much time could they really devote to the country's problems if they were constantly thinking about excrement? When I asked Mr. Dunkelman that question, he just barked out a laugh, but he did go for almost thirty minutes without mentioning the wrong end of digestion.

Instead what he talked about was how much things had changed since he was a kid. "I was a city kid," he said, "from a solid middle-class Jewish family. You know, I was ten when we got our first television. What do you think of that, huh? No Internet, no cable television, no car phones."

"Why would anyone have a car phone?" I asked with genuine curiosity.

He waved a hand to shut me up and continued with his monologue. "We used to go to the movies, my friends and me, one Saturday a month. Looked forward to it like it was the Super Bowl. It surprised me, to get to this age, see all this change in the world, the crazy technology, only to find out people haven't changed at all. People are exactly the same now as they were when I was a kid."

"People never surprise me," I said.

"Why is that?"

"Because," I said, "people can be relied on to always look out for number one. People think nothing about lying, cheating, stealing—as long as they see it as something they want or need, they're always willing to justify it."

Mr. Dunkelman nodded but said, "It can seem that way—when you're young. The older you get, the more you understand. There's a lot of hurt in the world. You know, your parents, they're just people. Like you. You think when you get older, you get things all sorted out, or you forget what it felt like to be young. That's not it. You get older, you learn a little about the world, learn what it is to love someone else more than you love yourself, and you think, if only I had it all to do over again, I could do it better. Be a better person. When you have kids, you see an opportunity to do it better through them, tell your kid all the secrets you wish you had known when you were that age. But it doesn't work that way." He chuckled mirthlessly as he said, "Because your kids don't give a shit. They think you're just a crazy old man who spends too much time thinking about his bowels. I'll tell you the secret. You'll ignore it. People your age always do. But when you get to be my age, you realize there's only two things that really matter in this world."

"Oh, shit. Hold on while I get a pen so I can write this down," I said, and patted my pockets as if trying to locate a pen.

"Shut up, you schlemiel," he growled. "I'm telling you. You won't listen to me—the same way people ignored Moses, treated him like he was some crazy old devil who was leading them in circles in the desert. Fifty years from now, you'll look back and realize I was right. The only two things in this world that really matter are the people who love you—and I don't mean your family. Sometimes the people who love you best have no blood relation to you. But in the end, all that will matter to you are the people who really love you . . . ," he said, then paused as the quarterback stepped out of the pocket and ducked a tackle to take a Hail Mary pass at the twenty-second mark. "The people who love you, and how often you shit. That's all there is."

"Jesus, that's depressing," I said. "No wonder your kids never come to see you. You didn't tell them that story, did you?"

He dismissed my comment with a wave of his hand.

"Maybe you just need to work on your delivery," I said thoughtfully. "You don't exactly come across as the wise old prophet. Maybe more like a really, really angry Regis Philbin."

"*Uch.* Don't even mention that schlemiel to me," Mr. D said with disgust. "Why is he famous?"

ELEVEN

THAT MONDAY SCHOOL WAS, AS ADVERTISED, too long and boring to keep my attention, but there was an interesting development at the end of the day. Peter Smalley was waiting by my car when I got out to the parking lot, slumped against the front quarter panel, his hand gripping two library books against his leg while he looked at his phone.

There wasn't enough wrong with him that it was immediately obvious. Until you studied him carefully, there was just a nagging sense that something was off, not quite right—his awkward gait, lopsided expressions, and, when he spoke, the mild speech impediment that made him sound slightly drunk.

Looking at him now, I got the sense that he was posed, his skinny ass irreverently parked on the cherry finish of my car, his hip hitched at an angle to give the appearance of indifference. He was an actor playing a role, Guy Casually Waiting for Friend at Car. Just like he had played the Betrayed by Life role while talking about his sister at the Siegel Center.

"Hey, Pete," I said as my car alarm chirped under him.

His face lit up when he saw me and I wondered how long he had been waiting.

"Hey, Jesse," he said with as much enthusiasm as a puppy greeting its master at the door.

"What's shakin'?" I asked.

"Nothin'," he said. "What are you doing today? Can you hang out?"

I tossed my bag in the backseat and shut the door. "I've got some errands to run."

His face fell, but since his face was already droopy on one side, the expression was pathetically reminiscent of a baby pug.

"You can ride along if you want, but it will be boring," I said.

The light behind his eyes returned. "That'd be great. I mean, that's cool. I'll just ride with you—keep you company."

"Suit yourself," I said, and he hurried around the hood of the car to get into the passenger side.

"Your car is awesome," he said as he settled into the passenger seat. "I can't believe your parents bought you these wheels."

"They didn't buy it," I said. "I bought it myself, had it fixed up."

"That's awesome," he said.

"Yeah. Awesome."

I drove to Digger's with the plan to get in and out of there early, before he was too high to transact business. He smoked all day at work, but once he settled in with his Miller High Life and his bong, it was hard to keep him focused. After he had been home for a few hours, spent some time in his own head, he started to get paranoid too. He'd keep moving to the front window to check the street from behind the curtain and would rock on his bony ass with nervous energy.

When I pulled up in front of Digger's trailer, I turned to Pete before I opened my door. "We're just stopping in to run an errand. You keep your mouth shut while we're here, got it?"

He nodded mutely, apparently good at following directions.

I knocked on Digger's aluminum storm door and waited patiently for him to look out from the top of the curtain covering the window right next to the door, probably with gun in hand—a Walther P38 pistol his grandfather took off some dead Kraut during World War II.

"Who's your girlfriend?" Digger asked as he opened the door.

"Who him?" I asked, feigning some surprise. "He's my kid brother."

"I didn't know you had a kid brother," Digger said as he eyed Pete carefully. "You never mentioned him."

"Yeah, well, he's retarded. I don't like to talk about him," I said as we stepped inside and shut the door behind us.

"What's your name?" Digger asked Pete.

Pete looked to me but kept his mouth shut. "His name is Pete," I said. "He doesn't talk much."

"I guess that's good," Digger said as he slipped the pistol into the waistband of his jeans. Pete followed me meekly into the room and sat next to me on the couch. Digger took his place in the recliner across from us and immediately started loading a bong hit. He held the bong out to Pete, who shot me a questioning look. I gave a barely perceptible nod and he took the bong and the lighter from Digger. "Shotgun," Digger said, and Pete flinched, ducking his head down between his shoulders.

"He means there's a shotgun on the bong," I said. "Here." I held the shotgun while Pete tried to light the shake in the bowl. He kept fumbling the lighter, couldn't hold the lighter and flick it with the same hand. An eternity passed while Digger and I tensely watched Pete struggle to light the bong. Finally I put a stop to the debacle by taking the lighter from him and holding it to the bong myself. When the tube was filled with thick blue smoke I removed my finger and told him to inhale.

Pete's coughing fit lasted for about three minutes, his face getting redder and redder. Digger got him a glass of water from the galley kitchen and Pete struggled to get his coughing under control while Digger and I each took our bong hits and discussed the likelihood of the Patriots making it to the play-offs that season.

I took a QP off Digger and stayed as long as was necessary to be polite. Pete did two more bong hits and had pretty much melted into a puddle on the love seat when I nudged him and told him it was time to go.

"Hey, you're all right, kid," Digger said to Pete. "For a retard, he doesn't say a bunch of stupid stuff," Digger said to me.

"Nah, he's all right," I said.

"You tell your brother," Digger said in a loud, succinct voice, as if Pete had a hearing problem, "from now on, he should bring you around more. Let you hang out."

Pete gave a noncommittal grunt that could be interpreted either way and gave me a look as if most of the time I kept him locked in a basement.

Back in the car Pete tipped his head back on the headrest and rocked it from side to side. "Shit, man," he said.

"What?" I asked.

"I'm fucking stoned."

"Yeah? Well, don't get used to it. That shit will make you stupid."

"I'm hungry," he said as he slid down into the seat and put a foot on the dash. I slapped his leg down, then put the car into gear.

"Yeah, let's hit the diner," I said as I backed the car out. "I could use something to eat. I missed lunch."

I drove us to Dan and Ethel's Diner on Main Street and we got a booth near the window. Pete ate corned beef and cabbage while I had potato pancakes and lox—the Jew in me taking charge when I was stoned. Genes are a crazy thing.

"So, how do you know that guy—Digger—was that his name?" Pete asked me.

"I met him through another guy I know," I said evasively.

"He's weird. You think he really believes all that psychobabble shit about the Colombians putting mind-control chemicals in the cocaine they export?"

I wiped my mouth, then tossed my crumpled napkin on the plate before pushing it aside. "Digger spent some time inside. It made him a little paranoid."

"Inside where?" Pete asked, his brow wrinkled in confusion.

"Inside, inside. In jail, dope."

"Seriously?" he asked, his voice breaking like a twelve-year-old's.

"As a heart attack."

"People call you Sway, don't they?" Pete asked. "I've heard that around school."

"Some do," I agreed. "But if you start calling me that, I'll knock you out."

"Why do they call you that?"

"I have no idea," I lied.

"Are you lying, or you really don't know?"

I leveled a look on him that would shut most people up but he just watched me and waited expectantly. If Pete didn't have many friends, it would not come as a surprise to me. He had a really annoying habit of asking questions, prying in a way that was almost an interrogation.

"Sometimes what we want to be and what the world expects from us are two different things," I said.

"*Tchuh*," he grunted, and laughed. "You don't have to tell me that. Welcome to my world," he said.

TWELVE

FOR THE NEXT WEEK, STUDYING BRIDGET BE-
came my full-time job, and not just because Ken was paying me to get to know her. I figured with what I knew
about her work at the Siegel Center and her brother, I had
enough to give Ken an in, but I didn't contact him to make
a report. With each day, I became more intrigued by Bridget,
the only genuinely nice person I had ever observed. With
knowledge of her class schedule, I could keep track of her
movements during the day and discovered some remarkable
things.

First, she smiled at everyone—not just the good-looking or popular people, but the rejects of society as well. And second, she never showed any interest in using her good looks as a tool or a weapon. Everywhere she went, she left a trail of yearning boys in her wake but she was mostly oblivious.

I managed to run into her accidentally on purpose two more times and each time she greeted me enthusiastically with a warm smile, and took the time to talk to me.

Sometimes I found my thoughts traveling back to Bridget by even the most unlikely paths. Just a glimpse of her in the hallway at school was enough to throw me off balance and disrupt my thought processes.

That was the same week Joey and I obtained access to Travis Marsh's locker. It was Joey who delivered the anonymous tip to Burke about illegal drug activity at Wakefield that inspired the school administration to take action. Travis was busted during a supposedly random search, the local police K-9 unit brought in to sniff lockers while the school was in lockdown.

No one was really surprised when Travis Marsh went down for drug possession, ten hits of X and half an ounce of pot divided into dime bags, all of it in his locker concealed under a duffel bag full of filthy gym clothes. Possession with intent to distribute requires mandatory expulsion from the school system.

Later I heard that Travis did six months at county lockup, but I figured if the nation's tax dollars were going to pay for Travis's care and feeding either way, he might as well spend some time in jail. At least there he had a better chance of earning a high school diploma than he did at Wakefield. Could be it was the best thing that ever happened to him.

I happened to be home from school with a stomachache and general malaise the day of Travis's bust, but kept an eye on the news throughout the day to see if the local media picked up on the police activity at Wakefield. It was just the kind of story the media loved, prompting terrified parents to wonder whether their child was in extreme danger every time he or she entered the halls of their public school, imagining Columbine-like possibilities that could threaten the beautiful and athletically capable. Anti-bullying, empowering the powerless, and parent involvement would be hot topics for a while, until everyone remembered they didn't really give a shit about the weaker kids with limited social skills.

It wasn't long after the school day ended when my doorbell rang, and even though I took my time getting there, the person didn't follow the ring with a knock. A large black guy, with the unlikely name of Carter Goldsmith, stood at the kitchen door. Always laid-back, he would probably have waited a full ten minutes without ever wondering what was taking me so long.

"What's shakin'?" I greeted him as I opened the door and stepped back to let him enter the house. Carter had a ribbon of scar tissue on his temple and short dreadlocks. His six feet four inches and 250 pounds of bulk were scary as shit on the football field, but he was the nicest guy I knew.

Carter was an important ally. His size and strength made him a good heavy, a physical threat that most people would never challenge. And as it was for me with many people, I owned his biggest secret, had guarded it carefully for a long time. He saw it as a debt, but I never really thought of it that way. He had long since repaid me for my services.

"Hey, Sway," he said as he squeezed his frame through the kitchen door and gave me a hand to shake as he gripped my shoulder in a man hug.

As Carter eased himself onto the leather couch, I aimed the remote at the stereo and it clicked on to one of my dad's old CDs. A lot of nights I came home and found Dad sitting in the dark, enveloped in a cocoon of the old folky music he preferred for heavy drinking. Usually Dad was drunk, and sometimes asleep, and I would rouse him from the recliner, encourage him to go to bed so I wouldn't have to look at him in the morning.

Carter began nodding his head in time with the music, "Cecilia" by Simon & Garfunkel. "This is nice," Carter said. "I like this. What do you call this?"

"Simon and Garfunkel," I said.

"Whatsa who?" he asked.

"The music. It's Paul Simon and Art Garfunkel."

"Garfunky? That's a white dude's name?" Carter asked with a chuckle.

"Uh, yeah," I said as I took up the bag of weed I kept stowed on the hidden ledge under the coffee table and started to fill him a bowl. "Yeah, he's white. Jewish, I guess, with a name like Art Garfunkel. It's my dad's music."

"Funny," said Carter, the football-playing philosopher, "you don't have to look at a man's skin but can still judge him instantly by his name. You think someone hears the name Carter Goldsmith they assume I'm black?"

"No, they probably think you're Jewish," I said, "which could help you or hurt you, depending."

"How do you know I'm not Jewish?" he asked, and he sincerely wanted to know.

"Are you?" I asked.

"No."

"Well, being Jewish myself, I can usually spot a tribe member right off. It's not just about the way you look, hard to define what gives it away."

He nodded and seemed to accept my answer. "Your old man's music is my music, my friend," he said as he took the bowl from me and hit it. He offered the bowl back to me and I just shook my head.

"It's good stuff. Creeper," I said as I headed to the fridge and got him a cold bottle of Gatorade, which I kept on hand specifically for Carter's visits. We sat in amicable silence for a little while, listening to music while Carter enjoyed his buzz.

Finally we got down to business and Carter bought three quarters, which I knew he would break into eighths to sell to the other guys on the football team, making a little finder's fee for himself. Nothing wrong with that and it saved me the trouble. Even if Carter got caught, he would never name his source. His word was as good as gold. We owned each other's secrets—a friendship, most people would call it, though caring about other people only promises misery. It's one of the laws of the universe.

It occurred to me that Carter would be the person to understand, the only person I spoke to on such a personal level other than Joey. So I asked him, "Have you ever been in love, Carter?"

"Sure," he said with his easy smile.

"What does it feel like?"

"Feel like?" he asked.

"Yeah, what did you feel like when you were in love?"

"Well, I suppose I felt the same way I do when I jack myself off, but ten times better. You know," he said with a shrug, even that simple gesture an impressive feat of physical strength. "I'm surprised to find you still got your V-card, Sway."

"I don't," I said. "I'm not talking about whether you've ever been laid. I mean have you ever been in love?"

"Oh. I guess if they aren't the same thing, then, no, I've never been in love. Not love like the way you love that guitar of yours."

"I don't play guitar anymore," I said.

"No? I guess that's right. Now that you mention it, I haven't seen you play guitar in . . . a while."

"I'm just wondering," I said, "because I'm not sure what it's supposed to feel like. Love. With a girl, I mean."

"I guess it's like coming," he said. "Until you do, you can't know what it feels like."

"Yeah," I said with a nod, "maybe. But you come, you know what it is. You're in love with a girl, there's no way to know it since you don't know what love feels like."

"I love this kind of bud," he said with a smile as he tucked an arm behind his head and settled back on the couch. "Leads to all sorts of interesting speculation."

THIRTEEN

DAVID COHEN WAS WAITING OUTSIDE THE
door to the library as I was leaving after fourth-period lunch.
He looked stressed and uptight, as was his usual. "Jesse, I
need to talk to you."

"It can't wait until after school?" I asked with a casual
glance at my six to see who might be listening.

"This will only take a second," he said, so I assented
with a nod and he fell into step beside me. "Heather agreed
to go out with me. I need to know what I should do. Where
should I take her?"

"I would suggest Paolo's," I said. "Anytime a guy spends that much money, it puts her in a good mood."

"I'm taking her out this Friday night. There's no way I'll be able to get a reservation on such short notice unless we eat at five thirty with the geriatrics."

I sighed. For a kid who was supposed to have a genius IQ, he wasn't very enterprising. "I'll get you a reservation for eight o'clock," I said.

His face broke into a grin and he said, "You're the best, Jesse."

"Yeah, well, you remember that when it comes time to get your work done."

"I'm on top of it," he called over his shoulder as he walked away.

When I turned around, Joey was blocking my path. "Ken's looking for you," she said as she fell into step beside me.

"I'm doing great, Joe, how are you?"

"I'd be doing a lot better if I didn't have to talk to Ken Foster." A shudder went through her body and she shook her head, as if clearing away a terrible thought. "He's so gross. How do girls find that guy attractive?"

"Tell him to meet me at the bleachers after school. I'll be at practice."

"I'm not your fucking secretary," she said, which I took for acknowledgment of my request. Joey's attitude didn't usually get under my skin, but the past week I had been on edge and couldn't really put my finger on a reason. I chalked it up to being busy, preoccupied with everything going on.

———

Girls' lacrosse offers the kind of raw aggressiveness that is rarely seen in young women, a display that is both sexy and viscerally satisfying. I tried to catch at least a few games during the season and whenever possible took my business meetings on the bleachers during practice.

Ken arrived with his posse in tow, but he told them to wait down by the practice field, then climbed the bleachers to come and sit beside me.

"Why are we meeting here?" Ken asked.

"I like to watch," I said with a nod toward the field. "I think better when I'm watching."

Ken's lip curled in distaste as he surveyed the thick thighs and broad shoulders of the athletic girls on the field. He didn't appreciate the power of their toned bodies, power that was more significant than any fleeting beauty.

"What did you find out?" he asked.

I knew then what had been bothering me, that I didn't really want to tell Ken anything about Bridget I had discovered during my weeks of reconnaissance. It was like capturing a wild animal and putting it in a cage—there was pleasure in the idea of owning the animal, making it tame, but Ken would never appreciate the beauty of the caged bird. After a while, he would forget to care for it properly, would lose interest in preserving what had originally made the pet attractive to him.

My gut tightened as I rattled through my report— filling him in on her brother and his condition, her volunteer work at the Siegel Center—not needing to refer to my written notes. "She's into theater and impressionist art—" I stopped as I saw his eyes start to glaze over. Ken was a stupid clod, the equivalent of pond scum in intellect, and the thought of his sweaty, jockstrap-wearing, buffoon body pressed against Bridget made a sick feeling rise in my gut.

"Wednesday after school, she'll be at the Impressionists in Winter exhibition at the campus gallery," I continued as my head started to hum with a dull ache.

"The what?" he asked with predictable ignorance.

"The impressionists. It's a group of painters from the nineteenth century—you know, Monet, Degas, Renoir," I said as I handed him my report, carefully typed and edited by Kwang, who took dictation over the phone. "I suggest you show up there, accidentally run into her. And I would go alone," I said, cutting my eyes meaningfully at the goon squad as they loitered on the track, shouting rude comments to the girls on the field and laughing at their own jokes. "Put her at ease instead of making her feel like she's about to be gang-raped. You'll just happen to be there, taking in the exhibit. Ask her out for a coffee. She'll say yes."

"How do you know she'll say yes?"

"You pay me to know these things. Just ask her. But look, and this is important, no matter how well your coffee date goes, don't ask her out for a real date."

"Why not?" he asked, exasperated.

"Because that's what she'll be expecting you to do. Hold back. Let her have a few days to think about you and we'll follow it up with the coup de grâce."

"The what?"

"Nothing," I said, suppressing a weary sigh. "Just keep it simple. Leave her wanting more. Got it?"

He nodded as he glanced through the notes on the page. "So, that's it?" Ken asked as he stood to go.

"One more thing," I said. "It's in the report but it's important that you remember it. If you could have one superpower for a day, you would want it to be the ability to heal people with a touch."

"What?"

I repeated myself, slowly, so that even Ken could understand.

"What the fuck are you talking about?" he asked.

"Just remember it," I said, weary with his idiocy. "It's just her thing. She's going to ask you, so remember it."

"Is this really going to work?"

"She's a nice person. If you show an interest in the things that interest her and are moderately charming, it ought to do the trick. Use the line about healing people with a touch and she'll be putty in your hands."

"What do I owe you?" he asked.

"Two hundred," I said, just throwing out the random figure. Normally it would be in my best interest to negotiate a favor from someone like Ken, but I let it go.

After my meeting with Ken, I needed to do something to deaden all self-awareness.

When I got home, I turned to the anesthetic my father relied on. Four shots of whiskey later and I had made up my mind what I would do. Our house, built in the late 1800s, was one of the original houses in town, built at the same time as the university. It was an easy walk to the historic downtown and the collection of restaurants and bars that stayed open long after the shops had closed.

Dad was playing with a trio that evening—one of several bands that he practiced with on a regular basis—at a small club. The doorman recognized me and let me in though it was a twenty-one-and-older crowd after the dinner rush. I sat in the back, hidden in a dark corner, and watched my father as a stranger would. Tonight he played the piano, one of several instruments he could play before he ever learned to read music.

By the time I was thirteen, I had accompanied him at small, intimate shows like this one, and large concert venues where ours was one of many bands. At first I had played only rhythm guitar, backing up his group, but after a while he would give me lead on some pieces, stepping back to hand over the spotlight, though careful always to announce to everyone I was his son. He couldn't stand the thought of letting me take an accomplishment for myself, wanted everyone to know my God-given talent had come from his genes.

It had never been clear if I was a true prodigy, born with some gene that gave me a gift for playing guitar, or if my father had simply made it so through uncompromising expectation and exposure to the broad possibilities of all music. Like my dad, usually if I heard a song once, I could play it back without ever seeing a sheet of music.

Listening to my father play, if my eyes were shut, I could focus on the feeling of the music, the swell of it rolling through my seat like a wave and traveling up my spine, filling my core. I sat in the worn, vinyl booth, the ghost of my mother occupying the seat beside me. I felt her presence the way you can sense another person in your house, even if you can't see or hear them—the groan of a floorboard, the movement of air, the vibration of breath on a heartbeat.

When I was a kid, I had spent many nights like this, watching my dad perform with my mom beside me. I used to resent the gazes of the men around us as their eyes stole my mother's quiet beauty, her willowy figure and thick black curls, for their own fantasies. She was my mother, they saw me with her, but it didn't stop their minds from wandering from her slender wrists to her full lips and mentally undressing her.

And even though he was a dickhead, my dad had always deeply loved my mom. I could see it in his eyes when he looked at her, his complete and total disbelief that this beautiful, soulful woman had chosen him above thousands of other options. I'm sure it had come as a major shock and disappointment when he realized that behind those brown eyes flecked with gold was a broken brain. Yet still he loved her, even after she had made it impossible to live with her.

When Dad stood to take his bow, I was already gone, my hands and face burning with the cold. At home I smoked a joint, then lay on my bed, naked and flat on my back with Weezer playing loudly enough that I wouldn't hear Dad arrive home.

FOURTEEN

MR. DUNKELMAN AND I WERE PLAYING A HAND
of rummy in the rec room of the old folks' home late one
afternoon. I studied the discard pile and made up my
mind to lift the entire pile for a forty-five-point play. He
was holding only four cards, so it was a risky move on my
part, but I liked watching him get pissed about me making a risky play more than I liked winning.

"It's crazy to me," Mr. D was saying. "They can draft you
and send you off to fight in a foreign war when you're eighteen, but they won't let you buy a beer or a bottle of whiskey."

His outrage was not inspired by sympathy for the plight of youth, but by his desire to have beer and whiskey delivered to him in Hell's Waiting Room—his nickname for the place he called home.

"They haven't drafted anyone since Vietnam," I said as I sat back and tried to wait patiently for him to make his move.

"Twenty-one to buy alcohol is absurd," he said, and I covertly rolled my eyes. At the rate this game was going, I'd be an old fart myself before either of us reached five hundred points. "By the time I was twenty-one, I had a wife and a job at a glass-cutting shop. And I sure as hell was drinking before that. That's how I ended up with a damn kid in the first place."

"I told you," I said, "if you want me to bring you some beer and whiskey I will, but I'm not going down to that damn VFW hall again. Those guys in the funny hats creeped me out. Why can't you drink at a normal place—like an Applebee's or something?"

"First of all," he said as he studied the cards already in play on the table while I drummed my fingers with impatience, "I'm not letting you bring me beer and whiskey here. If you got caught, we'd both get in trouble. Second of all, I wouldn't be caught dead in some place called Applebee's. Sounds like some damn queer joint." Mr. Dunkelman's social sense had halted development sometime during WWII.

"You sound like an old fart," I said, and he swore under his breath as I put down another thirty points' worth of cards.

My phone buzzed with a call from Joey so I answered it while Mr. D swore at me again for distracting him from the game. "What's up?" I said into the phone.

"Where are you?" Joey asked, her voice tight with strain.

"I'm at the Sunrise Assisted Living place."

"The what?"

I enunciated clearly: "Sunrise Assisted Living."

"What *the hell* are you doing there?" she asked.

"It's a long story." I was having a difficult time managing my oversized hand of cards as I pressed the phone to my ear with my shoulder. "What's up?"

"I need you to come and get me," she said, and from the muffled sound of her voice, I knew she was chewing her thumbnail with worry. Her voice had a strange echoing quality to it, as if she were calling from inside a well.

"Where are you?" I asked.

"At the moment, I'm locked in the bathroom at my house. I need you to come get me. Right. Now."

When I pulled up at the curb in front of her house ten minutes later, Joey came trotting out the front door and hurried down the concrete steps to the sidewalk. Joey's house was part of the historic downtown area, one of the large brick homes that had been divided into apartments for student rentals. I had seen the inside of the first-floor apartment only a half dozen times in all the years I had known Joey.

I climbed out of the car and leaned one arm along the roof of it so I could get a clear view of the glass storm door, where a man stood watching us. Clad only in a white undershirt and faded jeans, he wore his dark hair combed back off his high forehead. The white T-shirt strained against his beer belly and accented his budding man tits.

Joey's eyes were red-rimmed as if she had been crying, and a storm clouded her face. She hugged her sweater tightly around herself, and from the size of her bag I knew she wasn't planning to come home for a few nights.

The man and I watched each other for a minute, him eyeing me with suspicion and anger, me studying his face carefully so I wouldn't forget it.

"Who's that?" I asked.

"Roy Fucking Finnegan," Joey spat. "Mom's latest creepy, dumb-ass boyfriend."

"You okay?" I asked as she yanked open the passenger door.

"Get me out of here," was all she said.

"That his car?" I gestured to the yellow Chrysler at the curb. Joey only nodded, her lips pressed together in a crimped line. I took a moment to capture a picture of the license plate before we drove away.

After we stopped at the corner grocery store for a couple of forty-ounce bottles of Mickey's Big Mouth, we drove in silence to the riverfront park. In the summer, the park was a favorite spot for young mothers strolling with their babies or couples taking a romantic walk along the water. On this fall afternoon, the temperature steadily dropping with the approaching sunset, we had the park to ourselves as we sat on the hood of my car and sipped our beers. Etta James's "My Dearest Darling" poured out of the car windows and drifted on the wind to blend with the rush of water at the fall line of the river.

"I wish my life was like a Taylor Swift song," Joey said.

"Not me," I said. "It's got to suck to be that talented and good-looking."

"I don't mean I want to be like Taylor Swift. I mean that in her songs, the worst thing that ever happens is she breaks up with a boy or gets dumped. If that was the worst thing that ever happened to me, life would be a piece of cake."

I wasn't going to ask Joey what had happened with the guy, Roy Fucking Finnegan. She would tell me what happened if she wanted to, not because I asked.

We were both reclined on the windshield, watching the sky, Joey's head resting on my shoulder.

When she spoke again, her voice was dull and impossible to read. "A few weeks ago, he started coming by when my mom wasn't home. The first time I didn't think anything of it, but the second time I started to catch on. Before today it was just kind of creepy. Today it was . . . creepier."

"Did you tell your mom? About the other times?" I asked.

"You think she cares? She doesn't listen to me. Roy has a job and only hits her when he's drunk. That makes him Mr. Wonderful, as far as she's concerned."

"He put his hands on you?" I asked, keeping my tone neutral.

She shook her head by rocking it against my shoulder. "He stood blocking the kitchen doorway, making it so I had to squeeze past him to get by, you know. He got all close to me with his disgusting beer belly. I pushed him away, told him to keep his hands off of me. That's when I ran and hid in the bathroom." She stopped and took a deep breath, practically gulping air. "I'm not going back there. I'm not going to sleep with one eye open until he dumps her or kills her."

"I'll take care of it," I said as I put an arm around her shoulder and stroked her hair idly. "You stay at my place for the next couple of days, and I'll take care of it."

The sun began its final descent behind the trees, and the air turned suddenly cold. Joey's hot tears soaked the collar of my shirt, and her body quivered with restrained sobs.

"I'm going to take care of it," I said again.

FIFTEEN

"I'M COLD," DARNELL SAID FROM THE BACK-
seat, possibly for the seven hundredth time. "How much
longer do we have to wait?"

"Till the man comes out, dumb-ass," Carter said without
turning to look at Darnell. "Damn, stop talking so much."

Darnell sat back with a sigh, his fingers drumming on
the vinyl seat. Right when the drumming noise became
such a horrible irritant that I was getting ready to say something, the side entrance of the Cat's Eye Pub opened and
out stumbled Roy Fucking Finnegan.

"That's him," I said. We all reached up at the same time to roll our balaclavas down over our faces, the stillness of the night around us almost surreal as we watched him walk to the yellow Chrysler. Roy's breath gusted out as a cloud of steam and he swayed slightly on his feet as he dug in his pocket for his keys.

"Let's do this," Carter said as he opened the car door and slid out of his seat.

It was hard to tell what Roy Fucking Finnegan was thinking as he looked up from the lock of his car door and watched three figures dressed all in black and wearing black balaclavas approach him silently. The cloud of steam around his head dissipated as he held his breath in shock and fear, his eyes widening stupidly as he tried to process what he was seeing.

"Wha—?" Roy started to speak, but Carter lashed out with his improvised weapon, a sock filled with gravel, and took Roy down with a single blow to his shoulder. I glanced surreptitiously around the dark and near-empty parking lot as Carter and Darnell lifted Roy by the upper arms and dragged him quickly out of sight behind the pub.

In the alley, Carter and Darnell held Roy upright against a Dumpster as he moaned quietly, his head rocking from side to side. Darnell had Roy's left arm twisted up behind his back, but he wasn't putting any pressure on yet. Carter gripped Roy by the back of his collar, held him still.

"Hey, Roy," I said, dropping my tone to a low growl to disguise my voice. "We need to talk."

"Who—? Wha—?" He was still dazed from the blow to his neck as I dug in his pocket and pulled out his wallet. I flipped through the credit card holder to see if there was anything of interest and checked the cash pocket—seven bucks in ones. "Take it," he said, his speech slightly slurred, maybe from the alcohol, maybe from getting hit. "Just take the wallet."

"No, thanks," I said. "Look, Roy, I know you aren't exceptionally bright, so I'm going to say this slowly, because I don't like to repeat myself." There was a sickly sweet smell coming from the Dumpster. Instead of watching Roy, both Darnell and Carter were watching me through the eyeholes of their balaclavas, silently waiting.

"You've been stepping out with a woman named Cheryl McCabe," I said to Roy. Pause for effect. "But not anymore. I want you to stay away from her. You don't call her, you don't see her, you don't stop by her work for a drink after your shift. Are you listening to me, Roy?" He was still rocking his head, his eyes squeezed shut against the pain in his head.

"What's she to you, man?" he asked.

I slapped him across the face with his open billfold and he jerked in surprise. "Not relevant, Roy. I want you to stay away from Cheryl McCabe. Do you understand me? Yes or no?"

"Man, screw you. If you're not her boyfriend or something, what's it to you?"

I nodded at Carter and he gripped Roy by a handful of hair on the top of his head. Roy cried out in pain and surprise as Carter twisted his fist and pulled the hair harder. Carter cracked Roy's head back against the Dumpster, ringing it like a gong.

I waited while Roy got himself together and until he

stopped whining about the pain in his head, then said, "Look, Roy, if we're out here talking much longer, these guys are going to be into me for overtime, and you've already cost me too much time and money. So, here's how this is going to go: These guys aren't going to put you in the hospital tonight. They're just going to give you a little taste of what can happen if you don't take my advice."

"She never told me . . . She never said she was involved with anybody," Roy sputtered, his voice rising with fear. "It's her fault, man, if she was stepping out on you. I didn't know nothin'."

"We haven't even touched you yet and you're throwing her under the bus?" I asked. "That's a sign of poor character, Roy. Now, listen, I don't want to have to do anything else to you, but if I so much as see you look at Cheryl cross-eyed, I'm going to burn down that piece-of-shit house of yours. The house is crap, but that's a nice fifty-two-inch flat screen you've got. It would be a shame to lose that."

Finally he was quiet as he thought about what I'd said. I let it sink in for a minute, let him come to the realization that I had been in his house. If you're going to make somebody really angry, it's best to know everything there is to know about them first.

I leaned in to speak closer to his face, to compound his discomfort. "Tonight you're going to need that OxyContin you keep in the medicine cabinet, so I left you just a couple of pills, but those things are habit forming, Roy. I took the rest of them—for your own good, you understand?"

His breath was coming in ragged gasps now and he let out a small, nasal whimper.

As I waited for him to answer, I shot a glance at Carter.

"Man, who are you?" Roy asked.

"Stay away from Cheryl and her daughter," I said in almost a whisper, "or next time, I have you put to bed with a shovel."

I stepped back and gave Carter and Darnell a small nod. "Just give him enough to put him out of commission for a bit so that you can get to the car," I said. "And don't touch his face. Keep it to his body."

I didn't stay to watch, just turned and pulled off my balaclava before I stepped out of the alley. My leg bounced with nervous energy as I waited for Carter and Darnell in the car, the engine running.

A man and a woman came out of the pub, arm in arm, but it was cold enough that they didn't linger. They sat in their car for a minute as the engine warmed and I felt a pang of anxiety that Carter and Darnell might choose that moment to walk out of the alleyway.

"Come on, come on," I muttered to myself, urging the guy to put his car into drive and leave. From my vantage point, I could see Carter at the edge of the building, pulling off his balaclava as he watched and waited for the car to leave. "Good man," I said, again to myself. I should have known Carter was smart enough to think about making sure the coast was clear.

Most people tended to mind their own business, but unless you're actively breaking the law, chances are you would call the cops if you saw two huge guys in ski masks walking out of an alley late at night.

We maintained silence between us until we were far enough away from the pub that we knew no one was coming after us. Carter and I dropped Darnell at home first. I handed Darnell a roll of bills over the back of the seat and he hesitated for a minute before getting out of the car. "Man, that was some crazy shit," he said, but he was smiling. "What did that dude do to you, man?"

"There's nothing personal in it for me," I said. "It's just business."

"You keep your mouth shut," Carter said to Darnell.

"Psht, Negro, please," Darnell said with a swat at the back of Carter's head. "You think I'm stupid or something?"

"I know you're stupid," Carter shot back. "That's why I'm tellin' you."

"Kiss my ass, Goldie," Darnell said, and a gust of cold air signaled his departure.

"Man, that dumb-ass talks too much," Carter said as we pulled away from the curb. "Sorry 'bout that. I won't bring him along again."

"Darnell's all right," I said absentmindedly. "He knew enough when to keep his mouth shut."

"That Cheryl McCabe—that's Joey's mom, huh?" Carter asked. "She okay?" His voice was tight as he rubbed his hands together in his lap, as if trying to clean them.

"She will be. As long as you convinced Roy to stay away from her."

"Oh, we did that. I don't think she'll be having any problems with him anymore."

"Thanks, Carter," I said, and meant it. Violence cost Carter more than it did other people. Even though nobody would fuck with him now, he had already served a lifetime of fear living with his old man.

"No problem, Sway," he said with a nod. "It's no problem."

SIXTEEN

I DIDN'T USUALLY GO TO SCHOOL SPORTING
events other than girls' lacrosse. The Friday game would be
the first football game I had attended since sophomore year.
I stood with my arms rested on the fence that surrounded
the playing field, waiting for Ken and watching the cheerleaders do their opening spiel to get the crowd riled up. The
cheerleaders all wore too much makeup and it gave me the
creeps to see all the older guys at the game—teachers and
dads—watch the cheerleaders' perfectly toned midriffs with
undisguised interest. Cheerleading leads down a dark path

toward a future of working at Hooters, girls being conditioned to believe it was okay for their only social value to come from their looks.

As the team came trotting onto the field, the hum of the crowd rose to a roar and the school fight song pounded through the PA system. Ken caught the salute I gave him and jogged over to stand at the other side of the fence, his helmet resting under his arm. "What's up, Alderman?"

"How did your coffee date go?"

"Good," he said.

"Did she ask you about what superpower you would want?"

"Yeah, I told her the line you said to use."

"And?"

"It made her happy."

"All right, then. Ready for phase two?" I asked.

"Is there an eventual relationship with a girl in my future, or are you and I just becoming besties?"

"Patience, son," I said. "I talked to Bridget today and she said she was coming to the game tonight."

"Yeah?" His gaze drifted to the bleachers as he studied the crowd.

"You find me after the game," I said. "I'll bring her to you."

"What are you going to do?" Ken called after me as I walked away.

"Confidential," I said over my shoulder.

From my vantage point at the top of the bleachers, I saw Bridget when she arrived with two of her girlfriends about fifteen minutes later. Her hair was swept back in a French braid but she still reached up every once in a while to tug at the tendrils of hair that had escaped the braid. Her nervous habit, like everything else about her, was completely familiar to me now. As was the feeling I got in my gut every time I saw her.

At halftime I watched as Bridget and her friends went to the refreshment stand to buy drinks. A guy approached her as she waited in line, one of the kids from the drama club I had seen her with on a few occasions. I knew he was gay, even if he didn't make that fact public, so I didn't really pay it much mind. It bothered me that when I saw her talking to other guys, my hackles would rise. I didn't like the way men looked at her, because I knew what they were thinking when they did.

By the third quarter, a dull ache had started behind my left eye. The drone of the announcer's voice and the horrible selection of music were enough to make my teeth ache. It was no wonder high school students were regularly driven to take the lives of their classmates before taking their own. I mean, One Direction? Really? How does that not violate some child protection law?

When the countdown clock reached two minutes of the last quarter, the loudspeaker pumped out the inevitable Gary Glitter "Rock and Roll Part 2," and by then I thought I might throw up the hot dog I had eaten. I was glad Joey wasn't with me. She would have told me that this assignment wasn't worth any amount of money, and she would have been right. I hated it when Joey was right.

As the rest of the crowd watched the thrilling Wakefield victory, I was moving into position. Bridget stepped into the aisle to start down the stairs just as I was passing her row. The herd was choking the exit, so I'd have a couple of minutes to talk to her.

"Hey," she said with a smile when she noticed me.

"Hey, yourself," I said as we shuffled slowly down the stairs amidst the crowd. The back of her hand bumped mine and the shock it sent through my body almost made me stumble-trip down the stairs. In that brief touch, I felt the coolness of the night air in her skin, her softness. Had she been any other girl, I would have taken her hand then and made sure she knew that I wanted her.

But Bridget wasn't any other girl. She was *the* girl.

The people around us seemed to melt away and my headache dissipated.

"What are you up to?" she asked.

"I'm heading to a party after the game," I said. "What about you?"

She huffed out a little sigh and said, "My dad's picking me up in about thirty minutes. He doesn't like for me to stay out late. I looked for you yesterday when I went to visit my grandmother."

"Yeah?" I asked.

"Yeah," she said. "I was hoping I would see you."

"Why hoping?" I asked.

"I don't know," she said like it was no big thing, but I noticed color rise in her cheeks. Intriguing. "I thought maybe we could get together sometime. Go out for a movie or something."

"You mean like some kind of community service thing?" I asked. "Some kind of outreach program for a beautiful girl to give a totally average guy better self-esteem?"

"I don't think there's anything average about you," she said as she looked at me through hooded eyes. My heart palpitated crazily and I had to take an awkward shuddering breath. "Who are you here with?" she asked, but I was distracted by the sight of Ken looming ahead.

Ken's timing was just about perfect, and damn if he wasn't a ruggedly good-looking son of a bitch, the cut of his perfect physique accentuated by the football uniform. From his advantage of height, he had seen us approaching through the crowd, with eyes only for Bridget.

"Hey, Ken," I said, feigning some surprise at finding him in our path.

"Hey, Alderman," he said.

"Bridget, you know Ken, right?" I said.

"Sure. Of course," she said with a smile, and I could sense Ken's heart reacting to Bridget the same way mine had. "You played a great game."

"Thanks," he said. His smile was somewhat sheepish and he had perfected the "aw, shucks" tilt of his head to such a degree that I imagined it got him laid on a weekly.

"Ken was just saying to me before the game how he thinks the work you do at the Siegel Center is so great," I said casually.

"Really?" Bridget asked as she turned to look on Ken with new eyes. "How did that come up?"

"He was telling me about his cousin Jamie," I cut in before Ken could ruin the conversation. "She has Down syndrome and they were really close growing up."

Ken had started to sputter a little, but I salvaged the situation. "Don't be embarrassed," I said as I gave his shoulder a friendly smack. "I won't tell Bridget there were tears in your eyes while you were talking about how much you hated it when people made fun of your cousin."

Ken shot me a nervous glance, his eyes wide with a question as Bridget's heart started to bleed everywhere. "Jesse," she said with a warning in her voice. "That isn't funny."

"I'm just giving him a hard time," I said.

"You know," Bridget said to Ken. "You should come with me to the Siegel Center sometime. The kids would love it and you can get your community service hours for the President's Volunteer Service Award."

Jesus, people were so predictable. It never ceased to amaze me that I knew them better than they knew themselves. I had given Ken the impression that my plan was somehow premeditated. In truth, the idea for the fake cousin with Down syndrome had struck me during the game, during the third and unnecessary rendition of Queen's "We Will Rock You." Sheer brilliance.

"That would be great," Ken was saying. "It would—" He stalled by clearing his throat, but his hesitation came across as suppressed emotion, so it worked perfectly. "—it would really make Jamie happy to hear that I was doing something like that."

"You should totally bring her," Bridget said with such enthusiasm that I almost experienced a twinge of guilt. Almost.

Here's the thing—I was going to set Bridget up with Ken, fulfill my contractual obligation to him. Had I believed that I was truly capable of loving Bridget, I might not have gone through with it. And anyway, my theory was that once Bridget got to know Ken a little, she would tire of him quickly, would see him for what he really was. I'd just let nature take its course.

I could have used my powers to make her mine. And if you didn't already see where that would get us, you clearly haven't been paying attention up to this point. In the real world, Beauty doesn't fall for Beast and live happily ever after. In the real world, Beast deflowers Beauty. Beast breaks Beauty's heart. Beauty engages in self-destructive behavior like sleeping around too much in college, thereby furthering the negative emotional impact inflicted by Beast. It was a sad story.

"Yeah, well, she lives in Maine," Ken said, and I was impressed by his improvisational skills. Not bad for a meathead. "We spent summers there, when I was a kid."

"Oh, well, you should still come and volunteer," Bridget said earnestly. "You could teach the kids a few football moves. We're working on developing their gross motor skills and building their confidence through sports."

Wow. Baffling. Where did all that goodness come from?

"You too, Jesse," Bridget said, returning her attention to me, whether to keep me from feeling left out or because she really thought I had something to offer the Siegel Center kids, I couldn't be sure. Her lack of self-interest made her difficult to read. "You should volunteer. Pete would love to have you around."

And the Beast reared its ugly head, frightening the poor Beauty and driving her into the arms of her Prince Charming.

"Are you joking?" I asked her. "You think I don't have anything better to do?"

"Hey, easy," Ken said. A gentle warning for me to back off.

And then Bridget's doe eyes were on him and our fates were sealed.

"Whatever, man," I said, "I have a party to get to. You'll wait with Bridget till her dad gets here to pick her up?" I asked as I extended a hand to shake Ken's.

"Yeah, sure," he said as he stepped in closer to her to assume his role as protector.

"I'll see you around," I said to Bridget as I turned to walk away. "Tell Pete I said hey." My tone was casual and indifferent, but I could feel bile rising in my throat and I was sick to my stomach. Truly sick. Even though I knew that giving Bridget the blowoff was the right thing to do, I still hated walking away from her, leaving her with Ken.

SEVENTEEN

SATURDAY MORNING I WOKE IN A STRANGE
bed and for a disorienting moment could not remember
where I was. I felt the weight of another person on the bed
beside me but I didn't open my eyes to see who it was.

After a few minutes, the previous night's events started
to come back to me. A kegger at the Phi Delt fraternity
house featuring some lame local band—more sorority
girls with low self-esteem and spray tans than you could
shake a stick at. The one who lay across my arm was petite
and raven-haired, her face puffy and smeared with makeup.

The old coyote ugly joke came to my mind as I carefully slipped my arm out from under her head.

I switched over to the local radio station as I drove home that morning. I hardly ever listen to regular radio because the music is mostly crap and listening to the radio in a car is like my own personal version of hell—strapped to a seat and forced to listen to the same shite music on a continuous loop. But this morning I was curious to get an update about how things were going at the car wash.

The announcer was a woman speaking with way too much enthusiasm for 11 A.M. on a Saturday, broadcasting live from the Suds 'n' Shine on Main. The Wakefield senior class fund-raiser featured DJ Kiddush, a well-known DJ on the Boston club circuit, who was spinning his mixes of the latest dance music.

Sam Kline had been a student of my dad's, a musician with an incredible talent to play any stringed instrument. He had always been on the small side and was kind of a sickly kid with a slight stammer. His junior year of college, Sam had shaved his hair into a Mohawk, pierced his lip, got contacts to replace his glasses, and started wearing obscure anime T-shirts. He renamed himself DJ Kiddush, bought a MacBook, and flooded social media with his remixes of popular dance tunes.

I pulled up at the car wash to check on my investment and was satisfied to see a dozen cars waiting on line, guys lined up against the side of the building to leer at the university cheerleaders in their skimpy uniforms.

I was in conversation with DJ Kiddush when Gray Dabson approached me with a broad smile, his Adam's apple protruding grotesquely out of his shirt collar. "Hey, Jesse. This is unbelievable," Gray said with such enthusiasm, it made me wince in my hungover state. "Half the town has turned out to get their cars washed by the university cheerleaders. I guess I got the right man for the job when I hired you."

Gray was apparently in his element when he was taking credit for the work of others, one of the most telling signs of a poor leader.

"There's a forty-five-minute wait right now for a wash," Gray continued, oblivious of the fact that I still had not said a word. He was puffed up with his own inflated sense of self-importance. "But not for you, of course. We'll put you right at the front of the line. It's the least I can do." He practically snapped his fingers at a freshman kid who was hovering nearby and called him over to us. "Miles," Gray said, his tone now weighted with some imagined authority, "tell the guys Jesse's car is next and to see that it gets the full treatment."

"Miles," I said, clapping a hand on his shoulder and giving him a slight shake, "if I see you, or anyone else, touch my car, I'll rip off your arm and beat you with it. Understand?"

Kiddush barked out a laugh and shook his head as he put his headphones back over his ears.

"Uh, sure," Miles said, shooting a glance at Gray, who now had beads of sweat on his brow though it wasn't unseasonably warm.

Kiddush held out a fist for me to bump but was already back in his BPM world as I turned to leave. As I strolled away, Gray fell into step beside me and shooed Miles with a discreet flick of his hand.

"The Jammin' Java guys have been selling coffee and pastries all morning to people who are waiting on line. Inviting them to set up coffee and food sales was a stroke of genius," Gray said.

"You're due a thirty percent cut of whatever business they do during the wash," I said as I walked over to say hello to the cheerleaders. "Make sure you get an accounting from them before they leave for the day."

"Yeah, sure, no problem, Sway," Gray said quickly.

"Don't call me that," I snapped.

"Okay . . . uh . . . Jesse, no problem."

The university cheerleaders were laughing and chatting gaily as I approached, searching for the familiar head of auburn hair. Courtney. She was bent over, scrubbing the fender of an Acura; two guys with potbellies, their poor life choices evident from their wardrobe, stood to one side, watching her with undisguised lust. I didn't fault them for it. I had spent most of my formative years under the same spell.

"Hey, girl," I said when I was still about ten feet from her.

Courtney wore an impish smile as she stood to greet me. "Hey, Jesse," she said sweetly. "Long time no see."

"Did you miss me?" I asked, and she laughed and tossed her head back, her auburn hair casting a shimmer of red in the sun. Courtney was one of those good-looking girls made impossibly beautiful by sheer force of personality. As a fourteen-year-old, I'd get a rock-hard boner anytime I got within fifty feet of her. Her parents, close with mine from the time she was four and I just a baby, had spent many evenings at our house. While our parents drank and talked late into the night, we had watched Disney movies in our pajamas on the living room floor.

Courtney was my first love. I loved her in the way only a nine-year-old boy can love a twelve-year-old girl, the first girl I had ever seen naked in person. The first girl who had ever kissed me, even if it was just on the cheek and her lips had been greasy with popcorn butter. The first and only girl to break my heart when she fell in love with a soccer-playing WASP who moved to our town from Baltimore when Courtney was fifteen. At twelve, I had been filled with so much hope, knew that soon my voice would change, I'd grow hair on my balls, and we'd finally be together. But it didn't happen the way I imagined it would. Life never does.

No, she fell in love with the WASPy guy who could bounce a soccer ball on his head like a trained seal, not a twelve-year-old with a Jewfro who played classical guitar.

I was older now, no longer awkward in the presence of the opposite sex, but I felt a flutter in my belly and a chill in my bowels under the glow of her smile.

She came to throw a possessive arm around my neck and held me close. "Guys," she called out to the other cheerleaders working on the Acura, "this is my little brother, Jesse."

The girls all smiled and said hello and I put an arm around Court's waist to give her a brief hug. I was taller than she was now, a small triumph. "How've you been?" I asked her.

"Good. It's good to see you," she said as she reached over to fluff my hair with her slender fingers.

"Yeah?" I asked.

"Yeah. I think about you all the time. I was really glad that you called. I always think about calling but—" She hesitated as she searched for the right words to say, but then gave up. "—well, you know."

"Sure, yeah. You don't have to explain."

"I always think, maybe I could just call him and not mention it, not mention anything about his mom," she said. "But then I start to think maybe that would be weird. You know, you can't just call someone and *not* talk about it."

"And if you don't talk about it, it's still hanging there, like the elephant on the veranda, everyone too polite to mention it," I said, finishing the thought for her. "Damn, girl, you think you need to tell me any of this? I know it. I've been living it."

She squeezed my hand as we moved away from the others to have some privacy. "I see your dad sometimes," she said. "You know, he still sees my folks occasionally. I always look for you when we go to the symphony."

"Yeah?" I asked.

"Yeah."

"Well, I guess it's good to be missed," I said.

"Of course I miss you," she said, giving my shoulder a gentle shake. "I love you like a play cousin."

"Which is why," I said, "I knew I could count on you for today."

"Yeah, I guess there's a sucker born every minute," she said with a smirk and a wry twist of her eyebrows. "You know, instead of going to college, you should think about just running for Congress or something."

"Please," I scoffed, "politicians don't accomplish anything. I would never go into such a futile line of work."

"Then the world will miss out on one of the best bullshit artists to ever play the game," she said.

"Can't bullshit a bullshitter," I said. "You're the best in the business. I stand in awe. Besides, now you can feel good about yourself—supporting your alma mater, the poor, disadvantaged kids who go to Wakefield who will now get a decent homecoming dance and senior class trip."

She laughed and slapped my arm, but it was gentle, like a bird lighting briefly on a branch. "So, what have you been up to? You seeing anybody?" she asked.

"No. You?"

"Not really," she said with a sigh. "I've been hanging around this one guy who's very big into the Greek scene."

"Huh. I thought frat guys were all gay," I mused.

"Oh, you're very subtle," she said, then punched me in the gut and dropped a kiss on my forehead as I bent double to absorb the impact. As she turned away, I found myself studying her, comparing her beauty to Bridget's. Thinking about Bridget in the presence of such charm and beauty was not a good sign.

EIGHTEEN

I DON'T KNOW THE WHOLE STORY ABOUT HOW
things went down between Bridget and Ken. I didn't ask.
Didn't want to know any details. But I started seeing them
walking the halls at school together. I knew from Pete,
who over the ensuing weeks had inserted himself as my
very own sidekick, that Ken now volunteered with Bridget
on Tuesdays at the Siegel Center and was helping her to
organize a 5K to raise money for a therapeutic garden, whatever that is, for the kids she worked with.

Ken was like Frankenstein's monster, reformed into

Mr. Nice Guy under Bridget's influence. Suddenly the worst bully to walk the halls of Wakefield became an advocate for the deformed and powerless. Had I believed that people could change, I would have said Bridget made him a true convert, but knowing people, which is what I know best, I knew the change had to be superficial.

David Cohen accosted me after chemistry again one day that week, looking worried and strung out. It was my habit now to walk the long way to the cafeteria after fourth period so I could pass Bridget's locker. She and I both had early lunch while Ken was stuck in late lunch, so I knew I would see her by herself after fourth period. Sometimes I was caught up in the throng of students moving to the cafeteria and she wouldn't notice me; other times she would see me, her face breaking into a smile. If she saw me, I usually just gave her a nod or a wink, but I never stopped to talk.

"I need money," David said as we strolled along the first-floor hallway.

"I gave you a hundred-dollar advance last week," I said at a volume only he could hear.

"I know, but I need more."

"I'm not running a charitable foundation, David," I said, letting my tone convey a warning. He needed to be put in his place. In truth, I was done with him and had been shopping around for a replacement. There was a freshman in senior calculus I had started to cultivate as David's replacement—a nerdy girl named Hilary. I had assumed she would be vulnerable, easy to take under my wing given her mousiness, but she was driving a hard bargain, demanding almost twice what I had been paying David. I tried to explain to her that the market couldn't support the kind of prices she was quoting, but so far she was unwilling to budge. Eventually Hilary and I would reach a compromise—the hunger was in her eyes, so I knew she wouldn't let the opportunity walk away, and I respected her negotiating skills—but in the meantime I was still relying heavily on David.

"The labs you handed over last week were the sloppiest I've seen from you," I said. "I couldn't even charge full price for them."

David rubbed nervously at the bridge of his nose and shifted his shoulders to redistribute the weight of his backpack. "I was out almost every night last week with Heather, and homecoming is going to set me back four hundred dollars—tux, limo, dinner."

He was full of excuses, which is a sign of poor character. David had been in my pocket since sophomore year but I was wiser now and knew to avoid his type. His intelligence was shallow, useful only for churning out the work high school teachers demanded, but there was nothing original or creative in his work. He cared only about reputation and empty rewards, cared nothing about the satisfaction of a job well done.

"David, I can't keep advancing you money if you're going to turn out a shitty product," I said, stating the painfully obvious.

"I know," he said too quickly, telling me that he wasn't really listening. "I get it. It's just that I bought Heather a really expensive necklace with money from my college savings. My dad found out and cut off my access to the account. The hundred bucks you gave me last week barely paid for dinner and a movie on Friday. I had to tell her I was going to my cousin's bat mitzvah on Saturday because I didn't have any funds to take her out."

How had this happened? Suddenly I'm the guy's shrink, his loan shark, pimp. His behavior was totally unprofessional and now I was getting sucked into a situation where I had to invest time in counseling his personal life.

"Jesus, she's bleeding you dry," I said with disdain. "She's going to ruin you if you don't get out now." We were approaching Bridget's locker and my mind was straying from David's problem.

"No!" he yelped, then checked himself and, after a furtive glance to see if anyone was paying too close attention to our conversation, lowered his voice to say, "No way. I'm getting laid like once a week. She went down on me in the car after I gave her the necklace. Heather is the best . . . the only . . . thing that has ever happened to me. I'm not giving her up."

I stopped to face him in the hallway so my next words would sink in. We had passed Bridget's locker and I caught only a glimpse of her gilded hair over David's head. Now he had ruined the one moment of the day I looked forward to and I was done with his weakness, his lack of self-respect.

"I'm going to give you another hundred against the assignments due in two weeks, but the next time you give me a product I can't sell, I'm cutting you loose." He reacted with a relieved smile, like a junkie who just got a fix.

I held up a hand to silence him and continued, "Now, I'm going to give you some advice, free of charge, and if you're smart, you'll take it. A girl like Heather is poison. She looks fierce and she'll treat you right as long as you're paying for it, but she'll ruin you and never look back. Get out now while you still have a little dignity left."

He wasn't listening to me—had stopped listening as soon as I'd said I would give him some money—and I knew that it was only a matter of time. It was time to get to work on securing David's replacement. In business, emotional attachments are a liability. David had been compromised by his relationship with Heather and was no longer of use to me.

NINETEEN

"DO YOU KNOW HOW BEAUTY IS DEFINED?"
Pete asked me as he thoughtfully contemplated a bite of
omelet on his fork.

"Is this a trick question?" I asked. It was a rainy Saturday afternoon and we were killing time before I stopped
off at Skinhead Rob's to stock up on party favors for an evening of teenage drunken debauchery.

He ignored me and kept talking. "Anthropologists have
done studies to figure out what makes people perceive
someone else as beautiful. It was discovered that in cul-
tures around the world, from Bushmen in Africa to alpaca

herders in Bolivia, the more symmetrical someone's face—
the more even a person's features—then the more beautiful they are considered. It's a universal truth."

"Really?" I asked with a slight frown. "People herd al-
pacas? I thought they were hunted in the wild."

Pete ignored my comment, was really good at ignoring
me, in fact. Even when I was actively trying to irritate him,
he either didn't notice or didn't care.

"Of course, there are other factors," he continued as his
gaze shifted to the window. "With some people it's more
about attitude, the way they carry themselves. Like you. I
mean, you're not ugly—"

"Thanks for saying so." I tipped my water glass at him
in a mock toast.

"—but most of what makes up your appeal is the fact
that you carry yourself with confidence, come across like
you're the man."

"Who says I'm not the man?" I asked as I sat back and
put one arm along the back of the booth and gestured to
the waitress that we were ready for the check.

"My point," he said as he turned back to look me in the
eye, "is that girls are biologically predisposed to be attracted
to a certain male archetype—a guy who has symmetrical
features, tall but not freakishly tall, broad shoulders, big
muscles. Speaking strictly from an evolutionary stand-
point, it just makes sense. No woman would want to mate
with a weak or sickly guy, end up having weak, sickly kids."

"Yeah, okay, I get it. If we ever get shipwrecked and
everyone is starving, you'll be the first one to get eaten. So,
what?" I asked him as the waitress set down our tab on the
table. "Thanks." I unconsciously directed a smile at her.

"Sure," she said. Her hand strayed to the back of her neck and she tugged at a lock of hair that had come free of her ponytail. As she walked away, she glanced back over her shoulder and caught me as I watched her retreating figure.

"See what I mean?" Pete said, almost an accusation.

"What?"

"If I put the moves on a girl like that, she would just roll her eyes, probably tell me to drop dead."

"I'm not putting the moves on anyone. All I did was thank her for bringing the check," I said as I pulled out my wallet. Pete moved to reach in his front pocket and I just gave a slight shake of my head and put my debit card on the table.

"Thanks," he said. "I'll get you next time. But I'm right. You were totally hitting on that girl and she was flirting right back."

"You're imagining things."

"Oh, yeah? When she comes back, ask her for her phone number—see what she says."

"What's your point, exactly?" I asked.

"My point is, no girl is going to look twice at a guy like me because my face is lopsided and I walk with a limp. No one wants lopsided, limping babies, so no one is going to want to sleep with me."

"So, you'll find a girl with low self-esteem and a sweet disposition," I said. "Worse things happen at sea, gimp."

"Ask her for her number," he said as the waitress was walking back to our table.

"You ask her," I shot back.

He just shook his head and looked out the window again as she came to take my credit card. When she brought the slip for me to sign, she hung at the end of the table awkwardly while I wrote in a 25 percent tip.

As she took the credit card slip, she thanked me and leaned a hip against the edge of the table. "I was, uh . . . Well, I was wondering if you're into music at all," she said to me as her hand returned to nervously stroke the wayward lock of hair. "On Wednesdays, there's an open mic night at the Hut, over on University."

"You play an instrument?" I asked her.

"Sort of," she said with a self-conscious laugh. "I play guitar but mostly I'm a singer. Do you play an instrument?"

"No," I said with a glance at Pete, who was muttering to himself as he stared out the window at the passing traffic. "But I am into music."

"Cool. Maybe I'll see you there sometime," she said as she took two steps backwards then turned to walk away.

"I told you," Pete said in a smarmy voice once she had gone. "She didn't even notice I was here."

"She was probably just being polite—ignoring the fact that you're a lunatic, over there muttering to yourself."

"You going to ask her out?"

"Doubt it," I said. "If she goes to open mic night at the Hut, she can't possibly have very good taste in music."

"I guess if you have girls throwing themselves at you all the time, you can just pick and choose the ones you'll grace with your presence."

"I think you're too hung up on the idea that people don't like you because you're funny-looking," I said pensively. "You should consider that it has more to do with your shitty personality."

"You're hilarious."

"I've got to split," I said as I checked my watch and stood.

"I'm going with you," Pete said as he reached for his bag.

"Not today, gimp. I can't take you where I'm going."

"Why not?" he asked.

"Because Skinhead Rob is bad news. Anything can happen when you're dealing with an individual as crazy as he is."

"You actually know someone whose name is Skinhead Rob?"

"He doesn't call himself Skinhead Rob," I said. "He's a skinhead whose name happens to be Rob."

"Why are you friends with a guy who's a skinhead?" Pete asked, his voice rising in the way it did when he was frustrated with me.

"I don't send him a Christmas card every year, Pete. I just buy things from him."

"But still," he said, frowning, "aren't you Jewish? Don't skinheads hate Jews?"

"Sure, they hate just about everybody who isn't a WASP—they even hate gays, and cripples like yourself." I acknowledged the middle finger he shot me with a small nod. "But he knows it would be impossible to get ahead if he dealt strictly with Aryans. Skinhead Rob may be crazy but he's a practical businessman."

"If he's so dangerous, why do you go there by yourself? Why aren't you worried that something might happen to you?" Pete asked.

"I don't trust him, because I'm not stupid, but I sure as

hell don't want to have you with me if the cops decide to-day is the day to take him down, or if Rob suddenly goes postal. Your sister would kill me."

He shot me an ugly look but didn't pursue the argu-ment any further.

"We'll hang out tonight," I said as I walked away. "I'll pick you up."

As I drove away from the diner, I felt my shoulders get-ting tight. Dealing with Rob was always unpleasant. I just hoped Grim wouldn't be there. Just the thought of seeing Grim made my testicles shrink into my abdomen.

TWENTY

SKINHEAD ROB LIVED WITH HIS MOTHER, A
petite woman with wiry, washed-out blond hair, who had
been broken by life. Rob was the product of her first marriage with a guy who had been in and out of prison since
Rob came out of the womb. His younger sister was the
spawn of a different man and was only about fourteen. Her
brother treated her like crap but was strangely protective
when it came to guys showing any interest in her. Not that
many guys would. She was small for her age and had a boy-
ish figure, her skin pale, a network of blue veins showing
in her forehead.

I went to the back door, which opened into Rob's basement room, dark and dank and smelling like musty laundry. Black light posters adorned the walls, and a large swastika flag hung suspended from the ceiling over the bed. There were several bookshelves filled with books, meant to demonstrate Rob's ideologies more than actual evidence he could read—*Mein Kampf, Eugenics, The Fountainhead,* and, oddly, the Narnia Chronicles.

"Hey, Rob," I said with a curt nod as I held back a hand to keep the storm door from slamming behind me.

"You're late," he said without taking his eyes from the forty-two-inch television that stood on a stack of plastic milk crates at the end of his bed. I knew without looking that he was watching a Mel Gibson film—Skinhead Rob's personal hero because Mel was an anti-Semite and a Holocaust denier. It seemed to me that wearing a mullet like Mel's was more of a crime than eating latkes, but I carefully guarded my opinions around Rob.

Though he called me out for being tardy, I wasn't convinced time had any real meaning for Rob. He didn't leave his basement lair very often. At least not during daylight hours. His skin was as pale as winter sunshine, his eyes such a dark blue, they looked almost black, like a shark's, devoid of all emotion. The strip of hair down the center of his head was wispy and too black for the color to be natural.

I didn't apologize for my lateness. Deferring to Rob would be a sign of weakness, and he preyed on the weak. I changed the subject to business, the only language Rob and I had in common.

"I'll take fifty hits of X off your hands if you've got it," I said.

"Where's that girl of yours? I like it when you send Joey to see me," he said as he reached for a pack of cigarettes and a lighter.

"I don't know. I don't see the girl socially," I lied.

"Yeah," he said with a nod. "She's the frigid type. Makes up half of her appeal."

I shrugged, feigning indifference, knowing I would never again send Joey to this place to run an errand for me.

"Hey, there's a concert I want to see—next Thursday night—but it's sold out. You think you could get tickets for me?" he asked as he stood and went to the large safe that stood in the laundry area and began working the combination.

"Yeah, sure," I said. "What's the show?"

"Voivod."

I nodded. "No problem. I'll make a few calls."

"You know," he said as he dug around inside the safe and counted pills into a bag, "you're all right. Grim's always saying I shouldn't trust you, you know, shouldn't trust a Jew, but you're not bad."

"Yeah, well, you know, I'm only half Jewish," I said.

"Oh, yeah?" Rob asked, oblivious of my cheekiness. "I guess that's not so bad, then. Not like you're black or a queer or something."

Jesus wept.

Suddenly the room felt small, like the walls were closing in, and I craved fresh air and sunshine on my face. I dug in my pocket for a wad of cash, wanting to speed things along and get out, the menace of this place palpable.

Just then, there was a creaking noise as the basement door opened and a pair of legs appeared on the basement steps. I quickly slipped the money back in my pocket and casually leaned back on the heel of my hand as if I were just hanging out.

Rob's sister appeared carrying a basket of laundry. Clad only in shorts and a skimpy tank top, the outfit on her scrawny frame was indecent. I directed my eyes at the floor, as if just by looking at her, I was somehow in violation. She watched me, her expression blank and stupid.

"Hey," I said with a nod, resting my gaze anywhere but directly on her.

"What the fuck?" Rob swore as he slammed the door of the safe.

I jerked at the sound of his voice but his anger barely registered with his sister. She was still watching me, like a rabbit hoping if it didn't make any sudden moves, it wouldn't end up as someone's dinner.

"I told you to knock, you dumb-ass!" Rob shouted.

She kept her gaze fixed on me, as if asking me to step in and say something to calm Rob. For a long minute I was rapt, seeing her entire pathetic existence through the windows to her soul. Like an animal raised in a cage, she had never known anything different, yet there was a longing for salvation all the same. Then the shutters came down again and her expression took on the bovine acceptance of a life that offered only the promise of pain.

Rob knocked the laundry basket roughly from her hands and gave her a shove. She cried out, more from fear than from pain, and lurched halfway back up the stairs before turning on him and screaming, "I'm going to tell Mom!"

"Go ahead!" Rob shot back. "And then I'll black both your damn eyes, you worthless little shit."

She was crying as she slammed the basement door, Rob growling and muttering to himself as he went back to the safe. In a moment he returned with a wrinkled brown paper bag and tossed it into my lap.

My feet itched to be moving as I waited for him to count the wad of cash and I didn't take the time, as I usually would, to verify he had given me the correct number of hits.

As I emerged from Rob's lair, I took a deep breath, had not realized until that moment that I had been taking only small sips of the toxic air in Rob's basement. I walked to my car knowing it was the last time I would visit this place.

TWENTY-ONE

THAT NIGHT DAD HAD A GIG, SO I HAD THE
house to myself. My phone had been buzzing with texts
since early in the evening but I ignored them. They could
wait. There was an incoming call as I stood at the sink
combing my hair after a shower. Pete. I answered.

There was a brief pause after I answered, then Pete's
voice, low, almost a whisper. "Jesse?"

"Yes."

"You told me we were going to hang out tonight," Pete
said, sounding pissed.

"We are. I just finished getting ready," I said as I smoothed my hair forward with the palm of my hand and took one last look in the mirror. "I'll come pick you up."

"It's nine o'clock!" he cried.

"So?" I asked.

"My parents aren't going to let me leave at nine o'clock at night. Where would I tell them I'm going?"

"Shit, I don't know, Pete," I said. "They're your parents. Tell them whatever you want, or don't tell them anything. Whatever."

"You mean sneak out?" he asked, his voice rising in alarm.

"Or just walk out. Jesus, relax. I'll be there in ten," I said, and cut the connection before he could start whining about something else.

When I pulled up in front of his house, Pete was sitting at the curb, concealed by a parked car. "Where are we going?" he asked as he fastened his seat belt.

"To a party."

"What kind of a party? Will there be alcohol there?" he asked, grilling me, which was just his way.

I frowned. "What other kind of party is there?"

"Why are we going so late?"

"This isn't late, Pete. Ten o'clock is early unless you're four or forty," I said as I turned the volume back up to listening level.

"What the hell are you listening to?" he asked.

"*Faust,*" I said. "An opera by Gounod."

"You listen to opera?"

"Doesn't everybody?" He couldn't tell if I was being

ironical so just shut his mouth for the ten-minute ride to the party, which was some kind of personal record for him.

I didn't need the GPS to tell me we had arrived at the house, since there were a half dozen guys staggering around the front lawn shouting and carrying on as two of their buddies wrestled on the ground engaged in some kind of pseudo-homosexual mating ritual.

A small crowd of girls in too-short skirts huddled around the front stoop, oblivious of the fact that the guys were too preoccupied with touching each other to notice them. The house was thumping with bass from music that was un-identifiable from where we sat.

"Man, I've got to stop showing my face at high school parties," I said with a weary sigh. "This is a shitshow."

"Is a shitshow good or bad?" Pete asked.

"Nothing is either good or bad," I said absentmindedly, "only thinking makes it so."

"What's that? Like poetry or something?" Pete asked.

"You talk a lot," I said, but he ignored my observation, his usual MO.

"Looks like we're the last ones to get here," he said as he waited for me to open my door first. I didn't, just sat back in my seat while I surveyed the scene on the lawn.

"It doesn't matter," I said. "The party doesn't start until I get here."

"Oh, yeah?" he asked smartly. "You're just so god-damn popular, they couldn't possibly have a party without you there?"

"I bring all the party favors," I said. "They're all waiting for their hits of X, their dime bags."

"What do you—? You mean you're a drug dealer?" he asked, his voice rising to a squeak. "Are you serious?"

"What did you think I was doing at Digger's?" I asked. "Buying a quarter pound of pot to smoke myself?"

"I don't know," he said. "I didn't think you were a dealer. Oh man, you're going to get my ass arrested."

"I'm feeling a lot of judgment coming from a kid who drools and has a bum leg," I said.

"Fuck you," he said, his voice dropping back down a couple of octaves, his hand unconsciously straying to his lower lip to test it for wetness.

"Attaboy," I said.

"You can be a real asshole, you know that?"

"Yeah. Come on."

The house was a disaster—the ubiquitous red Solo cups covering every surface, girls dancing badly on the couch, and the detritus of a respectable home scattered on the floor—but people seemed still sober enough that things were mostly under control.

We were only about a dozen steps into the house when Carter's voice boomed across the open living area. "A-yo!" he called out. He was a full head taller than anyone else in the room and from his vantage point he had seen us right away. The crowd parted and Pete fell into step behind me as I made my way to Carter's side. Once I was within reach of Carter, he pulled me into a tight hug—not a man hug, a real hug—giving me a slight shake before letting me go. "Hey, Sway," he said as he steadied me on my feet.

"Hey, Carter," I said, and pulled a dime bag from my inside pocket and palmed it to him. "My compliments."

"Man, I love this guy," Carter said to Pete, who was now standing beside me, trying to appear casual and failing miserably because his mouth gaped in astonishment at the sights around him. The music was loud, Katy Perry it sounded like, though most of that shite pop music sounds the same to me. Girls were dancing with each other while guys stood around in a circle watching them, leering and making rude suggestions. Sadly, these were the guys who would end up getting laid that night. It's one of the laws of the universe that if you make a move on every girl you see, a certain percentage can be counted on to put out. Some guys are more into quantity than quality.

Two girls came dancing up to us as we stood talking to Carter, giggling and yanking the hems of their short skirts down, and the necklines of their low-cut shirts up. "Hey, Sway," the shorter, prettier, blonder one said to me and then snaked an arm around my neck. Her breath had the sickly sweet smell of a malted beverage and her lip gloss was laid on like cake icing.

"Don't call me that," I said, and twitched a shoulder to shrug her off.

"You have any X?" she asked me. "I want to feel sexy tonight." As she said this, she rubbed herself against me like a cat.

"If you've got twenty dollars, I've got a hit of X for you, Maria," I said.

She stuck her lower lip out but reached into her bra and pulled out two crumpled twenties. "I want two. Who's the freak?" she asked, finally noticing Pete, who was studying her cleavage so closely, I don't think his eyes had made it to her face.

"This is Pete," I said. "He's my cousin. He goes to boarding school in Switzerland, but he fucked up his knee in a snowboarding accident so he came back stateside to recuperate."

"For real?" Maria asked, now eyeing Pete with genuine interest.

"For real," I said.

"Switzerland?" she said, talking to Pete now. "You rich or something?"

"No, Maria," I said with a grin for Carter's benefit, "it's one of those charity Swiss boarding schools for poor kids."

Pete still hadn't said a word but Maria detached herself from me and went after Pete, throwing herself on his wealth like a soldier protecting his platoon from a live grenade.

"I'm Maria," she said, but Pete still hadn't looked up from her cleavage so maybe didn't catch her name. "Come on," she said, and pulled him along by the arm as she walked away.

Pete looked to me, his eyes wide with uncertainty, but I just turned back to my conversation with Carter.

It was about an hour later, while I was looking for a bathroom that wasn't being used as a vomitorium, when I ran into Bridget at the bottom of the stairs. She had a red Solo cup in her hand but she seemed steady enough.

"Shouldn't you be home polishing your halo?" I asked her.

"I thought I told you, Jesse," she said, deadpan, "I'm determined to like you even though you don't want me to."

"You were serious about that?" I asked.

"Very. Pete talks about you nonstop—Jesse said this, Jesse did that—he practically worships you."

"Yeah?" I asked, feigning some surprise. "Where is he tonight?" I was not taking any responsibility if she saw her baby brother out drinking with the delinquents.

"Home. My parents have a pretty strict curfew," she said, her nose wrinkling slightly in distaste. "I'm staying over at a friend's house, the only reason I'm out this late. My parents would freak if they knew I was here."

"They won't hear it from me," I said earnestly.

She laughed and poked me in the chest playfully and, *Jesus,* I had to fight the urge to grab her and cover her mouth with mine. "Who are you here with?" she asked.

"I came alone," I said, hoping Pete didn't choose that moment to make an appearance. "What about you?"

"I came with Ken," Bridget said just as he walked up behind her, his eyes widening when he saw she was talking to me.

"Hey, Alderman," Ken said as he put a hand on Bridget's hip and then let his hand slide down so it rested on the rise of her perfect butt cheek.

"Hey, Ken," I said, studiously avoiding even a glance at his hand while my blood simmered.

"I was just telling Jesse that he's become Pete's new personal hero," Bridget said wryly as she turned into Ken's embrace and leaned against his perfectly cut torso.

"Is that right?" Ken asked, his tone friendly enough but his eyes narrowing with suspicion as he studied my expression.

There was a sudden commotion in the room as people started to chant encouragement for a guy who was shotgunning a can of beer. Ken was distracted by the activity but I caught Bridget's sidelong glance of reproach. She and I exchanged a look full of meaning while Ken laughed loudly at the spectacle.

Ken moved to join the crowd cheering on the douche bag as he shotgunned the beer. "Good times," I said.

"Yeah," Bridget said with a sigh. "I guess. I never really came to parties like this until I started hanging out with Ken."

"I didn't know you and Ken were 'hanging out,'" I said casually. "Are you seeing each other?"

"He's been helping me at the Siegel Center with the kids so, yeah, we've sort of been . . . seeing each other."

"I thought you were only interested in dating ugly guys," I said. "Ugly guys with a good heart. Isn't that right?"

"Yeah, okay, Ken's good-looking. But he's also a good person. At least he's not afraid to tell me how he feels about me. You know, it doesn't really matter if a guy likes you if he doesn't *tell you* he likes you." She delivered this challenge with a sweet smile.

We played the silent game again.

Seriously, I was usually a world-champion silent-game player. But I lost. Again.

"What's that supposed to mean?" I asked.

"I'm just making conversation," she said, all innocence.

"You know," I said, "you might like to think you know

me, but you don't. You're not as smart as you think you are."

"I know enough," she said. "I'm not as naïve as you like to think I am, *Sway*." I hated the sound of my nickname in her voice.

"I don't like to think about you at all," I said.

She opened her mouth to respond but before she could get a word out Ken interrupted her. "Hey, Bridge!" he shouted, and I found myself bristling at the unflattering nickname he used for her.

For a few heartbeats she hesitated and I thought she might ignore him and stay with me. Ken called her name again and waved for her to return to his side. Ken was unsteady on his feet, swaying slightly as he held on to the couch and waited for Bridget.

"I guess I should go," Bridget said.

"Is Ken driving you?" I asked.

"This is just a Coke," she said as she tipped her cup at me. "I'm the DD."

"I wasn't worried," I said. "I'm just making conversation."

I winked at her and continued up the steps in my search for a bathroom.

TWENTY-TWO

BY ABOUT 2 A.M., THE PARTY HAD WOUND down to the slow-dancing, date-rape part of the event. Once Ken and Bridget left I went in search of Pete since I hadn't seen him for a couple of hours. I finally found him in the master bedroom, lying spread-eagle on the king-size bed, asleep but, thankfully, not dead. His eyelids fluttered open when I nudged his leg and he looked at me, dazed, maybe not remembering where he was.

"You loaded?" I asked.

"I think so," he groaned, "unless the room is really spin-ning."

"Let's get out of here," I said, helping him to locate the missing articles of his clothing and get dressed. I supported his weight as he stumbled down the stairs.

Carter was waiting for us—I had said I would give him a ride home—and he smiled broadly when he saw Pete struggling to keep his feet.

"And a good time was had by all," Carter said.

"I don't feel so good," Pete moaned.

"You'll feel better after some breakfast," I said as Carter took Pete easily under the armpit and together we steered him toward the door.

Carter deposited Pete in the car, then folded himself into the front seat.

"Oh, God, I can't even think about food. I think I'm going to throw up," Pete said as he started to roll down his window.

"There's a plastic bag under the seat," I said with a nod toward the passenger seat. "If you need to be sick, do it in there. Some cop sees you heaving out the window, you'll get me pulled over for sure and I'll be in jail until I'm too old to get accepted to a decent college."

He fumbled under the seat for a minute, then spent the rest of the ride with the bag gripped in his lap, his eyes closed and head tipped back against the headrest.

I drove to Dan and Ethel's Diner, where Pete and I ate corned beef and runny eggs with coffee, and Carter ate a pile of pancakes smothered in an obscene amount of maple syrup. Pete put so much milk and sugar in his coffee, it might as well have been a milk shake, but the caffeine seemed to help him. Carter sat next to Pete, who was crammed against the inside wall of the booth with Carter's bulk filling three-quarters of the space.

"That was . . . incredible," Pete said.

"Yeah?" I asked absently. "She let you into her lady cave?"

"They were both there. It was dark, the room was spinning. I'm not really sure what all happened, but I think I fooled around with both of them."

"Oh, man," Carter said. "The trifecta. It's every man's dream."

"It's the X," I said around a mouthful of corned beef. "Makes people horny."

"But now they think I'm some rich kid who goes to boarding school in Switzerland," Pete said as he carelessly wiped his mouth with a paper napkin and tossed it on the table. The first couple of times I ate across from Pete, I had been put off by the ever-present drool that pooled at the left corner of his mouth, but I was used to it now.

"So?" I asked. "What do you want to do, marry 'em?"

"Well, no"—and his face broke into a lopsided smile— "but I wouldn't mind doing it again."

Carter and I both laughed and Carter pounded Pete on the back with the flat of his massive hand.

"What I'm trying to figure out," Pete said as he shoveled another forkful of food into his mouth, "if that's what sex is like, why people aren't doing it all the time. Why do people do anything else?"

"One of the mysteries of the universe," Carter said in agreement.

"Yeah, you're screwed now," I said. "Won't be able to think about doing much else."

"It's not like I was thinking about much else before I did it," Pete said with a sly grin. "It's possible I hold the world record for jacking off the most times in one day—"

"I doubt that," I said. "There are some sick fuckers out there."

"—but now that I know what it really feels like to be with a girl . . ." His eyes started to glaze over and we were losing him.

"Eat up," I said. "Sun will be up soon and I seriously don't need to have you in my car if your parents wake up and have the cops out looking for your disabled ass."

Carter laughed. "Sway, you are one messed-up dude sometimes."

"Why do you call him that?" Pete asked. "Sway?"

"Because he is sway," Carter said simply.

Pete looked at me but I just shook my head and turned to stare out the plate-glass window at the deserted main street.

"But what does it mean?" Pete asked.

"You never heard of sway?" Carter asked, baffled by Pete's question.

"No."

Carter shrugged. "Sway isn't something you can define. A dude who's got sway is the man—doesn't have to try to be cool, just . . . is. Jesse's as cool as the underside of my pillow. He's so slick, he could convince you that I'm white, have you believing it like it's gospel." Carter turned his attention to me as he said, "I thought you were schooling this boy?"

TWENTY-THREE

IT WAS BITTERLY COLD BY THE MIDDLE OF October. The sky assaulted us almost daily with stinging rain or sleet, and the gloom of a Massachusetts winter started to set in hard. The Wakefield microcosm was rocked by one of its worst football seasons since the Eisenhower administration. Ken, captain of the team, was too preoccupied with coaching the kids at the Siegel Center, and trying to get into Bridget's pants, to pay much attention to taking the team all the way. The first game against crosstown rival Buford High was a blowout. They delivered a punishment of 42–0.

Wakefield's star student, David Cohen, who after the midterm grade report would drop to a disappointing fifty-first in his class, fumbled the annual Battle of the Brains regional academic competition. David was too busy getting hand jobs from Heather in his dad's old Volvo to care about the academic reputation of Wakefield, a bafflingly dim reputation considering more than half the student population had at least one parent who taught at the college.

Since it was the major employer in town, most of the kids who grew up here had at least one parent who worked at the college, but Buford High, for the most part, hosted those students whose parents served food to, or collected the garbage of, the literati. That its student body consistently outshone Wakefield in almost every measurable academic marker had confounded the school system patriarchs for decades.

David had been one of Wakefield's few shining lights, eclipsed only by the football and hockey programs, which were known for graduating its players to acceptance at schools like University of Michigan, Ohio State, and Nebraska—schools where, if news reports were at all reliable, middle-class girls with impossibly blond hair were frequently roofied at frat parties.

For a while Principal Burke had been flying high after Travis Marsh was expelled. Burke tried promoting a new vision of a Wakefield High School where school spirit could be expressed through the jelly bracelets that went out of fashion in 2006. The school spent close to a thousand dollars on the plastic bracelets in the Wakefield colors of green and white, the words WARRIOR PRIDE inscribed on them. The students refused to wear them, as did most of the faculty, and all but a few ended up in the local landfill. Pep rallies became a regular venue where Burke talked about Wakefield Warrior pride and other ridiculous concepts. I used the assembly periods to catch up on my e-mail and texts.

Now Principal Burke was at a low point and anarchy threatened his reign. Burke's moment of glory after Travis Marsh's demise had been an illusion, his control of the student body only superficial. Battle of the Brains was a disappointment, a minor letdown, but when the football team started a downward spiral, a losing streak of six games, you could see Burke was starting to feel the strain.

When I shut my locker door I found a skinny kid standing there, just watching me, a hopeful look on his face. I cocked my head in question and waited for him to speak. He didn't for a minute, just shifted his backpack, which seemed to weigh more than he did, to his other shoulder and cleared his throat. I took the time to notice him, figuring most people didn't. He was the kind of kid who faded into the wallpaper, lost amid the beautiful and athletically capable, with oily brown hair and a smattering of freckles on his nose, unremarkable in every way.

"Can I help you?" I asked.

"You're the guy they call Sway," he said. Not a question.

"Some do," I agreed.

"You've been hanging around that special needs kid. Pete Smalley."

"I didn't know about the special needs part," I said. "He never mentioned them."

"You friends with him?" he asked, squinting one eye with judgment.

"I've got a class to get to," I said. "Is there going to be an eventual point to this conversation?"

"I heard Pete got laid," he said.

"Not by me."

"Suddenly he's one of the chosen," the kid said, sounding like he was on the offensive though I still couldn't figure what his angle was. "You start hanging out with him, he gets laid, he goes to all the parties—I even saw a cheerleader say hi to him in the hallway."

"And?" I asked, trying to keep the weariness from my voice.

"My parents went out of town last month," he said, "and I had a party at my house. I got two kegs and made a hundred Jell-O shots with vodka. You know who showed up?"

"I don't," I said thoughtfully, "but I have a bad feeling you're going to tell me."

"The guys from my LARPer club. That's it. The six of them and one fat chick who's a sorceress."

"A sorceress? Like she can do magic?" I asked. I pride myself on the fact that virtually no one can take me by surprise, but this was a new one on me.

"Yeah, magic, spells and potions."

"If she can do magic, why is she fat?" I asked.

He searched my face to gauge whether I was putting

him on. "She can't really do magic. She plays a sorceress when she does role-playing. Anyway, she put out, but not for me. The whole thing was a freaking bust."

"Huh," I grunted noncommittally. "Well . . ."

"Andrew."

"Well, Andrew. I'm late for class now so I'd better hit it. It's been . . . interesting talking to you." I started to walk away but he fell in step with me like a puppy tripping at my heels.

"Wait," he said. "Everyone says that you can get things, do things for people. I want to hire you."

"I don't know where you're getting your information, but anyway, I'm busy. Senior year, college applications, all that stuff," I said.

"I heard you got early acceptance to Harvard," he said, "that you know someone and got early acceptance because the person in charge of admissions owed you a favor."

My face broke into a smile but I didn't look at him as I said, "I hadn't heard that rumor before. It's a good one."

"So, it's not true?" he asked, sounding a little disappointed.

"It's not a bad idea—Harvard," I mused aloud. "Lots of kids with money there. Person with the right kind of connections could make a fortune. Course, then you're stuck going to school for another four years with a bunch of douche bags."

I stopped outside the science and math wing and pulled open the door just as the final bell was ringing. It was quiet now, Andrew and me the only ones still in the hallway.

"Wait," he said again, his voice a strangled cry. "I want

your help. I can pay you." He held up a roll of cash the size of my fist. "It's seven hundred fifty dollars. Everything I saved from working over the summer."

I let the door drop shut and looked back over my shoulder to see if there were any witnesses. "You stupid or something?" I asked. "Put that away."

Chastened, he shoved the money back into his pocket, his gaze dropping to the tops of his shoes. I suppressed a weary sigh when I saw his chin quiver. He sniffled loudly and wiped a sleeve across his nose in a childish gesture.

"What do you think I can do for you?" I asked.

He was silent, searching for an answer, but none seemed to come.

"I can't help you if you don't know what you want," I said.

"I want . . . I want to be popular," he said.

"I don't work miracles, Andrew," I said. "My abilities have human limitations."

"I just want people to like me," he said in that same whiny way Pete would get. "What makes everyone like you, but not me?"

I had the hall door open again and was halfway through the doorway when I stopped to ask, "You think people like me? Is that what you think?"

"Everyone knows you, invites you to all the parties," he said lamely. "All the girls want to date you."

"That's not what I asked you," I said, wondering why I was even making the effort with this kid.

"Who cares if they like you? They want to be you," he said, now talking to me like I might be simple.

"Don't be an ass," I snapped. "You've made me late for class."

"Are you going to help me?" he asked.

"I'll think about it," I said, and let the door fall shut between us.

TWENTY-FOUR

IT WAS A FRIDAY NIGHT AND I HAD MADE MY
usual rounds, hit the frat parties where I had regular cus-
tomers. I ended up at the diner for a late-night meal with
Carter and Darnell, who were shooting the shit after a round
of burgers and fries.

The guys were causing a bit of a ruckus, people around
us starting to look our way, including the owner of the
diner, who shot us warning looks whenever he looked up
from the cash register.

Darnell, who was always the loudest in any group, caught
the ugly stares of the owner and shook his head. "Man,

Asian people are always hatin' on black people. We just spent thirty dollars in his restaurant and that dude's been giving us dirty looks since we sat down."

"What are you talking about? Not all Asian folks hate black people. Look at Jackie Chan. He's down with the brown."

"Wu-Tang Clan's tight with the Asian folks," Darnell said with a stoner's nod, his eyelids sleepy from the kind bud. "All those West Coast rappers've got an in with the kung fu dudes."

"Wu-Tang Clan is East Coast," Carter said with a chin thrust to make his point.

"I think I know my rappers, Goldie," Darnell shot back. "Isn't that right, Sway?"

"Carter's right," I said as I sipped at my coffee. "Wu-Tang was East Coast."

"Man, what d'you know about it, white boy?" Darnell said with a dismissive wave of his hand.

"He knows enough to know Ghostface Killah wasn't hanging around no Tupac," Carter said before I could respond to Darnell's accusation of being white.

"Whatever, man." Darnell sucked sharply at his teeth. "Forget you, forget this place. There's a billion other Asians who hate black folks."

"Man, what'd I tell you?" Carter said with a lazy gesture toward Darnell. "This boy talks too damn much."

"Some white girl is looking over here," Darnell said with a frown. "White people are haters too."

"Man, I'm right here," I said, and Carter laughed.

"It's a compliment," Carter said. "You and Jackie Chan are both down with the brown."

After I dropped Carter and Darnell off at Carter's house I drove home, so tired I just wanted to climb into bed and fall immediately into unconsciousness. I was brushing my teeth when my phone rang. I recognized the number though I had never programmed the owner's name into my phone to prevent myself from ever drunk-dialing it.

"Hello," I said in a voice that suggested I didn't know who was calling.

"Jesse, it's Bridget. Did I wake you?"

"It's eleven thirty," I said in a tone that clearly implied eleven thirty was absurdly early.

"I know," she said. "Sorry to call so late."

I didn't ask her why she was calling. Girls don't like it when you ask them obvious questions like that. I had learned that well enough from hanging out with Joey. But when you didn't ask, they liked to get in a huff because you weren't being sensitive to them when they wanted to talk.

Still, if you were going to lose either way, it's better to lose without saying anything so it can't be held against you later.

"Aren't you going to ask why I'm calling you so late?" she asked after a brief silence and I smiled at her predictability.

"Okay," I said. "Bridget, why are you calling me after your bedtime?"

"I just needed to talk to someone. Is that okay with you?" I had never heard Bridget sound so snide before and was curious what was wrong with her, though I didn't ask, because of the aforementioned rule for getting along with women.

"Have you been drinking?" I asked instead.

"So, what if I have?" she asked, uncharacteristically surly, and I knew then for sure she had been drinking.

I flipped off the bathroom light, leaving only the glow from the display on my iPod to light my way to my bed, and kicked my discarded clothes into the corner. As the sound of David Bowie's "Heroes" filled the room, I collapsed onto my bed and rested my head on the pillow, my eyes shut and my phone pressed to my ear.

"Are you listening to David Bowie?" Bridget asked. "I love David Bowie. This is even my favorite David Bowie song."

"Well, then you have better taste in music than your brother."

"*Uch*, don't get me started," she said. "I had to take him to a Maroon Five concert over the summer."

"I'm sorry," I said. "I didn't know."

"It's okay," she said with a small laugh. "I'm over it, but that's three hours of my life I'll never get back."

"Where are you?" I asked.

"I had a fight with my parents tonight," she said. "We had a big argument and then I left without even telling them where I was going. I've never done that before. They've called me like fifty times but I don't want to talk to them. God, they make me crazy sometimes. Anyway, I'm staying at a friend's house tonight. Her parents are out of town so her boyfriend's staying over. I didn't feel like being the fifth wheel anymore so I came upstairs to go to bed, but I can't sleep."

I wasn't going to ask why she was calling me instead of Ken. "So, what happened with your parents?" I asked as I folded one arm and tucked it behind my head. Lying in bed in the dark, with her voice in my ear, it was like having her there with me in bed. I could almost imagine the weight of her body on the mattress beside me.

"It seems stupid now," she said with a sigh. "Sometimes I really hate my parents. Life has been such a goddamn disappointment for them, I just can't bring myself to disappoint them about anything. It's fucking exhausting." She didn't usually swear this much but I let it pass without comment.

"Why a disappointment?" I asked.

"Oh, everything," she said. "My dad would never say it, but sometimes when he looks at Pete I can see him thinking that he wished he had a son who could throw a football or hit a home run. And we're poor. My parents are always fighting about money. I think my dad makes a decent salary but Pete has had a lot of medical bills and the insurance hasn't always covered everything. They can't hate him for it so they hate each other instead. Sometimes they fight about it late at night when they think we aren't listening. But Pete hears it. I know he does."

"There are worse things than not having enough money," I said. "At least your parents care about you. Care about what happens to you."

"I suppose so," she said, not wanting to be convinced. "I thought you'd be on my side in this."

"I am on your side," I said. "I'm on whatever side you want me to be."

"I mean," she continued without really listening to me, "I want my parents to be happy. Pete too. It's just too much fucking work to be in charge of making sure everyone else is happy all the time. It's like they all *need* me to be perfect. Not just my parents. Everyone. Perfect student. Perfect sister. Perfect daughter. It's exhausting."

"I don't think you're perfect," I said, "if it makes you feel any better."

"Much. Thanks," she said. Most people didn't know that Bridget was sarcastic, because she never gave it away with the tone of her voice. I realized in that moment it was one of the things I liked about her. Listening to her talk was like listening to a perfect minor chord progression in a song.

"You're welcome," I said, matching her nonsarcastic sarcasm.

"Why is it so easy for me to talk to you?" she asked.

"Maybe because you don't care what I think of you," I said.

"No, I think maybe it's because you don't expect me to be anything but myself." She laughed suddenly. "I think perfection would be boring for you."

The sound of her voice had started to lull me to sleep and I tried to prop the phone against my ear so I wouldn't have to use the strength of my arm to hold it in place. My breath became slow and even as my body settled toward sleep.

"Jesse," she said, so softly that for a minute I thought I had only imagined it.

"Bridget," I said, savoring the feel of her name on my lips.

"Do you think that there is only one soul mate for every person in the world? That there is only one person we're meant to be with? That once you find the person you're supposed to be with you never have a doubt about it, ever again?"

"I don't know," I said hollowly. "I hope not."

She murmured in agreement and there was the muffled sound of her hair and face against the phone. "My parents have been together since they were sixteen. My mom's never been with anyone other than my dad. At least that's what she told me. They're not exactly an advertisement for early marriage."

"Mm."

"What about your parents?" she asked absently. "Were they like that? Married really young?"

"My mom was young," I said as I suppressed a yawn. "Early twenties. My dad was a little older."

She cleared her throat then, a soft *ahem* that made me conscious of her being halfway across town from where I was at that moment, and forever distant from me.

"What was your mom like?" she asked quietly, apologetically.

For a long time I thought about just not answering her. If it had been anyone else, my first reflex would have been to end the call.

"My mom—" I stopped, the words completely foreign on my lips after not speaking them aloud in so many months. "My mom was . . . incomprehensible," I said. A pounding had started up in my head, a heartbeat of pain behind my eyes.

"What happened to her?" she asked. "The paper just said that she died from a possible overdose."

"Is that like your hobby or something?" I asked. "Googling other people's personal tragedies?"

"I wanted to know," she said simply.

Again she waited through the long silence, her breath in my ear. "My mother was not well," I said. Dramatic understatement.

Even when my mother had been present she wasn't much of a presence. For most of my childhood she had lived in a twilight of depression and functional alcoholism. Artistic or eccentric is how people described her when they were being polite, which most of the time people aren't. My mother had been distant from me for so long before she left this world that I hardly felt anything about it at all when she checked out for good—I neither loved nor hated her by the time she died. Shit, if I was married to someone like my dad, I might be tempted to take my own life too. He's the quintessential douche bag.

In the summer between my sophomore and junior years she ate several bottles of antidepressants and pain medications. They were all prescribed, just not prescribed to be taken all at once. She chased it with half a bottle of whiskey. My dad was the one who found her. Thank God.

"The rumors are true," I said dully. "She killed herself."

"Jesus," Bridget said, then, "Jesus," again since there wasn't really anything else to say. "Suicide. Such an awful word."

"They didn't call it that," I said, finding it almost easy to talk now, speaking to the darkness and music that enveloped me like a cocoon. "Not to our faces. They were very polite about it—the police."

"And now you carry that around with you," she said.

"In the place where the Wizard would put a heart if he gave me one," I said.

"You do have a heart, Jesse. Even if it's broken. I'm so sorry."

"Don't," I said quickly. "I don't like pity."

"I'm not giving you pity."

"Good, because I don't want it."

The silent game again. And, shit, if I wasn't going to lose. Again.

"Have you ever had a concussion?" I asked.

"No," she said, her voice sleepy now.

"I did, once, when I was about twelve. I wasn't looking where I was going and rode my bike right into the corner of a moving van. No helmet," I said, unconsciously lifting my hand to touch the side of my head where a three-inch scar was hidden by my hair. "I was knocked out for a few minutes. The next day when I woke up I couldn't remember anything that happened right before the accident, didn't remember the accident at all. My friends were with me, saw the whole thing and described it to me, to my parents, but I never could remember. It's as if that piece of my life was just lifted out and taken away."

She didn't interrupt, didn't ask me the point to my story, just listened in silence, making me wonder if she had fallen asleep.

"It's like my brain decided to protect me from the whole experience, didn't let me remember the crash, how it felt,"

I said thoughtfully. I had contemplated that incident many times in recent months, trying to decide if that biological mechanism was at work within me now—my brain trying to protect me, not allowing me to feel things that were too awful to examine in the light of day.

"I don't remember how anything felt before a year ago last month," I said to the dark. "Just like that period of time that was wiped out when I was knocked unconscious—my mind won't let me feel anything," I said, grasping for the words that could never adequately explain. "I don't know what it was like when I had feelings—it's lost and I can't remember it."

There was nothing appropriate or helpful that she could say and she seemed to know that. Most people don't. They forge ahead, filling the moment with meaningless chatter.

"You won't say anything?" I asked. "Not even to Pete." I hated this, the knowledge that she now owned a part of me. Secrets were power, but I was banking on the fact that Bridget had no use for power.

"You know I wouldn't say anything," she said. "If you have to ask, you don't even know me."

"Nobody really knows anyone," I said, knowing it was a lie as I said it. I knew Bridget. And now she knew me. Fuck.

TWENTY-FIVE

PETE AND I WERE SITTING ON THE SIDELINES
watching as Bridget conducted after-school practice with
her team of knuckleheads. She had begged us to come so
we could give the kids empty encouragement in the form
of cheers and applause while they ran through their practice
for the Special Olympics–knockoff event she was planning.
We were in constant peril from the balls flying in every direction but their intended, downfield toward a hoop that
was big enough a legally blind person could hit it.

There were lanes set up with cones for the kids to run
short sprints and relays, half the time ending up in a big

pile of arms and legs at the finish line when they all crashed into each other. Bridget wasn't daunted by their extreme lack of coordination, giving the kids pep talks like a real coach, always praising their efforts.

Ken showed up not long after and came to where we sat to deposit his backpack. "Hey, Pete," he said in a tone that implied Pete was slow or hard of hearing, or both. "What are you doing here, Alderman?" His question was friendly enough but there was underlying tension in his tone.

"Just watching the debacle," I said, letting boredom register in my voice. "Bridget wanted us to come and cheer them on."

"Yeah?" he asked. "She didn't mention to me that you were coming."

"I didn't tell her definitely either way," I said. "You know how it is."

"Sure, yeah," he said uncertainly. He wasn't going to say more with Pete there but I knew Ken's hackles were up and he didn't like me being around his girl. I didn't blame him. I didn't like it when other guys looked at her either.

Ken went over to join Bridget then. He leaned in to kiss her on the mouth but she turned her face to accept a kiss on the cheek, her eyes darting nervously to the kids to see if they were watching.

A few minutes later the courtyard door opened again and out walked a real big girl with long, full brown hair pushed back from her face with a headband.

Bridget waved to the girl and flashed her signature angelic smile. Even out of earshot I could tell the girl was cool toward Ken, but she greeted him with a nod and favored Bridget with a brief hug. I caught Ken's expression of distaste as his eyes passed over the girl's lumpy, over-sized figure.

Though she was overweight she was unapologetic about it, in tight red jeans and black ankle boots with a platform heel. She wore an oversized sweater covered in beads and sequins that made your eyes hurt if you studied it for too long.

"Who's that?" I asked Pete.

"Theresa. A friend of Bridget's," Pete said without much interest. "She comes sometimes to work with the kids."

Theresa wasn't much of an athlete, but she huffed and puffed around the courtyard retrieving balls and cheering like a lunatic. The kids loved her and showed as much affection for her as they did for Bridget.

Ken put on a good show for Bridget but after a while he had trouble hiding his boredom, kept studying his phone every time he thought Bridget wasn't paying attention. He was always all smiles for Bridget and never missed an opportunity to put a possessive hand or arm on her. At one point he put an arm around her shoulder and she rested comfortably against him. I looked away as he leaned in to plant a kiss on her forehead. Jesus, I hated seeing them together.

After Ken, Theresa, and Bridget had cleaned up the gear, Bridget came to talk to Pete and me. "Hey, guys. We're going to get something to eat. Want to come with us?"

"Sure," I said before Pete could respond. He glared at me but I ignored him.

"Man, why did you say we wanted to go?" Pete asked when the others had piled into Ken's car.

"I'm hungry," I lied.

He sighed but just climbed into the passenger seat of the T-Bird. I slapped Pete's hand away from the radio controls as he tried to change it from the classical station and he sighed again.

The diner where we ended up was a popular hangout for most of the douches from school. Half a dozen tables were taken up by people from Ken's clique and the satellite cliques that form around football players and cheerleaders. People were talking across the aisles or moving from one table to the next to visit with each other. This wasn't a place where I would find any of my people, but all of Ken's posse was here.

We sat in a booth—Ken and Bridget on one side, Theresa next to me, and Pete hanging awkwardly at the end of the table in an extra chair.

"Theresa, you know Jesse, right?" Bridget said, making introductions as we slid into our seats.

"How you doing?" I asked with a nod.

Theresa appraised me coolly, seeming to size me up in one long glance. "Sure," she said without much enthusiasm.

I had the best seat in the house, across from Bridget. My foot bumped Bridget's under the table and came to rest against hers. She didn't look at me or acknowledge that our feet were touching, and she didn't pull away. Even that insignificant physical contact was enough to make my body hum with desire. Pete moped and Ken shot me wary glances while Bridget and Theresa kept up a steady stream of meaningless chatter and I savored the feel of Bridget's foot against mine. Had I been stoned, it would have qualified as one of the most surreal moments of my life. By the way she behaved toward me, it was unclear how much Bridget remembered of our conversation from the other night, though I had replayed it in my mind so many times, I could almost watch it like a film reel in my head. I wondered if Bridget's mind was on me too, or if she thought nothing of our feet pressed together under the table.

Pull yourself together, Alderman.

After a few minutes, Ken tugged at Bridget's sleeve and said, "Babe, let's go over and say hi to the guys."

"Uh—" Bridget glanced uncertainly at the three of us and didn't move to follow Ken as he started to slide out of the booth.

"Go ahead," Theresa said as she sipped on the straw of her milk shake. "Don't worry about us."

"We'll be back in just a minute," Bridget said. As she slid her foot away and broke our physical connection, our eyes met and I detected disappointment in her gaze. She ruffled Pete's hair with her fingers as she slid out of the booth and took Ken's waiting hand. Annoyed, Pete jerked his head away from her and smoothed his hair.

With Bridget gone I turned my attention to Theresa and Pete. Theresa's wide thighs took up more than her fair share of our bench, and my leg was hot where it touched hers. The waitress dropped our food at the table a minute later—a huge burger piled high with bacon and cheese and a mountain of fries for Theresa. It surprised me that she ordered so much food—basically a public announce-ment that her large size was not due to some rare metabolic disorder, that she really did eat like a pig. But she didn't show any shame about it.

Pete and I both watched as she squeezed a glob of ketchup onto her plate. "So, what the hell is wrong with your sister?" Theresa asked Pete, her eyes on her food. "She could date just about any guy in school and she chooses to go out with that loser? What does she see in him?"

Pete shrugged. "I have no idea."

"I mean, I know he's popular," she continued, talking around a mouthful of food. "He'll get voted homecoming king, of course, because people don't have sense enough to vote on any other merit besides how well someone can throw a football. But he's the biggest turd in school."

"He's probably not worth much emotion—love or hate," I said as I traced a pattern in the condensation on my glass.

"Believe me—" Theresa licked ketchup from her thumb. "—if Bridget knew what he was really like, there is no way she would go out with him. No. Way."

"Yeah? What's he like?" I asked.

"A bully," she said with feeling. "Since middle school I've had to listen to people like him with their stupid fat jokes. The only thing worse than fat jokes is having people look at me like they feel sorry for me, telling me I have such nice hair and skin." She laughed ruefully as she plucked at the ends of her hair. "You know, people always tell a fat girl she has lovely hair or skin because they can't think of anything else nice to say."

"Maybe fat people really do have nicer hair and skin— because they eat more . . . protein or something," Pete suggested helpfully. Theresa considered his comment for a minute while I bit my lower lip to suppress a smile.

"Anyway," Theresa continued, unfazed by Pete's comment, "Ken and his friends are so stupid. They're like in kindergarten or something. And I'm such an idiot, I actually used to have a crush on that douche bag. I mean, he's gorgeous but it's not as if I think he would ever want to sleep with me or something." She waited until the silence had reached awkward status before she spoke again. "But I suppose that's obvious to you, since someone like Ken would never want to sleep with a girl like me, right?"

I just waited, hoping the question was rhetorical, but Pete forged ahead with the complete lack of social prowess that was his trademark. "I would sleep with just about any girl," he said. "Unless she smelled really bad. Or had VD or something. I don't really care so much what a person looks like. I mean, look at me, right? My face is crooked and I've got a limp. I talk funny. . . ." He trailed off, suddenly frustrated with itemizing a list of his own shortcomings.

Theresa's eyes were narrowed appraisingly as she considered Pete's monologue. "You know, maybe you shouldn't spend so much time talking about your . . . disabilities," she said. "You're just asking for negative attention."

"Look who's talking," Pete shot back. "You keep talking about how fat you are. You think I wouldn't give anything just to be fat? *You* can lose weight. I can't change who I am."

"Well, at least people feel sorry for you," Theresa said. "People love to hate on a fat person. They figure if a person is fat, then they're just lazy, or they eat too much. They don't think maybe a person has a medical condition that makes them that way. At least you people feel sorry for. They know it's not your fault that you walk with a limp."

"So, that's why you're . . . overweight?" Pete asked. "Because you have some kind of medical condition?"

"No, stupid, I eat too damn much," she said with a shit-eating grin that made both Pete and me laugh out loud. Theresa was like Mr. Dunkelman's dream girl. Suddenly I found myself cataloging her physical traits, assessing her desirability. She really did have nice hair.

"So, what did Ken do to you?" I asked.

Theresa sighed impatiently as she studied her burger to plan her next bite. There was a smudge of ketchup in the corner of her mouth as she said, "Like I said, even though he's a total D-bag he's also totally gorgeous. So, earlier this year, before he started dating Bridget, I was walking into school one day and he was looking at me so . . . I smiled at him. He smiled back at me and I thought he was actually being nice for once. Because I'm an idiot. Then he starts saying all these mean things about me being a lard ass and a whale, making a big show about it in front of his friends. God, what an A-hole."

"What a creep," Pete said glumly, and Theresa just nodded.

"You didn't tell Bridget that story?" I asked. Leading the witness. What I wanted to ask is *why* she didn't tell Bridget that story.

"Whatever," Theresa said with a flutter of her hand as she returned to her burger. "Bridget's not an idiot. And if she's happy with Ken, then I'm happy for her."

"You're a better person than most," I said to Theresa. "At least a better friend."

"I don't know about that," Theresa said, "and fat lot of

good it does me anyway." She shot us a quirky smile at her pun. "Fat is all people really see. And my awesome hair, of course," she quipped.

"I would love to tell Bridget that story," Pete said, "about what Ken said to you. She'd drop him in a second if she knew."

"Don't you dare," Theresa said as she put a handful of fries in her mouth. "It's my story and mine to share if I want to, which I don't."

"I don't think you're fat," Pete said with such intense solemnity that I wondered if he was experiencing some stir of feelings for Theresa.

Theresa gave up a smile for Pete's efforts. "Thanks," she said. "And I don't think I smell bad, and I definitely don't have VD, so maybe I still have a chance at homecoming queen, huh?" she asked with a wry twist of her eyebrows.

"You do have good hair," I said as I flipped one of her waves with my finger.

Her response was to shove me in the ribs with her elbow.

Theresa's loyalty to Bridget impressed me, even though her unwillingness to rat out Ken struck me as irritatingly naïve. Still, she deserved to be rewarded.

TWENTY-SIX

JOEY AND I CORNERED GRAY DABSON IN THE hallway the following week. We had given him sufficient time to settle his accounting and it was payday. The posters littering the halls to advertise homecoming-week events were a good indication the car wash had been a major financial success.

"Hey, Jesse, I've been looking for you," Gray said by way of greeting.

"Must not have been looking very hard," I said, standing a little closer to him than was socially acceptable, close enough that he felt compelled to take a step away.

His laugh was fake and forced because nothing I'd said was funny. "Well—" He cleared his throat as I waited expectantly. "—I wanted to talk to you because the thing is . . . if I want to disburse any money from the student council account, I have to have some sort of invoice. You know, Mr. Burke manages the account, is the signer on it, and I can't just withdraw money to pay you."

"Are you saying you want an invoice from me?" I asked, letting my voice rise to express my incredulity. "Is that what you're saying?"

"What I'm saying," he said, lifting his hands in supplication and giving a helpless shrug, "is I'm not really sure how I can get your money. Mr. Burke took all of the cash the day of the car wash to deposit and I don't have any way to pay you out of the student fund."

"So, what you're telling me is that you don't have my money, have no way of getting my money. Is that it?" I asked. This was information I already owned, but I had to drill it in to get the result I wanted.

He shrank away from me, wincing as he waited for me to hit him.

"We had a contract," I said.

"Technically speaking, it was a verbal agreement and probably not one that is legally binding," he said, and I watched his Adam's apple in fascination as he spoke.

"I could have you put to bed with a shovel," I said. "I know people."

"Jesus!" he yelped, and hunched his shoulders as he took a step away. He shot a questioning look at Joey but she just crossed her arms over her chest and cracked her gum.

"I'll figure something out," he said, his voice shaky. "You'll get your money. It just won't be right away."

I shook my head slowly and fought the urge to rub my forehead in frustration. "Here's the deal," I said. "You owe me. You. Personally. Your payment is already past due and if you can't make good, I'm going to take it out in-kind."

"I don't really know what you—"

"Shut up and listen," I said. "As student council president you oversee the election of homecoming king and queen."

"I mean, I wouldn't say I oversee it so much as—"

I interrupted his senseless babble. "Theresa Mason. She's already been nominated. You're going to see to it that she wins homecoming queen and Ken Foster will be king."

"You want me to fix the election?" he squeaked.

"I'm not telling you how or what to do," I said. "I'm telling you that you owe me, and the outcome I want is for Theresa Mason to be crowned homecoming queen."

"Jesse, we've already collected a ton of ballots. Bridget Smalley has it by a mile. I hardly even know anything about this Theresa girl. Her nomination came out of nowhere. You have to get at least three nominations to make the ballot. I assumed the nomination was some kind of cruel joke, if you want to know the truth."

"A joke? Why do you say that?" Joey asked. "Just because she doesn't look like a Barbie doll? Because she doesn't fit society's narrowly defined ideal of beauty?"

"Is that what this is about?" Gray asked with a confused frown. "You're making some kind of social statement?"

"You don't need to know why and you don't need to know anything about Theresa," I said slowly, clearly, so there would be no misunderstanding. "All you need to know is that she's the next homecoming queen."

"What about Bridget Smalley?" Gray asked. "She's perfect."

Joey snorted at his use of the word "perfect" but didn't interrupt his monologue.

"She's smart, beautiful, but still approachable and down-to-earth. And she's already dating Ken. It's not just about the dance, Jesse. The king and queen have other appearances they have to make together and homecoming night they're expected to kick off the dance by dancing together. It's tradition."

"What's wrong with Theresa as homecoming queen? Are you a fattist?" I asked, only because I knew it would amuse Joey.

"No, God no, Jesse," Gray said quickly. "I have nothing against fat people. My own mother is fat. I just don't think Bridget can be equaled when it comes to the perfect person to represent Wakefield both now and in the future. You're asking me to fix the election. I—it's—it's dishonest."

"Oh, please, nut up, Gray," I said with contempt for his cowardice. "It's not like she's going to be the new governor, for Christ's sake. You find a way," I said, pointing a finger at him, "or you'd better start watching your back."

"What was that about?" Joey asked as we walked away from Gray.

"Just business," I said.

"Usually I can see the big picture you're working toward," Joey said pensively, "but this time I'll admit it. I'm baffled. Come on, tell me. What's your angle?"

"Maybe Theresa's a friend of mine," I said.

"First of all," Joey said, "you don't have any friends. I'm not even sure you like me. Second, if you were going to have a friend, it certainly would not be Theresa Mason. And third, since when do you do things for people, friends included, when there's no cash incentive?"

"Who says there's not?"

"This is it, isn't it?" she asked, and turned to walk backwards so she could study my face. "You've officially lost your mind. You planning some kind of stunt for homecoming? A vat of pig's blood? An Uzi, maybe?"

"You watch too much television," I said.

"Okay, fine. You aren't going to tell me but I know there is something going on with you," she said, reading me in the way only Joey could. "I've just been thinking—I mean, if you've got some kind of terminal illness or Rob's got a hit out on you—you could take the time to formally document your intent to leave me your car and other worldly possessions once you're gone."

"Fuck off, Joey," I said, taking a quick detour into the boys' bathroom to avoid further conversation.

TWENTY-SEVEN

I WENT OUT OF MY WAY TO AVOID BRIDGET AT
school. Pete didn't usually mention his sister and I never
brought her up. Not that it kept me from thinking about
her. By now I had a mental list of love songs that I would
play her if (1) I still played guitar and (2) I was willing to
pursue a relationship with Bridget. Which I wasn't. Because
it could only end one way. As long as I didn't see her or talk
to her, ours was a perfect love.

Two weeks before homecoming Dad left on a road
trip—"going on tour," he called it, which made it sound a

lot more grand than what it really was. In reality it was four middle-aged guys who had never bothered to get a real job or invest regularly in haircuts. They would stay up late drinking every night, spending most of the money they earned on cheap hotels and cheaper women before they even made it back home. He left me some spending money, money that would still be sitting out on the kitchen counter when he got home, unless Joey helped herself to it.

It was while I was visiting Mr. Dunkelman, dropping off his weekly supply of junk food, that I saw more than a glimpse of Bridget for the first time in weeks. She was sitting in the rec room with her grandmother, who, Mr. Dunkelman had informed me, had recently been plotting her escape from the Nazi concentration camp where she was being held. Apparently, there was an underground tunnel that would provide the conduit for her escape. She had invited Mr. D to join her in her liberation.

"Concentration camp?" I asked. "She Jewish?"

"No, I think she just identifies with Jewish persecution mania," Mr. D said absentmindedly as he dealt the cards.

I never visited Mr. D on Thursdays, Bridget's usual day with her grandmother. Today was Wednesday and I noticed as soon as I saw Bridget that there was something wrong. Usually her face was set naturally with the corners of her mouth turned up slightly, her eyes bright with a smile even if she wasn't showing any teeth. But not today.

Bridget sat quietly beside her grandmother with her hands tucked between her thighs, shoulders slumped and head down, her mouth set in a grim line. My feet carried me to her without any direction from the sense center of my brain. She looked up at me as I stood before her and that was when I saw the tear that quivered on the brink of her lower lid.

"What's the matter?" I asked, jumping immediately to the conclusion that Ken had done something unforgivable, something that demanded application of Icy Hot in his jockstrap, or maybe even a malfunction of the braking system in his car. "Did something happen between you and Ken?"

Bridget shook her head and wiped at her eyes. "No, nothing like that. It was me. I did something really stupid and now—" A shudder seemed to pass through her before she continued. "—and now I have to disappoint the kids at the Siegel Center."

"What could you have done that was so terrible?" I asked, fighting the instinctive urge to take on the tone of voice usually reserved for injured kittens.

"You know, we've been planning that Special Olympics event for the kids but there's really no space big enough at the Siegel Center, no gym where we can set up and people can come watch. So, I told the kids that I would arrange for us to host the event at Wakefield. I thought it would be no big deal. It's a public building, you know? But Mr. Burke said that we can't use the building on the weekend. Something about budget cuts or liability for the school, I don't know. Now I have to go to the Siegel Center and tell the kids—" She paused as she swallowed back a small sob. "They've been so excited about it, practicing and telling their families. God, I'm such an idiot. I never should have told them we could do it until after I got permission."

"It's not your fault," I said. "Burke is a douche."

The corner of her mouth twitched with the hint of a smile. "Pete's new favorite word," she said as she cut me an admonishing look. "Being a bad influence seems to be your specialty."

"I had nothing to do with the new haircut," I said defensively. "I told him it makes him look like Ellen DeGeneres but he thinks the girls will be crazy about it."

My comment elicited a small laugh and Bridget shook her head. "Can't you be serious for one minute? This is really, really bad. Stop making jokes."

"Why do you always think I'm joking?" I asked. "That haircut is nothing to joke about. It's seriously awful. You know who has a haircut like that? Justin Bieber."

Now she laughed for real and I was inwardly pleased with myself for making her forget her worries, if only for a minute. She seemed to suddenly remember that she had nothing to be happy about and her face fell again. Dorothy was mumbling to herself in the wheelchair next to her and Bridget idly rubbed the old woman's hand.

"Mr. Dunkelman keeps an eye on her," I said.

"You call your grandfather Mr. Dunkelman?" Bridget asked with a small frown and I stiffened as I realized I had forgotten about the ruse that had brought us together.

"Yeah, well, we weren't close when I was growing up. In fact," I said, warming up to the lie, "we didn't even really know each other until recently."

"He wasn't close with your mom?" she asked, her voice quiet and apologetic.

"No," I said curtly as we treaded into muddy waters.

"Still," she said, "it must have been hard for him." She sighed and rubbed her forehead with her fingertips, the nail beds perfect, pink half moons. "I don't even want to face those kids on Tuesday. What am I supposed to say to them?"

"When's the event supposed to be?" I asked.

"The first weekend of December."

"I wouldn't say anything," I said. "Burke might still change his mind. Give it a week and if he still won't let you do it, then you can tell them. Until then, I'd keep it to yourself."

"You're crazy," she said. "He's not going to change his mind."

"Just wait a week before you tell the kids," I said, and gave her my best reassuring smile. "No reason to break their hearts right away."

The next day I didn't find Burke in his office until after the second lunch period and by then I had thought through how I would handle him. "I need to see Mr. Burke," I said to the pudgy receptionist with the foot-high beehive hairdon't.

"Well, I'm sorry," she said, not sounding the slightest bit sorry as she took a pencil and scratched absently at her scalp with the point of it. I imagined that her scalp was covered with little lumps of powdered skin under the hair helmet and contemplated the wedding band on her chubby ring finger. Disgust rolled in my gut as I thought about the kind of man who slept beside her every night. "Mr. Burke is very busy right now," she said with a crack of her gum. "You can talk to someone in guidance or make an appointment to see Mr. Burke another day."

"You tell him Jesse Alderman is here," I said. "He'll make time."

She glared at me, and the rolling chair groaned in protest as she pushed herself back from the desk. She didn't argue, just waddled into Burke's office to confer with him. Only a few seconds passed before she returned and gestured to Burke's door with a sneer. "He'll see you now."

"Alderman," Burke said by way of greeting as I entered his office and shut the door behind me. He held an unlit pipe, which he was cleaning with a pocketknife, and I could see Candy Crush on his computer monitor reflected in the framed diploma behind him. "I guess today is payday since you have chosen to grace me with your presence."

His head was swollen with ego now that no one overtly challenged his authority on campus. Travis Marsh, by all appearances worthless in the high school ecosystem, had served a vital function—had been Burke's daily reminder that his authority was insignificant compared to the will of one thousand students.

"You guessed right," I said, keeping my tone level, because anger isn't appropriate. You can't let emotion interfere with business. I had to remind myself that this was business, not a personal vendetta, not an issue that should interest me personally at all.

"And what is it I can do for you?" he asked, condescending now. Truly powerful people know better than to treat others the way Burke did.

"You're going to open the school gym on a Saturday for the kids from the Siegel Center to have their very own Special Olympics event," I said. "Whatever Saturday they want. That's your payment for Travis."

Burke sighed impatiently and rolled his eyes. "Look, I told that Smalley girl who's been moping around my office that my hands are tied. We've had budget cuts, I'm short-staffed, not to mention the liability if someone gets hurt. Jesus, she wants to let a bunch of cripples try pole-vaulting and shit. I'm probably saving them from serious injury."

"Cry me a river, Burke. I don't care about your problems," I said, placing my hands flat on the surface of his desk and leaning in so he had nowhere to look but into my face. "You signed a contract and I'm cashing in. You make it happen. I don't care how. If you don't, I'll make you very sorry."

"By doing what?" he scoffed. "Don't you threaten me, Alderman. Your fingerprints are all over that stunt you pulled to frame Travis Marsh. If I go down, you're going with me. You think if you go to the authorities, anyone will believe your word over mine?"

I turned and went for the door while he was still blustering behind me. "I'll tell you one thing," I said, my hand on the doorknob, the door still shut, "if you go down this road with me, you'll lose. I'll make what happened to Travis look like a cakewalk. The public can forgive just about anything, but they'll never forgive a pedophile. You think about that, but don't think too long. You've got until the end of the school day." I opened the door and was two steps out when I turned back to add, "And make sure you deliver the news to Bridget with a smile. No sulking. I want her to enjoy the moment."

I gave the receptionist a friendly nod on my way out of the office. Burke would probably waste the next ninety minutes stewing in his office before his inner spineless coward bowed to my demands and he went in search of Bridget to deliver the news.

When I was on my way to seventh period that day I was stopped by Bridget, who called out to me in the crowded hallway.

"I can't believe it!" she cried as she ran up to me. "Mr. Burke called me out of class, said he had changed his mind and we could use the campus for our event. Can you believe it?"

"That's great," I said, basking in the warmth of her smile.

"I don't know why he changed his mind but he did and I can't wait to tell the kids at the Siegel Center," she babbled happily. "They're going to be so excited." She said this with a clap of her hands and a bounce in her step and I felt my face spreading into a smile.

What she did next shouldn't have been any real surprise. Bridget was the most loving and effusive person God had ever made. It shouldn't have been a surprise, but when it happened I wasn't prepared. When she threw her arms around my neck, my bowels felt loose, my heart hammered in my throat, and Jimi Hendrix counted in "Little Wing" in my head.

The hug lasted a good ten seconds—and I mean a really

good ten seconds. I pressed one hand into the small of her back and savored the feel of her body against mine, the clean smell of her hair. Then she was pulling away, but not before dropping a kiss on my cheek.

I had just wasted a Get Out of Jail Free card for a hug from Bridget and to give some dopey kids a track-and-field venue. Was it worth it?

Does the pope shit in the woods?

TWENTY-EIGHT

FRIDAY NIGHT I LEFT THE HOUSE EARLY BE-
cause it was almost an hour drive to a club on the outskirts
of Boston called Plant Nine. Pete wasn't waiting outside
when I got to his house so I knocked at the door. It was a
few minutes before Pete came, his face clouded with anger
as he slammed the front door on his way out.

"Unfuckingbelieveable," he spat viciously as he stormed
past me and didn't wait to see if I followed him to the car.

Once we were in the car and pulling away from the curb
he spoke again, his voice tight with anger. "My parents are

giving me shit about how much time I've been spending out. Said they think you're a bad influence on me."

"Yeah, well, your parents are right," I said with a thoughtful nod. "I am a bad influence."

He kept up his tirade without stopping to listen to me. "They don't say jack shit when Bridget goes on dates or out with her friends. She's such a fucking saint, they don't believe she would do anything bad anyway."

"I don't know why you fight with them," I said. "The way to handle parents is to tell them what they want to hear— stay on top of your schoolwork so you don't have to listen to any shit about it, keep your head down and your nose clean, let them believe they're doing a good job. You take the fight to them, you'll lose every time."

"That's really great advice coming from the delinquent who hangs out with drug dealers and skinheads," he said.

"You finished?" I asked as we sat through a red light.

"Yeah. You got any weed?"

"Yeah, I got some."

"Well, can I have some?" he asked impatiently.

"I just gave you a dime bag last week."

"Yeah, and it lasted all of about two days," he said, talking tough now. "Let me have a hit of X."

"Forget it," I said. "You don't need to be messing with that stuff."

"Why?" he asked, his tone insolent. "I just want to try it. You've done it, haven't you?"

"Once or twice."

"So, let me try it."

"Ain't gonna happen, so stop asking me," I said.

"You suck," he muttered as he sank even lower in his seat. "What happened? Did you suddenly get a morality chip?"

"A what?" I asked with a frown.

"A morality chip," he said with some impatience. "You know, like a robot, programmed to learn emotions."

"It's amazing," I said with a shake of my head. "Somehow you always manage to outnerd yourself. What is that from? One of your stupid sci-fi books?"

He ignored my questions and continued his attack. I was used to it by now, the way he took out his bad moods on everyone around him. His cerebral palsy was more of a disability than he realized. No one had ever bothered to tell Pete what an asshole he could be, so he wasn't really aware of it. I figured any time I called him out for being an asshole it was helping him, molding him into a functioning member of society.

"So, what you're saying," he asked with a smart-ass tone, "is that it's okay for you to sell pot and X to people, but not for me to use it? That makes a whole lot of sense." He sounded like a little kid, trying to come off sarcastic and cool but really just sounding like a whiny twelve-year-old.

"I don't sample the merchandise unless the situation requires it, because I don't want to get stupid and work scooping ice cream for my entire adult life," I said because he needed a lecture, though I'm not sure why I bothered since he never listened to me anymore. Was too caught up in feeling sorry for himself lately to pay attention to much else. "You look at a guy like Digger," I continued. "He grazes on the grass all day long. That's why he's messed up in the head. Can't even see straight. You want to end up like him?"

"Whatever," Pete said with a dismissive wave as he leaned his seat back and stared out the window. "You sound like my old man."

"Oh, shit—" I choked on a laugh. "Did you really just say that to me? I'm telling you that stuff will bring you nothing but trouble. Your old man doesn't know shit about it, but I do."

"Yeah, yeah. I hear you," he said with a sigh.

"I'm serious."

"Yeah, I got it," he said, raising his voice to get the last word. "I got it, I just don't want it," he muttered to himself.

We rode for the next thirty minutes without talking much. Plant Nine was in the old warehouse district near the water, far from the bustle of the city. I pulled into an empty parking space at the curb and shut off the engine. "Be cool," I said, my hand resting on the door handle. "Keep your mouth shut and be cool."

By habit I slowed my gait to match Pete's as we walked along the crumbling sidewalk, though the pace at which he moved made it difficult to ever stay in step beside him. I always found myself a couple of steps ahead, even when I consciously slowed to a saunter. We crossed the deserted street and approached the club from the end of a long line of people waiting to get in. Pete stopped like he was going to hop in line, but I just shook my head and kept walking and he fell in behind me.

The lone bouncer was the kind of guy you only ever see in a movie—a giant redneck, tall and fat, his pale skin covered in tattoos—and looked like the kind of person who might torture kittens for recreation. Big D was an imposing figure, his massive frame swallowing the leather-topped barstool that sat outside the club door, his face fixed in a sneer. The aluminum stool groaned under his weight as he stood to greet me with a fist bump and a hug. I introduced him to Pete, who squawked when Big D ignored his outstretched hand and embraced him with a big squeeze. Pete stumbled back a step when he was let go.

"How you been, Sway?" Big D asked as he tugged his pants up at the waist and straightened his System of a Down T-shirt.

"I'm good, D," I said, giving his shoulder a slap. "How've you been?"

"Oh, I'm staying out of trouble," D said. "This your little brother?"

"Not by blood. Pete's part of that Big Brothers Big Sisters program. I'm like his mentor," I said with a humble shrug.

D's face split into a grin and he let out a guffaw as he slapped Pete on the shoulder with a paw as big and meaty as a baseball mitt. Pete cried out in surprise as he barely kept his footing. "I gotcha," D said with a chuckle. "You're like a positive male role model." Pete recovered himself and subtly edged out of Big D's reach. "Look at that face," Big D said to Pete as he grabbed me one-handed under the chin and squeezed my face in Jewish-grandmother fashion. "This boy could sell hell to a bishop."

D was still chuckling to himself as he lifted the rope and let us walk in. There were some subdued mutters of protest as Pete and I got into the club while a line of partygoers still waited for their turn, but no one would directly challenge D or question his right to play favorites.

"Ow," Pete said once we were out of earshot. "I think he dislocated my shoulder."

"Just be glad he likes you," I said over the thump of the bass music.

We made our way through the labyrinth of rooms that had once been a factory of some kind, the original purpose for the building long forgotten. It had been converted to a club, each room filled with pastimes to appeal to any audience—pool tables in one room, a bar with stools in the next, and multiple dance floors on two levels with a different DJ spinning in each space. There weren't many lights, which helped to conceal the disrepair and the peeling paint, the bare concrete floors painted black. Spotlights hung over the bars, allowing the bartenders to see to work, and the pool tables and dartboards had spotlights as well. Black lights illuminated the rest, casting an artificially healthy glow on the club kids.

Pete followed me to a courtyard with an outdoor bar and wooden decking for a dance floor. Industrial techno hummed from the giant speakers parked at two corners of the dance floor, an observation deck above it where people sat drinking, smoking, and talking as they watched the few dancers. The guys who danced to the industrial techno wore ripped jeans, black T-shirts emblazoned with the logos of bands I had never heard of, metal chains connecting their wallets to their pants or adorning their heavy black boots.

Pete and I were out of place, our clothes plain and conservative in comparison. It was always that way. I was here, in the middle of it, but somehow none of it ever had anything to do with me. I was an observer. Removed. Distant.

Most of the people here thought they were making some kind of social statement. Everybody getting their freak on. All trying to outfreak the next guy. More piercings, more tattoos—drawing attention to themselves so that . . . well, I wasn't really sure why.

Maybe without all that extra stuff, there was nothing worth mentioning about them. Or maybe they didn't get enough attention at home and wanted it from strangers on the street. Whatever the reason, they all seemed to pride themselves on being different, but in reality they all ended up looking the same, and treated anyone from outside their tight little clique like a leper.

Steve was where I expected to find him, leaning back on one elbow as he stood at the bar watching the crowd around him. His eyes traveled over the young girls who thronged at the bar, most of them sipping on Cokes because they were too young to buy alcohol.

There always seemed to be something a little off with Steve. Maybe it was that his eyes were open a little too wide, his grin too broad to be genuine, his speech too affected to not be rehearsed. He was part owner, or maybe just a manager, of the club, a detail he never clarified—probably because he wanted you to believe he was more of a rock star than he really was. Still, it was his playground and if I wanted to play, I needed to make nice with him. I didn't like him or trust him, but neither point was relevant.

Steve's blond hair was thin on top but he still wore it in a long ponytail, as if the hair in back could compensate and anyone who observed him would not notice his hair loss. His age was indeterminate in the low light of the club but the condition of his skin suggested he was much older than the girls he chose to date.

Steve's eyes never stayed fixed on any one thing for more than a second or two. His gaze traveled the room while he spoke or listened, never looking anyone in the eye. It could make a person uncomfortable but, on the rare occasion when he did meet your eye, you'd immediately wish he would look at something else. There wasn't much to see through the windows to his soul, but what was there was not pleasant to contemplate.

"Well, look who it is," Steve said by way of greeting as he untangled himself from a girl who was barely old enough for her tattoos to have been acquired legally.

"Hey, Steve," I said as I shook his hand, palming him a dime bag filled with a few hits of X and a large bud. "My buddy Pete," I said with a nod in Pete's direction. Pete nodded in greeting but kept his mouth shut—a small miracle.

Steve ignored Pete, which was the way I wanted it. Steve shouted for the bartender to bring us a couple of shooters and clinked his glass against mine before tipping his head back to slurp the cocktail. Etiquette dictated I take the shot. The price of doing business, though I didn't want to pay it.

"What are you looking at?" Steve asked suddenly, directing his comment over my shoulder to Pete. A grin was still plastered on Steve's face, but it was fixed like a grimace, no mirth evident.

"Who? Me?" Pete asked, pointing at his own chest.

"Yeah, you," Steve said, mimicking Pete's tone of surprise. "Who do you think I'm talking to?"

"I was—" Pete turned to me for help but I just watched him expectantly. "I was just watching the . . . people. You know, looking around," Pete said uncertainly.

"Well, that people you can't seem to stop looking at happens to be my girlfriend," Steve said.

"Hey, I didn't mean . . . I mean, I'm not . . ." Pete looked to me again for help.

"What's with this kid?" Steve asked, turning to me.

I jerked my head to one side, indicating that Steve should step aside with me so I could speak to him without being overheard. Steve shot one last scathing look at Pete, then stepped over to where I stood waiting a few feet away.

"Look," I said in a hushed tone, "the kid's okay. He's just spent some time in juvie. He was all kinds of messed up on hallucinogens—shrooms, LSD, you name it—when they sent him down state for almost an entire year. Guards messed him up a little bit."

"Yeah?" Steve asked, interest showing in his eyes as his gaze landed on Pete for a full ten seconds, longer than I'd ever seen him look at any one thing. "Guards messed with him?" he asked, the eagerness in his voice telling me he wanted more of the story.

"Yeah, he got his knee all busted up with a nightstick, hit in the head a few times. He's a little . . . off now, but he's cool," I said, shooting a furtive glance over my shoulder as if to make sure Pete couldn't overhear our conversation. "He hates cops now. Would probably kill one if he got the chance."

"That's messed up," Steve said, a newfound respect for Pete dawning in his eyes.

I shrugged. "Yeah."

It didn't take Steve long to lose interest in us and I gestured discreetly to Pete to follow me. A series of dark passages led to an interior space with a high ceiling and a dance floor the size of a basketball court, where hundreds of people moved under the flashing strobes and disco ball.

Kiddush was spinning in this room, the main and largest dance floor, and the crowd was loving it. He was playing an M.I.A. song and I nudged Pete's arm to get his attention. "Fall in and dig it!" I said in a shout to be heard over the music.

"What?" Pete shouted back.

"Let's dance."

"I don't know how," he said, sounding a little desperate.

"Nobody cares," I said over my shoulder as I walked into the crowd.

I moved to the center of the floor where a group of girls were dancing together and started to move. Kiddush was good at his job, playing his own remix of the song, and the crowd was pumped. I kept an eye on Pete to see how he was doing. What he had said was correct, he couldn't dance, but at least he was moving around, not standing in one spot and shifting from one foot to the other like most guys did.

As I watched him move under the flashing strobe, his movements seemed natural, almost fluid, and had lost their usual jerkiness under the shifting light. In the mix of shadows and movement you couldn't tell there was anything different about him. Suddenly he was the man, throwing his hips and arms around like he was totally lost in the music. The girls moved in closer to dance with him, feeding off his energy, while I paired off with an ebony-skinned Caribbean girl who could shimmy like nobody's business.

Pete was a hit with the ladies and stayed out on the floor long after I retreated to the bar and passed off party favors to my regulars. He was still dancing when I concluded business and I pulled him behind me to separate him from the throng.

I took Pete up to the DJ booth to meet Kiddush, who greeted us both with a man hug. He put on an extended remix of a Drake song and went down to the dance floor to amaze the crowd with some of his vintage breakdance moves while Pete and I watched from the DJ booth. Sam had spent many lonely Friday nights as a teenager practicing his music and his dance moves with no other company than a mirror and a collection of old-school videos on DVD.

I had to drag Pete out of the place. He would have been there until last call if I had let him, but it's best to always be the last to arrive and first to leave a party.

TWENTY-NINE

WHEN WE LEFT THE CLUB, IT WAS STILL EARLY
and I had one more stop to make.

"We're going bowling?" Pete asked with a frown as I
pulled into the lot of the local Games and Lanes.

"You can bowl if you want. I've got business," I said as I
climbed out of the T-Bird.

"Bridget and all of her friends have been hanging out
here lately," Pete said. "I'm not sure why. This place is a
dump."

I murmured a disinterested, "Mm," as we headed for

the entrance. A cop was stationed near the door. Now that most of the kids from the local high schools were hanging out at the Games and Lanes on Fridays and Saturdays, they kept an officer stationed here to make sure no one was drinking or getting pregnant in the parking lot.

"Hey, Jesse." The cop nodded to me as I approached.

"Stan, how've you been?" I asked.

"Well, I pulled the crap duty tonight, didn't I?" he asked as he cracked the knuckles of his left hand.

"Looks like," I said.

"You kids stay out of trouble," he said with a small salute as I reached for the door handle.

The noise hit us like a wall as we entered the alley, all twenty lanes filled with just about every clique imaginable from the local high schools. The sound of their conversation was a dull roar interspersed with the crescendo of balls striking the pins at the ends of the lanes. The brown carpet had once featured some kind of pattern of gold and red, long since worn away with the tread of many bowling shoes. The carpet held the smell unique to bowling alleys everywhere, the stale rot of spilled soda, beer, and ketchup. A faint reminder of the cigarettes people used to smoke inside still hung in the air, an odor nothing less than a full renovation would ever wipe away.

"I'll find you in a bit," I said to dismiss Pete as I headed toward the back of the house, to an unmarked office with a small window cut high in the door. I knocked once to announce myself, then opened the door and let myself in.

The owner, a man with the unfortunate name of Donald McDonald, sat behind a scarred wooden desk playing solitaire on an ancient desktop. Don was plump, his hands pale and doughy. He wore a handlebar mustache streaked with gray, his curly, grizzled hair receded far enough to give him a fivehead.

"Hey, kid," he said, barely sparing me a glance.

"Hiya, Don," I said as I helped myself to the folding chair across from his desk. "Looks like business is good."

"Yeah," he said with a noncommittal shrug, stringing me along. "It's okay."

"Looks better than okay," I said as he kept his gaze fixed on his computer screen, tried to make out like he was unconcerned about the whole conversation. "Every Friday and Saturday night the parking lot is full. Word around town is this is where the cool kids hang out on the weekends." I kept my tone light but was ready for the inevitable pushback he was going to give me. If Don wasn't such a cheap bastard, he might have considered a few upgrades to his bowling alley to attract new business instead of relying on me to build his clientele.

"What I meant is," he said, his tone world-weary, "sure I got a bunch of kids hanging out here on the weekends, but there are hidden expenses in that. You know, a lot more maintenance costs to keep the place up and running."

Here we go.

"I guess their money is as green as anybody else's," I said, starting in easy. "You didn't specify what type of crowd you wanted when we entered into this arrangement."

"Yeah, well, I'm just saying," he said as he held his hands out in supplication, finally spinning his chair to face me, "there are a lot more expenses when you have a crowd of kids coming in every weekend. The bathroom looks like a damn bomb went off in it at the end of the night."

"That sounds like a personal problem to me, Don," I said. It came off as a joke, though I was tiring quickly of our dance. "Are you trying to shine me on?" I asked, letting my impatience seep in at the edges.

His face composed itself into a look of innocence. "Shine you on? What are you talking about, Jesse?"

"Don't fuck with me, Don," I said.

He shrugged, but I could see beads of sweat forming on his upper lip. "I don't see what you're getting so upset about, Jesse. All I'm saying is maybe I don't have as much extra money as you think I do."

I leaned forward, tipping the chair onto two legs as I rested my elbows on my knees. "The way I see it, you've got two options open to you. You can pay me what you owe me and I'll go bowl a couple of rounds with my friends, or you can keep dicking me around and every kid with an allowance and a mode of transportation within ten square miles will take up a sudden interest in Putt 'n' Play."

"Jeez o' Petes, Jesse," he said, looking suddenly like a cornered rodent, his mustache drooping more than usual. "I didn't mean anything by it. I've got your money. Right here I've got it," he said as he reached into his top drawer and tossed an envelope on the desk.

I didn't thank him. Thanking someone for money you've earned is a show of weakness.

"I'll see you next week, Don," I said as I rose to go. "Spend a little of that extra money on getting the carpets shampooed, huh? The stink is enough to knock someone out."

"Yeah, sure, Jesse. Hey," he called me back as I was reaching for the door. "What did you do? To get everyone to start hanging out here, I mean?"

"Don," I said with a pained look, "if I told you that, I wouldn't have a job, now, would I?"

"Yeah, no, I get that. Thanks, Jesse. And, hey, if you want to bowl a round, you tell Jason at the desk, your shoe rental is on the house. The least I can do."

"Thanks, Don," I said, though the irony in my tone was lost on him.

As I wandered through the bowling alley, greeting people and taking the time to stop and talk to a few of them, I ran into Heather Black. She was sitting back near the low wall that separated the bowling lanes from the arcade and snack bar, scrolling through her phone. Her friends were all either huddled around the scoring table or taking turns up on the lanes, but Heather's attention was obviously elsewhere.

"Hey, Jesse," Heather said as she tossed her hair in a practiced way, her gold hoop earrings swinging against her cheeks.

"Heather, how've you been?" I asked as I leaned my elbows onto the ledge behind where she sat and watched the kids enjoying America's favorite pastime.

"Okay, I guess," she said without much enthusiasm.

"Where's your boy David?" I asked as I glanced around for a sign of him and moved to sit in the molded plastic chair beside hers.

"His parents have permanently grounded him since his last report card," she said as she lifted one foot onto the seat and hugged her shin. "So lame. He's saying they might not even let him go to homecoming."

"Sucks," I said.

"Has David said anything to you?" she asked. "About me, I mean."

"I haven't really talked to him much lately. Why?"

"I'm just curious." She paused and bit her lower lip, then said, "I was just wondering if maybe he wasn't inter- ested in me anymore or something. Was just using his parents as an excuse not to see me."

"Why would you think that?" I asked with a confused frown.

"I don't know," she said casually, but she couldn't hide her blush. "Maybe he's just not that into me."

"Are you joking?" I asked with a chuckle but stopped suddenly as I realized she wasn't. "Wait. You really think David isn't into you?"

"I don't know what to think," she said with a shake of her head, and she wouldn't look at me, feigned complete interest in the bowling action to avoid my eye.

"You're a beautiful girl, Heather. David would be crazy to not be into you."

"Yeah?" she asked.

"Sure," I said as I leaned back and put my arms along the back of the seats, my legs stretched out in front of me and crossed at the ankle.

"But just because I'm pretty," she said, sounding disap- pointed. "You don't think he would be into me because of my personality."

"I didn't say that," I said, which, I suppose, didn't mean I wasn't thinking it.

"Yeah, well, David's different, you know? He's not like other guys," she said as she slid an accusatory glance in my direction. "He treats me like I'm a princess."

"Of course he does. David Cohen is thanking whatever god he believes in every day that he gets to go out with a girl like you," I said.

She smiled thinly but her eyes remained dim with knowing. "I know you never really cared all that much about me when we were seeing each other," she said, pausing to give me a chance to deny it.

"I don't really care about anyone. You know that. And I never deserved you anyway," I said as I put an arm around her shoulder and dropped a friendly kiss on her cheek.

"I know," she said, and we shared a smile.

I found Pete hanging near the refreshment stand, a Coke in one hand, the other in his jacket pocket as he watched the people bowling. He was leaning against the wall, his eyes hooded with fatigue.

Bridget was down in the lanes with a group of her friends and Ken with his posse. I had hoped to be gone before Bridget spotted us but she waved happily from the lanes and came to say hi.

"Hey, guys," Bridget said as she threw an arm around Pete's shoulder and gave him a brief hug. "When did you get here?"

"Just a little while ago. We were at Plant Nine for a bit," Pete said, disclosing a lot more than I would have.

"Really?" she asked, looking to me as if to ask if I thought that it was a good idea for her kid brother to be out at a place known for its raves. I averted my gaze so I didn't have to meet her eye and pretended to have a sudden interest in something over my shoulder.

"We were just there to dance and watch the spectacle," Pete said. "We're not doing anything stupid."

"Still, I don't know, Pete. . . ." She trailed off and looked to me again for help but I refused to give her any.

"What about you?" Pete asked, gesturing to her. "You're out past curfew. I can't believe Saint Bridget would break the house rules," he said, putting a hand to his cheek in mock astonishment.

Her cheeks flushed as he said this and her lips drew into a grim line. "I'm not a saint," she said quietly.

Pete leaned in as he pointed an admonishing finger at Bridget. "I'll bet Mom and Dad didn't say shit about you staying out late with your friends but they tried to ground my ass."

"They're just looking out for you, Pete," Bridget said, which was exactly the wrong thing to say. For someone who was so sensitive to other people's feelings, Bridget wasn't very perceptive when it came to her own brother. He was like a volcano, just waiting for something to set him off. "They're just—" She glanced nervously in my direction then finished lamely, "worried." She didn't want to say the truth, that Pete's parents were concerned any time he left the house with me. She was protecting my feelings, which was sweet. And unnecessary.

"Let's get out of here," I said, slapping Pete's elbow. I

was trying to divert the coming storm, but he dug in his heels and refused to let it go.

"Why?" he asked Bridget, completely ignoring me. "Why are they so worried about me and not about you? Because you hang out with Mr. Homecoming King Superstar Football Player and I hang out with Jesse? Because you're so perfect and I'm such a freak?"

"I didn't say that," Bridget said quietly. He was hurting her feelings intentionally now, trying to make her feel as bad as he did.

I wanted to tell her not to take the bait, to just let it go. But it was too late. As she launched into an argument I grimaced and pinched the bridge of my nose.

"God, you know, I'm so tired of always being caught in the middle between you and Mom and Dad," Bridget said, her voice trembling with suppressed emotion. "They just want what's best for you."

Mental sigh of defeat.

"Why? Because I'm *special*?" Pete asked, his tone dripping with poison. "I'm not special and I'm not differently abled!" Pete was shouting now, spittle flying out of his mouth as he swung his arms crazily, like an excited chimpanzee. "I'm just fucked up! Okay? Do you get it?"

Bridget was keeping it together like a champion, her eyes open wide as she tried to hold back the tears. Her expression didn't waver but finally her lower lip trembled and a single, fat tear slid down her cheek.

"Why don't you stop trying to make me—? Agghh! Son of a bitch!" Pete cried out as he sat back hard on his ass, his face exploded in crimson as his nose started to bleed profusely. I shook the pain out of my hand; the knuckles had all popped when they connected with his face.

"You ever speak to your sister that way again, and I'll put you in a fucking wheelchair," I said as I took a menacing step in his direction.

"Jesse!" Bridget pushed me away from Pete, then sank to one knee as she reached out to touch his face. "What the hell is wrong with you?" Bridget asked me as she dug through her purse, then offered Pete a wrinkled napkin.

"Stay out of it," Pete said, taking the napkin from Bridget but pushing aside her hand as she tried to help him.

Bridget stood and took a step back, plucking nervously at the hem of her shirt with her slender fingers.

"You don't understand what it's like," Pete whined, "they all treat me like I'm some kind of charity case."

"You are a charity case," I said as I put my hands in my pockets to keep from hitting him again. "And an asshole if that's the way you treat the one person who's always looking out for you."

"*Stop it,*" Bridget said with a warning look in my direction. "I didn't ask you to stick up for me, Jesse."

"Stop letting him talk to you any damn way he pleases," I said, raising my voice to her.

Bridget opened her mouth to make a retort but was interrupted by Ken as he injected himself into the situation. I hadn't even noticed his approach but suddenly Ken was there, an arm out like a Heisman Trophy to hold me back. "Alderman, what the hell?" he asked, his face red with anger.

Pete lifted the front of his shirt to wipe his nose, sniffled, then coughed.

"Pete, you okay?" Ken asked.

"You fucking hit me, man," Pete said, ignoring Ken's question.

"No shit," I said. "You've been asking for it all night with your smart fucking mouth."

"Back off," Ken said, loud enough to make heads turn. "I swear to God, Alderman, I will rearrange your face."

"Ken," Bridget said, almost gently, as she gripped his arm. "Everyone just calm down, okay?" She wouldn't even look at me and her voice still trembled.

The guy behind the shoe counter was hurrying over to intervene, craning his neck around to look for Stan, the police officer, for some help. Stan, thankfully, was still hanging around outside to dissuade the dopers and drinkers and kids who just wanted to make out in their cars.

"Alderman, you need to get out of here," Ken said. I could see him struggling with his desire to pound me, all the while knowing that I held his secret, could turn Bridget against him with just a word. He was afraid to step over the line with me but, all the same, would go to the mat for Bridget if he had to and protect her little brother. I had my own internal struggle, wanted to fall to my knees and beg Bridget's forgiveness, explain myself to her until my words fell like verbal diarrhea. But I took a step away as the crowd waited breathlessly to see how our little drama would play out. Even the bowling-shoe guy seemed to be holding his breath.

"Fuck you, Ken," I said. "What's between me and the kid is none of your business."

If I had to be honest and tell you why I backed down then, I couldn't claim that it was because of Bridget's feelings or fear of a beat-down from Ken. I backed down because it all felt so futile at that moment. Who was I kidding? I was a monster. The kind of monster who punched a kid with cerebral palsy, who sold a sweet girl like Bridget to the highest bidder, who didn't have to care about how other people felt, because I didn't have any feelings of my own. The kind of monster who doesn't survive to see the end of the fairy tale.

Bridget started to come after me as I walked away, her voice calling me back, but Ken held her by the arm and told her to let me go.

"Night, Stan," I said as I walked out of the bowling alley into the crisp night air.

"You must suck at bowling if you're already giving up," Stan said as he rubbed his hands to warm them and rocked back on his heels.

"I suck at a lot of things, Stan," I said, and he laughed though nothing I had said was really funny.

THIRTY

PETE WASN'T SPEAKING TO ME. WELL, TECH-nically that was an exaggeration. I said hey to him in the hallway at school on Tuesday and he told me to fuck off. He was angry, which was understandable since I had punched him in the face, but I suppose if he truly hated me, he would have just ignored me. The best thing to do, I decided, was to give him a few days to cool down before I approached him again.

That same week, they announced the homecoming court over the PA system during first period. Named king, Ken Foster, royal douche. Queen, Theresa Mason. Excited murmurs filled the classroom until my history teacher, Mr. Smith—crotchety, old, and nails stained yellow with tobacco tar—barked for everyone to be quiet.

The halls were abuzz with gossip and speculation about Theresa's unexpected win. A win more unexpected by Theresa than anyone else. After the announcement, she stood with an entourage of cheerleaders and drill team members fawning over her in the main corridor, her smile putting the sun to shame.

I was curious what Ken's reaction would be when he heard the news, but I was in AP history during first period while he, I could only assume, was in woodshop or some remedial reading class.

It pleased me that Theresa was happy about winning homecoming queen, but really that wasn't the best part of the payout for my trouble. If I was being completely honest, it was the fact that Ken would be denied the glory of playing king, with Bridget on his arm as queen, that pleased me most of all. It brought a smile to my face every time I thought about it.

That evening I was asleep on the couch when the buzz of my phone woke me. The lights weren't on in the house and I fumbled for my phone in the dark. The call had gone to voice mail by the time I picked up, but it was Bridget calling so I dialed her back right away. Though I was still groggy when I placed the call, as soon as I heard the tone of her voice when she said hello, I was instantly awake and alert. "What is it?" I asked.

"Is Pete with you?"

"No," I said as I rubbed the stiffness of sleep out of my face. "Why?"

"He didn't come home after school and he wasn't at the Siegel Center with me. He's been acting really weird the past couple of days and I just . . . well, I'm worried."

My eyes shifted automatically to the clock on the DVR and saw that it was only seven o'clock, not late enough to jump to any extreme conclusions, but I knew the Small-eys followed a strict routine of dinner together as a family each night at six. I was already up and moving when she said, "He's been upset since your fight, has barely spoken to anyone since then. Have you talked to him at all?"

"No," I said, realizing as I did that I sounded guilty about that.

"Will you? Talk to him? I don't think you understand . . ." She paused and I could sense that she was holding back, keeping her emotion in check, "maybe you don't realize how important your friendship is to him. You're all he had. I don't want you guys to hate each other because of me."

"Stop worrying about him. He's doing this on purpose because he wants you to worry and be upset. Stop giving in," I said as I snatched my keys up from the counter and pulled the kitchen door shut behind me.

"It's not that simple," she said. "If anyone knows that, it's you. Find him, Jesse, and make this right. You make things right with him or I'll never speak to you again. Even if it kills me, I'll never speak to you again."

"Jesus, I thought your brother was the melodramatic one," I said, and ended the call.

———

It didn't take me long to find Pete. He wanted to be found, especially since the night was a cold one—a freezing stinging rain was blowing in from the north—and because he was mad and wanted to yell at someone. He was standing under the streetlight on the bridge, my bridge, so wet from the rain that water dripped from the end of his nose and his clothes stuck to the angles of his body.

When I left the house I was mad at Pete, pissed that he was doing it again, hurting his sister intentionally so he didn't have to be alone in his misery. By the time I reached the bridge and saw the shape he was in, my anger had abated and only impatience remained.

"What do you want?" he asked me sullenly as he watched the whitecaps on the river swirling around the rocks before passing under our feet. His eyes followed as each new whitecap formed and disintegrated into the dark current of the river.

"Your sister's upset," I said. "Worried about you. Again. You selfish little prick."

"And what? She sent you to find me?" He barked out a laugh. "Shit, I'm just upset. You're straight-up suicidal. Kind of ironic that she would send you to look after me."

"That's not what 'ironic' means," I said. "You're probably trying to say it's antithetical."

"Oh, please," he said snidely. "You trying to convince me you actually studied for the SAT?"

"I didn't have to study," I said. "I know what 'ironic' means."

His eyes narrowed into slits as he said, "What did you tell her?"

"I didn't tell her a thing." I held up my hands in a gesture of innocence. "She called me, said you were missing. Your parents are worried. So is she."

He looked back to the river as he said, "She doesn't know anything. Perfect brain, perfect body, perfect fucking life."

I didn't argue. My plan was to let him yell himself out, then convince him to get in the car, go home with me, and get out of the rain.

"Aren't you going to call her?" he asked. "Tell her you're a fucking hero?"

"I'll call her in a little while," I said. "Let her know you're okay."

"I'm not okay!" He shouted, but his voice was hoarse from the cold and wet. "I'll never be okay. I have to watch every time I meet someone new, them trying to figure out what's wrong with me—get treated like I'm simple-minded because I talk funny! I'm never—" He stopped and bit off the end of his sentence. During the pause that followed I could see how much he wanted to say more, but the words were going to burn on their way out. "I'm never going to get a girl who wants me—no girl wants to be with a freak."

"You're full of shit," I said with a dismissive wave of my hand and a shake of my head. "Those girls at the party were totally into you."

"Because you lied," he shot back, "told them I was someone I'm not. They wouldn't want the real me."

"So what?" I asked hotly. "What's so great about the real you? What's so great about Pete Smalley that a girl should want you?" I didn't wait for his answer. "You think girls put out because I'm being the real me? Fuck no. They like my money, my connections, what I can do for them. They don't give a shit about me."

"Well, maybe it doesn't matter to you, but I want someone to care about who the real me is. Maybe I don't want to be like you."

"What the fuck is the difference?" I asked. "Everybody is putting on a show all the time. Nobody's real. Maybe you can't hide things about yourself like the way you walk or the way you talk, but everyone is lying all the time about who they are, how they feel."

He wouldn't look at me, was still watching the river.

"I can't believe you hit me in the face," he said after a minute.

"Oh, God," I said wearily, "we're not going to relive that again, are we?"

"What if you had broken my nose?" he asked, like a girl with all his questions about hypotheticals that never happened, as if what might have happened mattered as much as what did.

"Oh, give me a break," I said. "You're acting like that was the first time someone ever punched you in the face."

"Of course it's the first time I've ever been punched in the face!" Pete's voice cracked as he shouted. "Only a psycho would hit a kid with cerebral palsy."

"Yeah, well, you were asking for it," I said, though not disputing the accusation of being a psycho. "You can't ask for it and then hide behind the fact that you've got cerebral palsy."

"God, you are such an asshole. You know that?" he

asked, though I took the question as rhetorical. "You have no idea what it's like to be me."

"Yeah?" I asked. "Do you have any idea what it's like to be *me*? You know what it's like to have your mom eat enough pills to kill a horse and chase it with a bottle of whiskey, then die on her own bathroom rug? Huh? You know what it's like to know that your mom vomited and shat herself when she died and was found in a pool of her own filth?"

He turned away from me violently, like he was going to throw up. Wouldn't look at me or give me his face, so I moved in front of him to force him to meet my eye.

"Come on, Pete. I thought you were so fucking smart. Nobody but you has any reason to be upset, right? You know all about what it's like for your dad to stay in bed for a month after your mom died, trying to drink himself to death."

He gasped and shook his head, his eyes squeezed shut.

"I didn't think so," I said, the anger leaving my body all at once, like a balloon deflating.

He rubbed at his eyes and sniffled, still refusing to look at me.

"So, what do you want to do?" I asked as I dug my hands in my pockets and hunched my shoulders against the wind. "You want to jump in the river or you want to go get a coffee or something? Because it's fucking cold and I don't want to stand out here in this shit anymore."

His face split suddenly into his signature lopsided grin and he shook his head. "Jesus, you're like an android or something," he said. "No emotional programming."

"I told you to stop talking that sci-fi shit to me," I said as

I gestured toward the car with an expectant look. "You coming or what?"

"Are you going to call Bridget?" he asked.

"No," I said. "Call her yourself. I'm not your god-damn babysitter."

He tried to shake the excess water from his jacket before climbing into the front seat and immediately adjusted the heater to warm his hands. We ended up at the Starbucks for a hot drink and a pastry.

"I used to think you were only nice to me because you wanted to get with Bridget," Pete said around a mouthful of Danish.

"What makes you think that's not true?" I asked.

"You've never even asked her out," he said, sounding cocky again now that he didn't have water dripping off his face and he wasn't shivering with the cold.

"How do you know?"

"Because she told me," he said. "She told me she liked you but you never asked her out. And I know why."

"Do you now?" I asked absently without looking at him. I was watching the guy working as the barista. Nice-looking, downtown MILFs with their stylish rain boots and North Face jackets got the full attention of the kid behind the counter—he'd cock his head and smile sweetly at them while he took their orders, nodding with a concerned frown as he carefully wrote out their special instructions on the side of the cup. With the grungy college kids, he didn't give the same consideration—now looking bored and put out as he served a young guy in a fleece jacket with tattoos on his neck.

"Yes," Pete said with a nod. He frowned with concentration as he lifted the hot drink to his lips, slurped loudly through the plastic lid, then carefully set the cup down. "Do you want to hear my theory?"

"Shoot."

"You don't think you deserve her," he said as he studied my reaction, "don't think you're good enough for her."

"That's an interesting theory," I said, refusing to give him my eyes.

"I know you're crazy about her. You love her. So, how come you've never asked her out?"

"Maybe because I thought it would affect my friendship with you," I suggested.

"Really?" he asked, his look of surprise mixed with hope so pathetic, it made me laugh.

"No," I said. "I couldn't care less what you think."

"Yeah, no shit," he said, but he was smiling.

We fell silent after that. I checked my messages and went for another coffee while he worked up the nerve to go home. Bridget had called twice and texted me once. I held up the phone for Pete to see the display.

"I'm calling her back," I said.

He just rolled his eyes but didn't say anything so I took that for agreement.

"Did you find him?" Bridget asked by way of answering her phone.

"Yes. I'm looking right at him and he's one ugly son of a bitch."

"Where are you?" she asked, ignoring my joke as Pete flipped me the bird.

"Just out for a coffee."

"Is he okay?" she asked.

"He's fine," I said as Pete's gaze wandered around the room, doing his best to look disinterested in my conversation. "I'll bring him home later."

"Thank you for finding him. My parents will be really relieved."

"Maybe not so relieved if you tell them who he's with," I said.

"Will you call me later?" she asked, ignoring my comment. "I want to talk to you."

Would I? I didn't want to, but not because I didn't want to talk to her. I didn't like listening to her voice on the phone, because it reminded me that I wasn't with her.

"Yes, I will," I lied.

I dropped Pete off about an hour later. He had softened toward me a little and we seemed to have forged a truce, though he was stubborn and would have to come back on his own terms. That night at home, I thought about not calling Bridget more than I thought about calling her, which I took for a good sign of my willpower. I was back in control, which is exactly what the captain of the *Titanic* thought right before it started its final plunge.

THIRTY-ONE

PETE AND I DIDN'T START HANGING OUT AGAIN after the night I found him in the rain. We would nod at each other around school or at parties and exchanged a couple of texts, but things were still strained between us. He owned me now, owned my secrets, and unlike his sister, would understand that it conveyed power. Pete could be spiteful and liked to abuse the people around him, but I knew he would never hold this over me. I trusted him at least that much.

The following Tuesday I didn't see Pete in school so I decided to go looking for him. He wasn't at the Siegel Center but Bridget was there with her crew of misfits. Bridget ignored me, pretended like I wasn't even there, so I just stood in Pete's favorite wallflower spot waiting for her to finish.

After a while she got the kids to help her pick up the hula hoops and other gear they were using for today's bastardized form of organized outdoor sport. Cynthia, whose name Pete had told me so I would have an alternative to Flipper Girl, came to stand before me and said, "Bridget told me to tell you that she's not speaking to you."

"Oh, yeah?" I asked. "Why's that?"

"I don't know," she said with an exaggerated shrug. "I guess you did something to make her mad."

"How am I supposed to know what I did to make her mad if she won't speak to me?" I asked.

"I don't know," Cynthia said again.

"You go tell her that just because she's the prettiest girl in school doesn't mean she gets to treat people any way she wants." Cynthia's eyes were wide with uncertainty but she turned to walk toward Bridget when I called her back, saying, "And hey, tell her that I don't appreciate being treated like a pawn in her ongoing war with her kid brother." Cynthia started to walk away again when I called her back a second time and said, "And tell her that I didn't come to talk to her anyway. I'm looking for her brother."

Cynthia looked more uncertain than ever but left to deliver my message. I watched as she tried to relay the entire content of my monologue to Bridget, who was now looking daggers in my direction. After another eternity Cynthia returned, a small smile on her face.

"Bridget says she's mad at you because you said you would call her and you didn't. And she said that you called her melodramatic and hung up on her so she doesn't have anything else to say to you until you apologize. Do you want me to tell her you're sorry?"

"Absolutely not," I said with an emphatic shake of my head.

"If I were you, I would apologize," Cynthia said. "She's super mad."

"How old are you?" I asked.

"Eleven."

"Well, you're not too young to learn this now. Apologizing is never a good idea. It's a show of weakness. Remember that."

"Even if you're wrong?" she asked.

"Right or wrong is completely subjective," I said as I crossed my arms over my chest. "There is no good or bad, only thinking makes it so."

"You're really weird," she said, which was kind of a mean thing to say, but I let it go since she had a flipper and all. Then she freaked me out by lifting the flipper and giving me a friendly pat. "I'm sure Bridget will forgive you. She's the nicest person ever."

One of the staff people was calling her, so Cynthia hurried to grab her backpack. She waved good-bye and I waved back to her as Bridget came over to talk to me.

"Where's Pete?" I asked.

"That's it?" she asked. "That's all you have to say to me? Where's Pete?"

"I thought you weren't speaking to me."

"You don't even know why I'm mad, do you?" she asked with a shake of her head.

"If you just tell me where Pete is, then you don't have to talk to me at all. I'll leave immediately."

"He's at the doctor with my parents," she said as she moved to retrieve her backpack but I beat her to it and lifted it onto my shoulder. We started walking toward the exit together. "They went into the city to see a specialist."

"Everything okay?" I asked, maybe too quickly.

"He's fine," she said as her eyes searched my face. "It's just his leg. It's been bothering him. You know, walking the way he does, it puts a lot of strain on his joints."

"He never mentioned it," I said.

She shrugged. "Normalcy is very important to Pete. He wouldn't want to draw attention to his disability by complaining about it."

"I haven't seen him much lately," I said. "He's still pissed at me."

"Yeah? Well, I'm pissed at you too. You said you were going to call me back the other night and you didn't."

"You want to walk and get a coffee or something?" I asked, changing the subject.

"Sure," she said as she tucked her hair under a knit cap. I held the door and nodded for her to go ahead of me.

We walked slowly, taking our time, down Congress Street in the historic district where iron benches and ornamental trees lined the street in orderly rows. It was just starting to get dark and the trees were filled with tiny white Christmas bulbs—the black branches were covered in a fine layer of ice, and the refraction of light created a dazzling display. When we reached the coffee shop the front window was smoky with condensation, the interior full of people on laptops and huddled around small tables. In silent agreement we kept walking, neither of us wanting to be among a crowd.

"Pete's birthday is this weekend," she said, breaking the silence between us.

"I know," I said. "I got him a bottle of raspberry vodka and a stripper for Saturday night."

"Can you be serious for two minutes?"

"This is me being super serious," I said, drawing my face into a somber mask.

"Anyway," Bridget went on, "he said he didn't really want a party so we thought we'd just take him out to dinner. It'll just be my parents and me, and Ken's planning to come."

Sure, I thought, just what Pete wanted for his birthday, to hang out with his parents and a douche.

"I know Pete would love it if you could come," Bridget said.

"I wouldn't be too sure about that. Do your parents know you're inviting me?" I asked.

"Yes," Bridget huffed impatiently. I seemed to be the only person who had that effect on her. It was strangely flattering. "And they promised me they'll be on their best behavior."

"What time is dinner?" I asked.

"We have reservations for seven. Please say you'll come," Bridget said, and I knew that there was no way I could say no to her, even though Pete would be furious.

"Sure, I'll be there."

"So, are we going to talk about what the hell that was all about the other night at the bowling alley?" Bridget asked with an expectant look. "I can't believe you punched Pete in the face."

I thought about making up some bullshit answer, but I was tired of lying to Bridget. There were so many lies to keep up with at this point, every conversation I had with her was full of land mines. "I didn't like him talking to you like that," I said, frustrated by this truth. "He should learn to treat you with a little more respect."

"My hero," she said with her trademark nonsarcastic sarcasm, but I could tell she wasn't really mad at me. "You're supposed to be looking out for him. Not punching him in the face."

"Look, I don't want to be the one to tell you this, but you babying him all the time doesn't help him. It makes him worse. He thinks he can treat people any way he wants and no one ever calls him out for acting like a prick."

"Yeah?" she asked wryly. "Well, you're like a prick role model."

I grabbed my chest as if shot by an arrow and grimaced. "Ow, my heart. Don't hurt me, Bridget." She laughed. Couldn't help herself. "I'm just trying to give him some space for a while," I said. "He'll be fine."

"I just wish he would talk to me. He never confides in me anymore. Maybe if he did . . . well . . . I don't know. I don't know anything anymore."

"It's not about you," I said. "He's got to figure things out for himself. You smother him."

"Do I?" she asked absently.

I shrugged one shoulder. "It's understandable. You're just doing what you think is best for him."

"I've always worried that he would be lonely—that people wouldn't be able to see what a good person he is, that all they'd see were his disabilities."

"The way you treat him," I said, choosing my words carefully, "I think you make it hard for people to see anything else."

She took a minute to digest my words as we strolled along. "I saw you kiss Heather the other night at the bowling alley," she said after a minute, her voice casual. "Are you dating her again?"

"Who wants to know?" I asked, savoring the jealousy I detected in her voice. I was curious where this line of conversation was going.

"I don't really think she's good for you," Bridget said. "For you to date, I mean."

"Are we giving each other advice about dating now?" I asked.

"I'm not giving you advice," she said with impatience. "I'm just saying I don't think Heather is good for you—that you need someone who cares about more than just lip gloss and celebrity gossip."

"You're very specific for someone who isn't giving out advice," I observed.

"Fine," she said with a toss of her hair. "I can tell you're going to be difficult, but you know what I mean."

"Why should you care about what I do, anyway?" I asked, nudging her with my elbow.

"We're friends. Of course I care."

We strolled along in silence for another minute but Bridget wasn't finished, saying, "What about you and Joey? I always see you with her."

"We're friends. That's it. Is it so hard for you to believe a guy and girl can be friends without it being something else?"

"With you?" she asked. "Yes, I definitely have a hard time believing that a girl would only want to be your friend. But, you're not in love with Joey?"

"No." I didn't ask her if she was in love with Ken. I didn't want to know.

She was silent for a while after that but when she finally spoke, I knew she had been thinking about Ken because she said, "Pete doesn't like Ken. Doesn't think he's genuine. I know it seems like all Ken cares about is partying and playing football, but he's got a really sensitive side. I ran into him at an exhibit at the campus gallery one day and we went out for coffee. He was really sweet, had such nice manners." My hands were clenched in fists in my jacket pockets as I resisted the urge to tell her to shut up. I didn't want to listen to this.

"He'd asked me out a few times before and I always said no, because I didn't really think we had anything in common. That day I asked him if he could have one superpower for a day, what would it be? Do you know what he said?"

"That he wished he could throw a football a hundred yards?" I hazarded a guess.

She nudged me with her elbow to quiet me. "He said if he could have one superpower, it would be to heal people with a touch. I thought that was really cool."

"Sure. Cool," I said.

"And the way he talks about his cousin Jamie, it's really sweet. He's been such a great help at the Siegel Center. The kids love him."

Hoo boy. This is your own doing, I told myself. I was the one who had set her up to fall for him. I tried to imagine the look on Bridget's face if I confessed and told her everything, told her she had ended up with a douche bag because I had given him all the right lines to use on her—had sold her for two hundred dollars like some moderately priced whore. I took a deep breath as I thought about how I should launch into my confession, prepared to tell her everything.

"You know," she said before I could get a word out, "my family won't be back until late, will probably stop for dinner on their way home. Do you want to go get something to eat?"

"You trying to get me killed?" I asked conversationally as I suppressed a sigh of relief. God help me, I had almost told her everything. "You know Ken would pound my face if he saw us together."

"I've told Ken that he and I are too young to just date one person. He's free to go out with anyone he wants to, and so am I." The way she said this reminded me that her good nature was tempered with a stubborn streak, the one thing she and Pete had in common. Pete. The thought of him made me want to pull away from her.

"Sure, you're free to date other people," I said, "but I'll bet other guys won't even get within fifty feet of you. They're all too afraid of getting pounded by Ken. Am I right?"

"Every guy except for you," she said.

"Well, I figure you're worth a couple of beatings."

She stopped walking so suddenly, I had to take a step back to recover my arm, which she held now by the crook of the elbow. "What are you saying?" she asked. "Are you saying what I think you're saying?"

Don't say it. Don't say it.

I clamped my jaws tight so no words could escape. I couldn't trust myself around her. My hand involuntarily lifted to tuck a lock of stray hair back under her hat. As I let my fingers trail down her cheek, she put her hand over mine and hers was surprisingly warm.

She took a deep breath before saying, "I get so screwed up when I'm around you." She laughed suddenly. "You punch my kid brother in the nose and I don't know whether to be furious at you or get all gushy because you punched him to protect my feelings. Why does everything you touch get so complicated?"

I took my hand away and put it in my jacket pocket, but she kept her hand on my forearm, squeezing it.

"There's nothing complicated about the way I feel about you, Bridget," I said.

"Don't," she said, giving my arm a shake. "You can't do this. You can't tell me that you care about me and then keep me at arm's length. You can't make me feel something for you and then constantly push me away. I get that it's difficult for you right now," she said, wading into the murky waters. "You know, I think that you're letting what happened with your mom prevent you from doing what you want. Like right now. I think you would kiss me if you would let yourself care about other people again. You can't go the rest of your life feeling nothing."

I stepped away from her, forcing her to let go of my arm. "You don't get to go there, Bridget," I said coldly. She winced as if I had slapped her. And just like that, the magic of our private world was shattered. "Just because I told you about my mom doesn't give you any special right to talk about her," I spat as anger bubbled up out of an empty abyss.

Now it was frigid when only a few minutes earlier it had been crisp, the lights on the trees now glaring when a moment before they had been a subtle dance of light. I looked into the distance, refusing to meet her eye.

"What did Pete tell you?" I asked angrily. "What did he say about my mom?"

She shook her head, her brow wrinkled in confusion. "Pete didn't tell me anything. I *know* you. Know you're hurting. Maybe if you could just talk about it—," she started lamely and I quickly cut her off.

Though I didn't want to, I was going to hurt her anyway. "You think you know something about it but you don't know shit." As the words left my mouth, icy and short, a sharp, stabbing pain went through my gut.

"Then what do you expect me to do?" she asked. "How can I care about you if you won't let me?"

"I didn't ask you for anything," I said dully. "I didn't ask you for anything and I don't want anything." My heart, already a dry, shriveled husk, turned to ash and collapsed in on itself.

"You're such a god-damn hypocrite," Bridget said. "You punch Pete in the face for hurting my feelings. What about you? You're just like him. You hurt me because you think I'll just always forgive you. Saint Bridget. Maybe this time I won't forgive you. Maybe I'm tired of forgiving people."

I sighed and rubbed my forehead wearily as she sniffled and wiped at her tears. After a minute I reached to pull her into a hug. Her arms were folded against my chest and her face buried between her hands as I held her and stroked the back of her head. I put my hands on either side of her face and pressed my forehead against hers. Her cheeks were hot and wet and I wanted to drink her tears.

As I stood there, smelling a faint mingling of peanut butter and oranges on her breath, I thought about kissing her. If I had kissed her right then, she would have let me. But I didn't. And so I lost her.

"I should go," she said as she pulled away, wiping the back of her hand across her cheek.

"I'll take you home," I said, but she shook her head and reached to take her backpack from my shoulder. I reluctantly let the strap fall into her hand.

"No. I want to be alone," she said as she pushed both of her arms into the straps of her backpack and settled the weight onto her back. "I'll take the bus."

"Bridget, knock it off," I said. "It's dark already. I'll drive you home. You don't have to ever talk to me again, just let me get you home safely."

"I'll be fine." She turned then and walked away, head down, shoulders bent under the weight of her backpack, her hand coming up to wipe the tears from her face every few seconds. The people passing her on the street turned to study her curiously as she walked alone, crying.

I followed her from a safe distance, waited in my car as she stood at the bus stop near the Siegel Center. The bus to her house came and left without her getting on it. I was starting to wonder if I should go to her and talk her into letting me drive her home when another bus came and she boarded it.

I followed the bus as it wound through town and turned up the hill toward a newer neighborhood of huge brick homes that sat back on immaculately landscaped lawns. By then I knew where she was going. My chest ached with it, but I would still watch to make sure she got there safely. I parked and cut my lights as the bus pulled to the curb.

Bridget said good night to the driver as she stepped off the bus and into Ken's arms. He was waiting for her, wearing frayed jeans and his letter jacket, had come to meet her instead of letting her walk alone at night. As they started to walk toward his house he put his arm around her shoulder and dropped a kiss on the top of her head. Though Bridget and I were almost the same height, Ken was a full head taller than she was. She looked small and delicate beside him.

The scar tissue on my soul was already there long before my mom's death. It was her life that had scarred me, not her death. I was beyond scarring when she killed herself, had been for a while.

THIRTY-TWO

"WHAT'S UP?" JOEY ASKED WHEN SHE STOPPED by my locker after lunch. "Skinhead Rob called me at home yesterday. At home," she enunciated carefully. "He wanted to know why he hasn't heard from you. Why you aren't calling him back."

"Don't worry about it. I'll call him today," I said.

"What's going on with you?" Joey asked.

"Why does there have to be something going on? I've just been busy."

"Busy with what? I mean, why are you avoiding Rob?

Digger too. You haven't moved any product in two weeks. I didn't know people like you could just hand in a letter of resignation. Blood in, blood out, all that creepy stuff."

"I told you not to worry about it," I said with an air of indifference I didn't feel. "I can handle Rob and Digger."

"*Tscha,*" she scoffed. "No one can handle Rob. But even Rob doesn't scare me as much as that guy Grim. He's an ogre."

"Well, Rob should scare you more than Grim does. Grim's just big and dumb and inbred—Rob is a true sociopath."

"You could have him killed," she said. "Surely you have a hit man among your circle of friends."

"It's not the worst idea you've ever had," I said.

"I'm not even going to ask what's going on inside your head right now," she said as she held up a hand to silence me. "The way your brain works is one of the great mysteries of the universe—like why people put ketchup on their eggs, or how anyone ever thought Tom Cruise was hot."

"I think it was because of that *Top Gun* movie. I've seen it. The woman who played his girlfriend looked old enough to be his mom, which is kind of hot."

"Ew. Let's not get into you and your Ms. Fuller fantasies. Please. I just ate."

The sound of someone crying out in fear or pain drew our attention suddenly to the end of the hallway. Clint Napier stood cornered by three guys, all at least twice his size. Clint was notable only because he was flaming. He headed up the drama club and consistently outgayed even the gayest stereotypes. From my reconnaissance work for Ken, I happened to know Clint was friends with Bridget, and the two of them ate lunch together a couple of times a week.

The three guys had taken Clint's backpack and were playing keep-away with it, like young bullies on the playground. Clint was shouting as they roughed him up, his voice high-pitched with anguish. His cries turned to real sobs as his situation turned to hopeless.

The guys threatening him were all members of Ken's posse, getting a little sport out of picking on a weaker kid. I watched them out of the corner of my eye as Joey and I were walking past. Just as we were almost beyond them, Clint cried out again in terror and pain and begged for them to leave him alone. This only prompted a round of laughs and high fives among the douche squad.

I stopped and sighed as I tipped my head back and squeezed my eyes shut. Was I really going to do this? Really? Why couldn't I just walk by and pretend like it wasn't happening? Bridget's face drifted into my mind then and all I could imagine was what her reaction would be to Clint's plight, fat tears welling up in her doe eyes and breaking the dam of her lower eyelid.

Crap.

I walked over to interrupt the fag-bashing party as Joey watched in puzzlement, her head cocked to one side like an inquisitive golden retriever.

"You guys got a problem?" I asked, directing my question to the biggest one. If one of them was going to hit me, I wanted it to be the one who had the best chance of knocking me out right away.

"No problem here," he said, his chin thrust out defiantly.

"Why are you messing with the kid?" I asked with a nod at Clint, whose eyes were wide with terror and shock.

"Why? Is he your boyfriend?" the guy asked, and his buddies howled in laughter as if it was the funniest thing they'd ever heard.

"Yes," I said. "He's my boyfriend. So, why don't you back off him?"

"What did you say to me, faggot?" he asked as his eyes narrowed and took on the same look you get from a wild animal—not intelligent, just wary and ready to kill you if you make the wrong move.

"I . . ." I paused, then shrugged. "I don't remember exactly what I said. Something along the lines of leave the kid alone." I turned to Clint, who had become a statue, his forehead creased with worry and doubt, hunched over and hugging himself, like he was trying to make himself as small as possible. "Get your stuff," I said, gesturing to his backpack, lying on the floor.

Clint's eyes shot to the face of his attacker, seeking approval.

"Well, come on. I don't have all day," I said impatiently.

"Hey, wait a second," the big guy said.

"What?" I shot back. "If you're going to beat him up, get to it. Otherwise this whole thing is just a waste of time." I waited for a few heartbeats to see what they would do but they all stood frozen, unsure how to address this non-threatening threat. Clint was hugging his backpack to his chest as he waited to see what would happen. I was curious myself but took that moment to turn and walk away.

"That was unbelievable," Clint said in a breathy voice, tagging along behind me as I fell into step beside Joey again. I felt the eyes of his three attackers following us down the hall but they didn't come after us.

"Get lost," I said to Clint.

"Seriously, you just saved my ass," he said, tripping at my heels. "Thank you so much."

"Yeah, okay, you thanked me," I said. "Now, go on. Get out of here." Clint looked completely baffled as he moved away from us.

"Oh, my God, what was that?" Joey asked as she laughed out loud and put her hands across her belly as if to hold in her mirth.

"I don't need him thinking we're besties all of a sudden," I said to cover my awkwardness. "He'll be like a stray dog."

"You are straight cray, you know that?" Joey asked.

"Zip it, Joe."

"You're like one of those real-life superheroes. You should get some tights and a mask. We'll have to think of a really good name," she said thoughtfully as she put a finger to her lips and squinted off into the middle distance.

"Keep it up," I said in a low growl. "I'm not above hitting a girl."

"Seriously," she said, "what was that about? Did you recently convert to Unitarianism or something?"

"It was just business," I said.

"Are you going to invoice him later for services rendered? Or was it *just business* the same way it was just business you arranging for Theresa to win homecoming queen?" Joey's voice was casual but there was the glint of amusement in her eyes.

"Just business as in it's my business and none of yours," I said, furious with myself now for doing something as stupid as getting involved in Clint's problems.

"And for a second there, I thought maybe the Wizard had given you a heart," Joey said. "But I know what this is about. This is all about that girl Bridget."

"Are you high?" I asked. "Is that why you're like this?"

"I should have known it was because of some dopey girl," she said, ignoring me. "I'm not blind, you know. That guy Clint is a friend of hers, isn't he? I've seen them around together. Is that why you hang out with that Pete kid? So his sister will think you're the bomb-diggity?"

"I don't know what you're talking about."

"God," she said smacking her forehead with her hand as she stopped in the middle of the hallway. "I can't believe I didn't see it sooner. You're totally in love with her. And she's like a Disney princess. Guys are all so predictable."

"Nobody asked you."

"Ooh, touchy," Joey said as she started to back away. "An Achilles' heel. I never would have believed it." Then she turned and walked away with an offhand wave over her head.

THIRTY-THREE

I HADN'T SEEN IT COMING, SO I DIDN'T FACTOR
the beat-down I got from Ken into my plans. That same
afternoon I saved Clint from torture at the hands of Ken's
posse was the day Ken cornered me on my way to my car
after school.

Ken's look of shock mixed with anger greeted me
when I strolled into the restaurant that Saturday evening for Pete's birthday. Ken was already with Bridget and
her parents when I arrived, so he didn't dare say anything, but he locked his gaze on mine and we exchanged

a silent battle of wills that went unnoticed by everyone else.

Pete's birthday dinner would have been mildly amusing had it only offered the entertainment of watching Ken suck up to Mr. and Mrs. Smalley and eye me suspiciously every time I opened my mouth to say something. It was made surreal by the fact that Pete's parents had chosen the Putt 'n' Play as the place to take us to eat, complete with arcade and people wearing funny hats who humbled themselves for five bucks an hour to sing "Happy Birthday to You" while clapping and marching in an impromptu parade. I counted eight renditions of the song while Pete stoically bit his lip, dreading his turn in the limelight.

I was still nursing a split lip and the dull ache in my head and chest, though it had been three days since Ken pummeled me in the school parking lot. From the look he was giving me across the table, I knew that if Bridget weren't witness, he'd have permanently disfigured my face the second I showed it at Pete's birthday dinner.

Ken was wrong, about a lot of things. It was arguable that my friendship with Pete had begun because I wanted an excuse to see Bridget on a regular, but our friendship had transcended her. And I had no intention of taking Bridget away from Ken. She belonged with someone like Ken, someone who would look after her and treat her like the angel she was. Someone not me.

I actually respected the fact that he had taken the initiative to kick my ass in order to protect her. It meant that he would keep lowlifes like me away from her at all costs, even at the risk of insulting the feelings of her little brother. Maybe I hadn't been able to handpick the guy for Bridget to make her avoid the likes of me, but I could have done worse.

That Ken touched her in such a familiar way made me wonder if they were sleeping together. In my mind I had convinced myself Bridget was a virgin, but there was no reason to assume that was true. Often we believe what we want to think is true, and in this I was no different. Ideally, Bridget would join a convent immediately after high school.

And even though I would never be with her, ever since I had held her in my arms after our fight, I knew that I would never love any other girl the way I loved Bridget. Lately I had started a playlist devoted to my favorite love songs—songs I would play for Bridget on my guitar if I could still play—and had burned it out on my iPod playing it so many times. The list may have included a song or two by Bruno Mars, but I would never admit it, even under professional torture. The soundtrack included Al Green, Otis Redding, Bonnie Raitt, Johnny Mathis, Billie Holiday, Marvin Gaye, Patty Griffin, Aaron Neville, Ray Charles, and it wouldn't be a list of love songs without Tony Bennett and Burt Bacharach.

Twice I caught Bridget's eye across the table and savored the way her mind lingered on me before Ken drew her attention away with a cloddish remark. When Bridget excused herself to the bathroom, Ken stood and held her chair, which almost sent Bridget's mother into a swoon. His chivalry grated on my nerves, and I finished two sodas only because I was often caught with nothing better to do than pick up my glass and draw from the brightly colored straw.

Sitting across from me as she was, I found it hard to keep my eyes off Bridget, but I didn't really try. Ken kept his gorilla mitts on Bridget at all times—his arm rested on her shoulder or his hand on her arm—like a kid protecting a toy he didn't want to share. Ken's displays of affection, his obvious obsession with their golden daughter, seemed to make the Smalleys happy rather than uncomfortable.

Pete's parents were grudgingly polite toward me, his mother making the effort by asking some questions about how I was doing in school. When she asked about my parents, Bridget cut her off quickly.

"Mom," Bridget said, the abrupt interruption delivered with a meaningful stare.

"Oh, uh . . . well," Mrs. Smalley said as she took a large gulp from her water glass to cover her awkwardness. "Sorry."

"Don't be," I said affably.

Silence followed and everyone watched the tabletop— everyone but Bridget, who bravely met my gaze and held it. I dropped her a wink and she looked away, her cheeks flushing.

"How are your grades?" Pete's mother asked me, the question weighted with her serious doubt that I would amount to much.

"I make honor roll usually," I said humbly, since Kwang was really the straight-A student.

"Which college are you hoping to attend?" she asked.

"I haven't really made up my mind that I'm going to go," I answered honestly.

"What do you mean?" Mrs. Smalley asked with a frown.

"I mean I'm not sure I want to go to college," I said.

She exchanged a knowing look with her husband and said, "Are you just trying to be funny?"

"No, ma'am. School doesn't interest me much. I'm not sure I want to commit to another four years of it."

A derisive snort emanated from Mr. Smalley and he said, "You'd better not get any ideas about not going to college when the time comes," directing his comment to Pete.

Pete's expression, already sour, twisted into a frown as he bit down on a sharp retort.

"Bridget's already applied to Dartmouth," Mrs. Smalley said, obvious pride in her voice. "They haven't given early decision yet but the admissions person we spoke to said she has a really great chance."

"Mom, please," Bridget said nervously. "Stop making such a big deal about it."

"It is a big deal, honey," she said with a smile, forgetting about her disapproval of me in light of her daughter's accomplishments. "Bridget was thinking about applying to Stanford too, but we're hoping she'll try to stay closer to home."

"Mom." Bridget's tone conveyed a warning.

"Where are you applying to college, Ken?" I asked curiously. Surely he didn't expect he could get into Dartmouth and follow Bridget after high school.

He glowered suspiciously. "A few of the state colleges— my dad wants me to apply to University of Vermont," he said, his tone uncertain, like he wasn't sure if he should be proud or ashamed in front of the Smalleys.

"Great business school," Mr. Smalley said knowingly. A point that would definitely not be proved by Ken's acceptance to the school.

"That would be so nice if you and Bridget were close enough that you could visit each other on the weekends," Mrs. Smalley said, beaming at Ken with a suggestive smile.

Ken's grin was sheepish, his "aw, shucks" routine that he usually employed to deflower virgins now on display for Mrs. Smalley. He cut his eyes to Bridget to gauge her reaction, but her expression was neutral.

Pete was quiet throughout all of this, the strain between him and his parents obvious. His folks liked to blame his rebellious behavior on me. It made them feel better, which was fine. Pete and Bridget were bothered by their parents' dislike of me, but I wasn't. The Smalleys needed me as an excuse, to make sense of Pete's behavior. If they could comfort themselves with the belief that I was a bad influence, then they didn't have to think of themselves as failures.

"It's time you started thinking about where you're going to apply," Mr. Smalley said to Pete. "Your sister won't get accepted to Dartmouth by some kind of miracle. She's worked hard for it."

"I gave up trying to compete with Bridget's perfection a while ago," Pete said—an open invitation to his parents for a fight.

Bridget visibly tensed at their exchange and looked at her hands, twisted in a ball in her lap. Ken was oblivious, sucking the last bit of meat off a short rib.

"Why can't you accept that Bridget and I are different people?" Pete asked. "Not because I'm wrong, or bad, or special. But just because she's her and I'm me."

Bridget's face clouded with anger and disappointment as Pete stubbornly clung to his childish resentments. Even though he deserved it, I knew Bridget wouldn't call him out for acting like a baby and ruining the birthday dinner.

"Hey, Pete," I said, hitting his shoulder with the back of my hand. "Come on, man."

"Stay out of it," he said to me.

I wiped my mouth one last time with my napkin and tossed it on the table as I pushed back my chair. "Fine, stay here and make everybody sorry they bothered to do something nice for you. Come on into the arcade when you're finished, and I've got twenty bucks that says I kick your ass at foosball."

Mrs. Smalley stiffened at my use of foul language at the table but my interruption was a relief. I pushed through the crowd to the bar and ordered two rum and Cokes in pint glasses. By the time I got to the arcade, Pete was there. I handed him his drink and knocked my glass roughly against his. "Cheers," I said.

"Unfuckingbelievable," he said. "They are so clueless."

"They're parents," I said. "They're supposed to be clueless. You got any quarters?"

"It's my birthday," he said, incredulous. "You want me to pay?"

"I just figured since it was like a special occasion, I'd let you pay for once," I said.

"You know what? Piss off. I'm going to the bathroom. Hold my drink."

"I'm not your date," I said. "Take it with you."

"You suck."

I smiled to myself after he had turned to walk away. Just like old times.

"Boy, you really know how to break up a party," Bridget said at my back.

I spun on my heel to find her standing alone, though I knew Ken couldn't be far away. "Hey, don't try to make that about me," I said, gesturing back toward the dining room. "I didn't create your family's dysfunction."

"God, sometimes the way they act makes me want to scream."

"So, scream at him," I said. "Scream at them."

She bit the inside of her cheek and shook her head as she dropped her gaze to the floor.

"You know," I said, "it won't kill him to get his feelings hurt once in a while. Everyone gets their feelings hurt once in a while."

"Except for you," she said.

"Except for me," I agreed.

Pete returned then, his usual scowl fixed in place, and stared hard at Bridget, as if daring her to say something about his outburst at the table.

I fed quarters into the foosball machine and retrieved the ball as it fell into the pocket at one end. Bridget stood beside me, apparently planning to watch the game, but I waved her away with a gesture of my hand. "No girls allowed," I said. If she stayed and she and Pete got into another argument, I would probably end up punching him in the face again and I was trying really hard to be the kind of person who didn't punch kids with cerebral palsy in the face, the leopard changing his spots.

Bridget muttered something under her breath but walked away and left us alone.

"You know," Pete said when she was out of earshot, "it's kind of pathetic how much you love her."

"I know," I said, most of my mind on the game now that Bridget was gone.

"I'd rather see her dating you than Ken, even though you're a prick."

"Mm-hm."

"You suck!" he shouted as I slammed a goal home.

"You gonna cry?" I asked.

"I'll tell you what I'm gonna do," he said as he spun the center stick in a patently illegal move, "is beat your ass."

"That's what your mother said to me last night," I said, and Pete howled with laughter.

"Uncool," he said. "You can't use 'your mama' jokes, because I can't say them back to you. That's like a rule. People whose moms are dead are not allowed to 'your mama' other people."

"I think you just made that up," I said. He executed another hard spin and I cussed at him. "Just because you're a cripple doesn't mean you get to cheat," I said.

"Cheap shot," Pete said as he retrieved the ball and rolled it absently between his fingers.

"You want to talk or do you want to play?" I asked.

"I want to get out of here," he said, as if all of a sudden making up his mind.

"Fine. I'm going to hit the head. You go break the news to your folks and I'll meet you up front."

On my way to the bathroom I ran into Ken. He stepped into my path so suddenly, I bounced off his chest and took a stumbling step back. "What now?" I asked.

"You were supposed to stay away tonight," Ken said.

"This isn't about you, Ken," I said in my most reasonable tone.

"What the fuck are you up to?" Ken asked as he bumped his shoulder against me and circled me like a dog inviting a fight. "I thought I told you to stay away."

"Ease up," I said, not willing to back down, but wanting to defuse the scene before it got out of hand. "I'm just here for the kid. If Bridget breaks up with you, it'll be because of your own miserable personality. Nothing else."

"What's your game?" he asked. "You expect me to believe you're suddenly biffers with Pete? That you're not trying to win Bridget's heart by being besties with her kid brother?"

"Look," I said, trying to reason with him, even though I know better than anyone if you're trying to reason with an idiot, you've already lost, "I was following her to get information for you when I met the kid. You paid me to get her to go out with you, remember? How else was I supposed to get to know her? Pete's a pain in my ass and he insists on tagging along wherever I go. What am I supposed to do? Tell him to fuck off?"

"What?" he asked. "Suddenly you're a humanitarian? What do you care?"

"I don't," I snapped. "What do you want me to say to

convince you that I don't give a shit about Bridget or her dopey brother?" I asked.

Ken's lips curled into an evil smile, and a look of triumph spread onto his face. Without asking, I knew what had happened. I turned and found Pete staring at me, the hurt and anger clear in his eyes. His lips parted and his breath started to come in gasps. Ken just hung back and enjoyed the moment.

"Get out of here," Pete said, his voice barely above a whisper.

"I'm already gone," I said.

THIRTY-FOUR

"THE THING IS," I SAID AS I LEANED FORWARD to reach for my drink, "he's proud, you know? Stubborn. Even if I could tell him the whole story about Ken and why I said what I did, he won't listen to me."

"Is it okay if I smoke in here?" Emerald (the name as fake as the green of her eyes) asked as she dug in her bag.

"Yeah, sure," I said. "You want another drink?"

"I'm good," she said as she blew out a match and looked for a place to set it. "I've got to drive and I've still got one more stop tonight. Some bachelor party in Belmont," she said, referring to the next town over, as I went to the sideboard to get a dish she could use as an ashtray.

"I don't know, hon," Mr. Dunkelman was saying. "This . . . lifestyle. It doesn't seem safe for you. Don't you worry about guys coming on too strong?"

"I always carry Mace with me, Mr. D," Emerald said with a reassuring pat on his hand, probably the most action he had seen from a woman since his wife died. "And most guys aren't so bad. Every once in a while it's a problem, but I can take care of myself."

By the time Emerald had gotten to my house the night of Pete's birthday party, neither Mr. D nor I were much in the mood to watch a strip show. My blunder with Pete weighed heavily on my mind, and Mr. Dunkelman said that it would creep him out to watch a girl as young as Emerald dance. "I'm old enough to be your grandfather," he said, as if she couldn't tell by the fact that the waistband of his pants was somewhere up near his armpits.

"Great-grandfather," I corrected him.

"Nobody asked you," he shot back, but then turned on the charm to politely offer Emerald something to eat.

I had been halfway through the story of what happened at Pete's birthday dinner, giving Mr. D the background on Ken and Bridget, when Emerald rang the doorbell and interrupted the conversation. Mr. Dunkelman sat and listened attentively to my monologue, stoically enduring a raspberry vodka mixed with orange juice. "Does he wear skirts too?" Mr. D had asked when I explained to him that raspberry vodka was Pete's favorite.

"If his friendship is important to you, then you have to

talk to him—you have to at least try to explain it to him," said Emerald. I found her surprisingly naïve for a woman who took off her clothes in front of people for money.

"Explain what?" I asked. "That I accepted money in exchange for spying on his sister? That I shared her personal details with some loser Abercrombie model so he could get in her lady cave?"

"Well, when you put it like that," Emerald said as she wrinkled her nose, "it does make it sound kind of bad."

"I think you should tell Bridget the truth," Mr. Dunkelman said. "Just explain to her that you're a little prick and you can't help yourself. I'm sure she'll be upset, but not nearly as upset as if she finds out on her own."

"Pete has probably already told her," I said, voicing what I had been thinking since I left the Putt 'n' Play.

"Maybe not," Mr. D said. "At least she can hear your side of it."

"Side? What side?" I asked. "This isn't a misunderstanding. I really did sell her personal information to a douche bag. Jesus, she probably lost her virginity to him because I played her like some fucked-up Cyrano de Bergerac. What else should I tell her? That the reason I decided to suddenly confess was because of some advice I got from a crazy old man who I paid to pretend he was my grandfather?"

"Crazy? Who are you calling crazy?" Mr. Dunkelman asked. "You can't keep telling lies to people, expect them to stay at arm's length. Either you're in the world and you have to learn to get along with the people who care about you, or you get out."

"Yeah?" I asked, my voice raised. "Well, maybe I'll just get out, then."

"Maybe you should," shot back Mr. D as our argument quickly degenerated into a playground squabble between five-year-olds.

"Hey, guys," Emerald said. "What are you getting so upset about?"

"I'm not upset," I said, carefully leveling my voice. "Nobody's upset."

My phone buzzed on the table and we all stopped to look at the lighted display. I could see without picking it up that it was a call from Pete.

It buzzed twice more before Mr. Dunkelman said, "Well, are you going to answer it?"

I picked up the phone and walked into the kitchen, away from their prying eyes and ears.

"Hello," I said into the phone, as if I didn't know who was calling.

"I didn't tell her what happened," Pete said without preamble. "She doesn't know what a dick you are."

"What do you want me to say?" I asked.

"Nothing," he said with a mirthless laugh. "There's nothing you can say to change the fact that you are a complete asshole. But I want to know the whole story. I want to hear it from you."

"There's nothing to tell. Ken wanted to date your sister. I'm in the business of getting people things that they want."

"So, you followed her? Spied on her? Pretended to be my friend so you could find out things about her?"

I thought about arguing with him, telling him that our friendship had nothing to do with it. My friendship with Pete had been completely accidental, an unintended side effect. Not that he would ever believe that.

I knew what I had to do, what was going to be best for everyone.

"That's right," I said. "I got to know you both so I could give Ken the information he needed to get in with your sister."

There was a long pause while he processed that, then said, "I don't believe you. I know you're all fucked up in the head, but there is no way any person could be that fucked up."

"Yeah, well, life is full of surprises," I said.

"So, that's it, then?" he asked.

"Yeah, I guess, unless you want to call me an asshole one more time."

"I trusted you," he said in a raspy whisper. "But however horrible a person you are for treating me like this, it's unforgivable the way you treated Bridget. She loves you."

"I have to go," I said, cutting him off. "I have company. I'll see you around." I cut the connection before he could respond and shut my phone off completely.

Mr. D and Emerald were waiting expectantly when I returned. "I told him we'd talk tomorrow," I said by way of explaining the phone call. Mr. D knew I was lying but didn't call me out.

"Well, it's been real nice hanging with you guys but I've got to get to that bachelor party. You want me to drop you at home on my way, Mr. Dunkelman?" Emerald asked.

"If it's not out of your way," Mr. D said as he shifted forward in his seat. Emerald offered him an arm to help him and he let her. I would have gotten my arm slapped for my trouble.

I slipped Emerald some folded bills and then watched from the door as they walked to the car, Mr. Dunkelman already starting in, complaining about his ungrateful kids. Maybe Emerald would be a more sympathetic listener than I was.

THIRTY-FIVE

I HEARD ABOUT PETE'S SURGERY IN A ROUND-
about way that same week. Bridget had told Mr. D all about
it on her weekly visit to Hell's Waiting Room. He relayed
the message over a game of cards in the rec room. Pete's
surgery was scheduled for Friday and he would be in the
hospital for a few days.

"You going to call him?" Mr. D asked as he picked up a
card from the stack.

I gave a noncommittal grunt in response and didn't
look up from my cards.

"It's been a week. You're not even going to try to talk to him?" Mr. D asked.

"What for?"

"I don't know," he said. "You could try apologizing."

"Apologize for what?" I asked as I looked up at him with a scowl.

"For being an asshole," he said impatiently. "That's not in dispute, is it? The part about you being an asshole?"

"Do you plan to discard sometime in the near future?" I asked with a meaningful glance at my watch. "Because you talk as much as a god-damn girl."

He discarded a ten of hearts as he *harrumphed* and muttered curses at me.

"You could have played that on my hand," I said as I scooped up the ten from the discard pile and lay it on the table in front of me. "You going senile on me?"

"Did you even hear what I said?" Mr. D asked. "He's having surgery."

"I heard you," I said.

"What's wrong with you?" he asked.

"I've got a lot on my mind. That okay with you? Christ," I said as anger bubbled over and I threw my cards down with a satisfying smack on the table. "Like I don't have enough shit going on and I got some old fart and a cripple riding my ass every time I turn around."

"You don't fool me, you little prick," Mr. D said, jabbing his knobby finger at me like a weapon. "However much that boy may hate you right now, he'll never hate you as much as you hate yourself."

I stood so suddenly, my chair tipped over with a crash

and I shoved it away with the underside of my foot instead of righting it. "Mind your own fucking business," I said as I snatched up my keys and phone and walked out.

My phone had been buzzing in my pocket all day long. Skinhead Rob and half a dozen other people were trying to get in touch with me. I ignored all of them.

I knew I would have to face the consequences with Rob but hadn't decided yet how best to handle the situation. Joey was right that I couldn't just put in a letter of resignation. And as long as Rob was pissed off at me, there was the real risk he would take it out on Joey. So far, every way I looked at it, the only way I could see to be rid of Rob completely was for one of us to die or go to prison. Neither was a simple proposition, and I was still working it out in my head.

That Saturday I went by the hospital to see Pete. I don't know why I went. It's not as if I expected him to speak to me, or if he did to say anything other than a string of angry profanities, which, I guess, was not much different from our normal relationship.

I hate the smell of hospitals—antiseptic misery and soiled socks. I made it through the lobby and waiting area okay and thought maybe it wouldn't be so bad, but once I got off the elevator and entered the corridors with patient rooms, I started to feel queasy. Pete's room was in the pediatric ward, where they had made the effort with colorful artwork and walls painted green and purple instead of institutional white, but the smell was the same.

Though it was still early, Pete's room was dark and he

asleep. The television cast blue light across his bed and his legs looked like sticks under the thin blanket. He looked about twelve with his skinny frame and stupid Bieber haircut.

I left the care package on his bedside table where he would see it when he woke—a Japanese porn magazine and some MoonPies. He would know who it was from, so would probably throw them away. As I stood watching him sleep, I wondered what the hell I was doing there and turned to go.

The hospital parking lot was full of cars but devoid of people. I was almost to the T-Bird when I heard a car door open and I spared a glance over my shoulder at the sound. Rob and his henchman, Grim, were just climbing out of Rob's GTO. A gust of air left my lungs in a rush and for a second I thought I might piss myself.

Rob was in a black trench coat and Grim in a camouflage military-issue jacket. I watched them as they approached me, like watching something on film. Maybe I had time to run for my car, could get it started and out of the lot before they were on me, but I didn't try. Just stood where I was and waited for the savagery that was headed my way in slow motion.

Grim looked bored and Rob's smile was genuinely crazy, if not genuinely happy.

"Rob," I said with a curt nod. "What are you doing here?" As if I didn't know.

"Does my presence offend you, Jew-boy?" Rob asked. He pulled a cigarette from his pocket and lit up as he parked one butt cheek on the edge of my car. Grim came to stand just behind me, arms crossed over his chest, while he waited for Rob to give him orders. This could end only one way and my gut felt hollow and light with air as I thought about the prospect of Grim pounding my face. I found myself wondering if he would kill me or just permanently disfigure me.

My life didn't flash before my eyes, but I imagined my broken, lifeless body being found by the security guard on the pavement later that evening. A sorry end.

"What do you want?" I asked.

"I haven't seen you around in a few weeks," Skinhead Rob said around his cigarette. "I was worried about you."

"Yeah?" I asked. "Well, don't be. I'm fine."

He laughed at that and gave Grim a chin thrust, a signal that Grim interpreted as instructions to laugh along with him. Rob pursed his rat face into a frown and gave a quick head shake.

Grim's laugh halted abruptly. "What?" he asked.

"Grab him," Rob said, exasperated.

Grim grabbed the back of my jacket collar and twisted his grip until the collar was tight against my throat. It was work to move air through my windpipe, but I tried to keep my breath steady and slow, not panic. It would all be over before too long. They would lose interest once I was unconscious. Or dead. There are worse things than being dead.

"So," Rob said as he studied the lit end of his cigarette, then blew on it to spark the ember, "you just decided you didn't want to work with me anymore? You hurt my feelings, Sway."

"I didn't know you had feelings, Rob," I gurgled through my constricted windpipe.

"I don't," Rob said as he narrowed one eye at me. "What I do have is a problem. I placed orders with some people for a whole lot of party favors, counting on you to move them for me. I've got thousands of dollars tied up in your abilities, Sway. Now, I don't know what is going on with you. I know you've been a little weird ever since your mom chased a bottle of Xanax with a liter of booze. At least that was what they reported in the paper. That true?"

"Close enough," I said as my head started to pound from lack of oxygen.

"Did she do it on purpose?" he asked. "Did she really hate you that much?"

He paused, as if he expected me to answer. The silence stretched on for a long minute while Rob smoked and Grim studied the fingernails on his hand that wasn't holding me by the neck.

"Like I said," Rob continued when it became obvious I wasn't going to say anything, "I don't know what's going on with you, but I'll tell you what I do know—today Grim is just going to mess you up a little. Next time we have this conversation, your dad's going to be planning another funeral. We clear?"

"Crystal," I wheezed, and Grim dropped his hold on my jacket. As I rubbed my throat, Rob flicked his cigarette in my direction, then stood and leaned casually against the grille of the T-Bird. His face was impassive while he watched Grim work me over. Grim mostly took body shots, punching me in the gut and kidney. Body shots hurt less than a blow to the face at the time of impact but hurt more later. I guess at least if you get punched in the face enough times, you get knocked unconscious. With body shots, there's no real hope of passing out.

Finally Grim did land a couple of punches on my cheekbone and mouth and then a nice coup de grâce right on my nose. He didn't break anything, but when I felt the pressure behind my eyelids I knew immediately I would end up with two black eyes. I windmilled my arms as I tried to keep my feet, my legs jelly and useless beneath me, and sank to the ground, hard on my ass, but I didn't feel it.

Grim grabbed me by the front of my shirt and pounded a few quick jabs to my face. I saw an explosion of stars and then, mercifully, nothing.

I don't know how long I was unconscious. Long enough that by the time I woke, Grim and Rob were long gone. I fought with my jacket to remove my phone from my pocket. Once the phone was in my hand, I was so exhausted that I rested for another eternity before holding up the lighted display so I could see it. My arm swayed as the muscles couldn't respond to my brain's directions and my vision doubled as I searched my contacts for Carter's number. I struggled to remain conscious while I waited for him to answer.

"Hey, Sway," he said into the phone, sounding glad to hear from me.

"Carter," I said, my voice hoarse and strained, like the sound of a creaky screen door.

"Sway? That you?"

"I need your help."

"Tell me where you are," he said, "and I'm already there."

———

Somehow I made it into the T-Bird and slumped across the front seat before passing out again. My world went to black and the next thing I knew Carter Goldsmith was standing over me.

"Sway? You in there, bro?" he asked.

"Yeah, I'm here, Carter," I croaked. My busted lip split again when I opened my mouth to speak, and hot blood poured into my mouth. I started to gag on it and Carter helped me to sit so I could spit the saliva and blood onto the pavement.

"Who did this to you?" he asked.

"I had it coming," I said, avoiding the question. "I can't drive. But I need to get out of here."

"Sway, I hate to be the one to point out the obvious," Carter said, "but you're in a hospital parking lot. Seems to me the thing to do is go inside, ask for some help."

"No," I said, but it came out as a groan. "They see me like this, they'll call the cops. No cops."

"You want me to take you home?"

I shook my head and immediately regretted it. "No. Not home. Joey's, if you'll take me. Her mom will be at work."

"Of course, I'll take you, baby. Scooch over."

Carter commandeered the T-Bird and my phone while I slumped against the inside of the passenger door. Street-lights burned into the car window, a continuous streak of painful light as we passed beneath them on the drive to Joey's house.

"I told him," Carter was saying into my phone, "but he wouldn't let me take him into the hospital."

Pause.

"I'm bringing him to you," Carter said, the direction of his voice telling me that he had turned his head to look at me. "Best you be prepared. It's bad."

At Joey's house she was waiting for us on the front stoop and came out to the car to support one side of me while Carter managed the other. A light rain had started to fall and the coolness of it felt good on my beaten face. They put me on Joey's bed as she ran to get some ice and a washcloth. I curled into the fetal position on my side as Joey placed a bag of frozen peas wrapped in a dish towel across my eyes and wiped the blood and gore from my face.

I was dimly aware as Carter removed my shoes and jacket and placed his enormous hand over the back of my head as a comfort. "I'll fuck the dude up if you tell me who it was," Carter said, and Joey shushed him.

"He doesn't want that," she said as she wiped gently at the split skin on my cheekbone.

In the haze between consciousness and oblivion I mumbled crazy shit and started to shake with cold. Joey covered me with a blanket, then curled up on her narrow bed beside me and held me close as she stroked my hair. Carter sat behind the bend in my legs and they warmed me with the heat from their bodies.

"I wanted to die," I said into my chest, my voice a grunt as I jerked with another shudder of cold. "I want to die."

"I know," Joey said, and shushed me and kissed me on the forehead. "I know. But you can't die. If you die, I'll be all alone."

"Shit," Carter said, and I felt him start to shake with quiet sobs as I drifted into the black.

Neutral Milk Hotel's "In the Aeroplane Over the Sea" drifted through the air from Joey's iPod, and I remember thinking how appropriate it would be to die listening to that song.

THIRTY-SIX

I PUT THE CAR INTO PARK AND TURNED OFF the windshield wipers. The rain was coming down in sheets and I didn't move to get out of the car, just sat back in my seat and idly rubbed my lower lip as I played possible scenarios over in my mind.

"When we get inside, you let me do the talking," I said. "You don't say a word. Just be cool and play it the way I told you. With a little luck he'll be in a good mood."

Andrew's eyes were wide. He was scared, which showed he at least had some sense.

"Are you sure this is a good idea?" he asked as he squinted through the rain at the forlorn trailer, the torn and grimy screens on the windows.

"You said you wanted to be popular, right?" I asked dully.

Andrew swallowed audibly. "Yeah. Yeah, that's what I want."

"Well, then, let's go."

The rain drummed on the siding of Digger's trailer, a hollow sound magnified by my uneasiness. I rapped hard on the aluminum screen door before I had time to convince myself this was a bad idea.

Digger's smile was forced and fake, but he beckoned for me to come inside. "Who's this?" he asked as he shut and locked the door behind us. "Your other retarded kid brother?"

"This is Andrew," I said. "Just a friend of mine. Not retarded," I added for clarification.

"Randy's here," Digger said with a gesture to the living room suite, as if I hadn't noticed the hulking giant lounging on the velour love seat a mere five paces away.

Randy was Digger's very large, very inbred cousin who also happened to be very dumb and very mean. My scrotum shriveled. If Digger had invited Randy to our meeting, I didn't expect things to go down well for me, but I played dumb, feigned indifference to Randy's presence.

"Hey, Randy," I said with a nod.

The ape only grunted as he shoveled a handful of Cheetos into his mouth and wiped the cheese dust from his hands onto his jeans. *Hoo boy.*

"What happened to your face?" Digger asked me,

studying the purple bruises that had started to green around the edges and the split skin on my cheekbone.

"I walked into a door," I said, and Digger hooted with laughter.

"Man," Digger said with a shake of his head as he moved to sit in his throne, leaving Andrew and me the only ones standing, "when you said you weren't going to be coming around anymore, I thought it was some kind of joke."

I nodded my head at Andrew, gesturing for him to sit on the unoccupied love seat while Randy kept a glare fixed on us.

Digger didn't move to fill a bong hit. Not a good sign. He just twisted his chair from side to side with his feet while he sat back looking at me.

I fought the urge to clear my throat before saying, "It had to happen sooner or later. I'm not going to stick around here forever. As soon as they give me that piece of paper in June, I'll be gone."

"Gone where?" Digger asked with an inquisitive frown.

I shrugged. "Anywhere. Not here."

"So, who's this kid?" Digger asked.

Randy shifted in his seat as the tension in the room became palpable.

"Andrew is my replacement," I said slowly. "I brought him here for a job interview."

The corner of Digger's mouth lifted in a half smile as he stole a glance at Randy.

"Job interview? You got any references, kid?" Digger asked.

Andrew just looked to me and didn't speak.

"He's a good kid," I said. "Knows how to keep his mouth shut. And he doesn't use, so he won't smoke his profits."

"And so? What? I'm just supposed to trust you on this?" Digger asked.

I shrugged. "I guess you've trusted me for this long and you aren't badly off for it."

Digger was nodding now in silent agreement but he still didn't look convinced.

"I'll train him, show him the ropes," I continued, speaking slowly so I didn't sound nervous. "He gets good grades, stays out of trouble. He's the last person anyone would suspect."

"And then what?" Digger asked. "I suppose you don't want to be my friend anymore either. You're going to stop hanging out?" As he said this, he cut his eyes away. I noticed his cheeks go a little red and I realized suddenly that Digger wasn't mad because I'd left him holding the bag; he was angry because I had hurt his feelings.

For once, I found myself speechless. There was an awkward silence while Digger tried to keep his face expressionless and I thought about how to handle this new development.

"Man, are you joking?" I asked. "I'm totally into that *Sons of Anarchy* show. I thought we were going to watch the rest of season one together. What did you think I meant—that I was never going to see you again?"

Digger's eyes brightened, and I swear he almost grinned. "Yeah . . . sure, yeah, of course I knew you didn't mean . . . well . . . you know," Digger said, playing it cool, but his obvious emotion was as awkward as a junior high school dance.

To cover his embarrassment, Digger reached for the tray of pot and started to load a bong hit. He offered the first hit to Andrew. Initiation. Andrew took it well. He was obviously clueless and had never smoked pot before, but he didn't show any hesitation or act too nervous about it. I started to relax by degrees and my heart slowed to a resting pace.

We ended up staying long enough to order a pizza and watch an episode of *Sons of Anarchy*. As it turned out, Andrew and Digger were into some of the same video games so they talked about Minecraft and other douchey things that were foreign to me. It made me think of Pete and his ridiculous sci-fi books.

When we finally left, Digger stood in the doorway, one hip leaned against the doorjamb as he watched us go. "So, I'll see you soon, right?" Digger called after me.

"Yeah, I'll see you, man," I called over my shoulder with a wave.

"He seems like an okay guy. Maybe a little nuts," Andrew said as he settled back into the passenger seat. "Do you trust him?"

"Wolves and lambs can never be of one mind," I said absently as I put the key in the ignition but didn't turn on the car.

"What does that mean?" Andrew asked, and as he did I was reminded that I missed Pete as my sidekick.

"You talk too much," I said as my phone started to play Joey's ringtone, Gnarls Barkley's "Crazy."

"How'd it go?" I asked by way of answering.

"It went okay," Joey said. "She's straight cray, but I think I can get through to her."

"You didn't go anywhere near her at her school, did you?" I asked. "If anyone saw you together, this isn't going to work."

"No one saw me," Joey said impatiently. "I was careful."

"How smart is she?" I asked. "Do you think she would understand the risk?"

"Maybe not," Joey admitted. "But I'm not sure she would care even if she did. She hates him."

There was a long silence while Joey waited and I made up my mind. "Okay. Do it. Call me and let me know how it goes as soon as you talk to her again."

A weary sigh. "Okay, fine. You realize you're putting yourself at risk with this idea. I'm not sure I understand why you're doing this—"

"You don't need to understand," I said as I started the car.

THIRTY-SEVEN

THAT SATURDAY WAS HOMECOMING. I MISSED
the parade around the outdoor track. I missed the game at
which Buford High delivered a crushing defeat of 35–7. As
I walked into the cafeteria, now transformed by Gray Dabson's homecoming committee into a theatrically lighted
landscape of papier-mâché and balloons and glitter, I saw
David and Heather having their homecoming portrait taken.
They both waved to me and I gave them a salute but didn't
stop to talk. I was only there for specific business.

I was hanging back in the shadows at the dance when

Bridget arrived on Ken's arm, looking like an angel in a simple, pale pink dress, her hair knotted in a French braid laced with a spray of tiny pink flowers. Soon after they arrived, Ken abandoned her to take up his royal duties for the opening dance. He left Bridget standing alone near the window where students dropped their dirty lunch trays on a conveyor. The window was discreetly covered by a cluster of balloons but still reeked of stale cooking grease and sour milk.

Bridget stood alone, her girlfriends all busy with their dates, and all other guys afraid to approach her and risk Ken's wrath. It had been a few days since she and I last spoke and I wondered if Pete had finally told her. He never could keep his mouth shut.

As I drew close, her smile told me that Pete had said nothing about the reason for our fight, which surprised me. Or maybe he told her and she had already forgiven me, which would not surprise me at all.

"You look beautiful," I said to her by way of greeting.

"Thanks," she said as her hand strayed nervously up to stroke a wayward strand of hair at the nape of her neck. "Who did you come with?"

"I came alone. I'm not staying. Just stopping by for a dance with you," I said honestly.

She laughed but sobered quickly as she watched my expression. "You're serious?" she asked.

"As serious as cancer. But we don't have much time," I said with a gesture to the dance floor. "Once Ken and Theresa are finished with their homecoming court activities, he's going to want you back."

I took her hand and she followed me onto the dance floor, where she put one hand on my shoulder; the other rested lightly in mine. Ken and Theresa were in the center of the dance floor in their plastic crowns, Theresa radiant, Ken as stiff as a virgin in a strip club.

"What happened to your face?" Bridget asked.

"Nothing, I was born this way," I said innocently.

"Very funny," she said in a tone that didn't sound as if she thought I was funny *at all*. "Were you in a fight?"

"Yes, with a flight of stairs. I lost."

Her expression was cool, her lips slightly pursed, as we started the silent game again. I was holding out, I was almost winning, when she took a deep breath and let out a quiet sigh, as if to convey her disappointment in me. And . . . fuck! I was going to lose. Again. She was like an Olympic-qualified silent game player.

"I got jumped by a couple of guys," I said. "It was no big deal."

"It looks like a big deal," she said, but let me off the hook by turning to look at Ken and Theresa in the spotlight. "She looks beautiful, doesn't she?" Bridget asked wistfully, her expression soft and difficult to read. Theresa was wearing a full-length black gown, the dress cut to accentuate her best features, a full bust and an hourglass waist. Her long, wavy brown hair hung loose around her shoulders. Theresa held herself with the kind of confidence that makes people beautiful.

"Are you disappointed?" I asked. "That you didn't win homecoming queen?"

She turned her attention back to me as she shook her

head. "Oh, no, not at all. I'm glad Theresa won. I mean, look at her. She's so happy. I was really excited when they announced that she was elected queen. People can be so superficial, especially in high school, but Theresa is awesome and I'm glad people can see that about her."

"I figured it would make you happy that she won," I said.

"Ken was disappointed, of course," she said dryly. "He wanted us to be king and queen together."

"Does he treat you right?" I asked.

She shrugged. "Sure. Yeah, I guess. He doesn't point out all of my faults the way you do. We don't have anything to argue about. And he never punches my kid brother in the nose. But other than that, he's a pretty good guy."

"Yeah, sounds like he's perfect for you," I said.

"Mm," she only murmured as she shifted closer to me and rested her cheek against my shoulder.

I rubbed my hand lightly up her back, then pressed the flat of my hand between her shoulder blades, consciously avoiding the small of her back or the rise of her hip. I didn't say anything, just took a moment to savor her smell, the warmth of her hand on my shoulder.

"I'm glad you're here," she said as she lifted her head. "I've missed you. We're okay, right? It's not weird between us?"

"No, not weird," I said quietly.

The song ended then but I held her for another minute and she didn't move away. "I'd better go," I said finally. "Ken will be looking for you."

"Thanks for keeping me company," she said, and gave

me a quick kiss on the cheek. I put my hand under her chin and kissed her softly on the lips—just once, to see what it felt like.

The apples of her cheeks flushed prettily as she stepped out of my arms and I turned to leave without a glance back.

I was almost to the parking lot when I ran into Pete, on his way into the dance with a group of people who before six weeks ago would never have noticed that he was alive. He was walking on crutches, still recovering from his surgery, but all things considered, he looked pretty good.

"Well, look who it is," Pete said, putting on a show for his audience. "I didn't think I'd see you here tonight, Jesse."

"I'm not staying," I said.

"I'll catch up with you guys," Pete said to his entourage, and they moved on and left us alone. "Man, you look like hell," he said once the others were out of earshot. "Who did that to you?"

"Skinhead Rob and his buddy," I said. "It was just a matter of time before I got on Rob's bad side."

"Yeah, I guess that's kind of your thing," he said with a smile playing at the corners of his mouth. "Eventually you end up on everyone's bad side."

"Yeah, well, enjoy yourself tonight," I said, and started to walk away.

"Alderman!" I glanced over my shoulder to see Ken moving toward me like a freight train, his plastic crown still in place on his perfectly coiffed hair.

"Uh-oh," Pete said gleefully. "He sounds pissed."

"I saw you," Ken said. "I saw you with Bridget. Man, I'm going to make you sorry you were ever born."

"I'm not looking for a fight, Ken," I said. "I was just say-ing good-bye. I'm not going to bother you or Bridget again."

"You're god-damn right you won't." Ken grabbed me by the front of my jacket and lifted me off my feet to give me a good shake, then threw me to the ground. I stood as he swung a fist but he timed it wrong and I felt only a puff of air across my face. He swung with his left and connected with my cheek. It wasn't his power arm, so I just staggered back a couple of steps but kept my feet.

"Ken?" Bridget called from behind him, and we all turned at the sound of her voice. She sounded confused, uncertain, but her voice hardened as she said, "Ken, what are you doing?"

"Nothing," Ken said quickly as he took a step away from me.

"Nothing?" she asked, her tone conveying a warning. "Did you just hit Jesse?"

"Don't worry about it," I told her. "We're just having a conversation."

"Pete, what's going on?" Bridget asked.

Pete eyed me carefully, watching for my reaction. From the gleam in his eye, I knew he wanted to punish me and this was the best opportunity he would ever get. I kept my face even, without expression.

"Ken's afraid Jesse will tell you the truth," Pete said.

"The truth about what?" Bridget asked.

"Do you want to tell her?" Pete asked as he turned back and forth between Ken and me, waiting for one of us to say something. "No?" he asked as we both stayed silent.

"Ken, what is he talking about?" Bridget asked.

"Baby, it's really nothing," Ken said. "You shouldn't worry about it. Pete just overheard a conversation, but he misunderstood and got the wrong idea."

"Ken paid Jesse to learn all about you so he could trick you into dating him," Pete blurted.

"What?" Bridget asked, looking more confused than ever. And really, when Pete said it out loud, it did sound ridiculous.

"Ken paid Jesse, for Jesse to fix it, so that you would go out with Ken," Pete said slowly.

"That doesn't even make sense," Bridget said. "Jesse had nothing to do with it. Ken and I ran into each other at the impressionist exhibit at the campus gallery. . . ." Her voice trailed off as she studied Ken's face closely. "He just happened to be there at the same time," she said, and as she said it she seemed to suddenly realize how unlikely it was that Ken had actually given up a Wednesday afternoon to tour the gallery on his own.

She turned to look at me, her expression still just confused, not angry yet. "Did you—?" She started to ask a question, then changed it to a statement. "You told him he could run into me there. Is that it?"

I just nodded but said nothing.

"What else did you tell him?" she asked, her eyes wide with shock, cheeks flushed red with anger.

"It's not important," Ken said. "What matters is how I feel about you, Bridge. I love you."

"Please," Bridget said as she closed her eyes and held up her hand to silence Ken. "What else did you tell him?" she asked me.

"I told him the things you like, your interests," I said, my voice trailing off as I stalled for time. Then I figured, what the hell, the jig was up. If she was going to hate me anyway, I might as well tell her everything. Be completely honest and bare my soul. "I told him he should tell you that if he could have one superpower for a day, he would want to heal people with a touch."

Bridget lifted a hand to cover her mouth as she realized the depth of our deception.

"That's what he does," Pete said with a nod at me. "He lies, manipulates people, for money. Jesse doesn't care about anybody but himself."

"Is it true?" Bridget asked me, a tremor in her voice.

"Which part?" I asked.

"Is it true that Ken paid you?"

"Two hundred bucks," I said with a nod.

Bridget took a step toward me and slapped me, hard, across the face. She was the third person in as many days to hit me in the face, but this blow hurt more than any of the others.

She turned to Ken and said, "Tell me you really have a cousin named Jamie with Down syndrome."

Silence. Ken hesitated just long enough that you knew the next words coming out of his mouth would all be bullshit.

"Tell me!" Bridget shouted while Ken stared mutely at his feet. "You *made up* a cousin with Down syndrome? Jesus, what is wrong with you? Both of you? You're . . . you're . . . ," she sputtered, gasping for breath as she started to lose it for real.

"Assholes," Pete finished for her.

With that, Bridget burst into tears and ran from all of us, back toward school. Ken hurried after her, calling her name. I wanted to go after her, but didn't. There was no way to recover from this. She would hate both of us forever.

"Feel better?" I asked Pete when they were gone.

"Much."

"You hurt your sister's feelings."

"I didn't do anything," he said emphatically. "You and Ken hurt her feelings. Don't try to make this my fault."

"I mean you didn't have to break it to her like that, the night of homecoming and all. You could have told her in private, spared her the embarrassment," I said.

"Spared her? Or spared you?" he asked in that tone he got when he was playing the betrayed-by-life role. "You really think you should be lecturing me about how to treat other people? She'll get over it. Better for her to know that you're both a couple of douches so she can move on."

"You're probably right," I said, and turned to go.

"Hey," Pete called after me. "That's it? You're just going to walk away?"

"That's it, Pete." I spoke without turning back to look at him, though I saw from the corner of my eye he was still standing in the middle of the parking lot as I pulled the car into traffic.

THIRTY-EIGHT

THE SIEGEL CENTER'S VERY OWN SPECIAL OLYM-
pics was held on a crisp Saturday afternoon in mid-
November on the campus at Wakefield High School. Half
the town turned out to watch the event. Though there were
plenty of people who just wanted to watch the spectacle of
the community's less coordinated throwing a Frisbee or
runing around the track, there were even more who wanted
to support the kids and make them feel loved.

As I walked along the sidelines to find a seat in the bleachers, a few of the kids from the Siegel Center recognized me

and attacked with their slobbery hugs and goofy smiles. An anonymous donor had provided the funds to buy all the kids uniforms and a medal on a ribbon for each participant, plus the money needed to install a new therapy garden in the courtyard at the Siegel Center.

The generous cash donation was made with the restrictions that the funds could only be used to help Bridget's kids and not to support the work of anti-Semitic terrorist cells, or programs endorsed by Oprah Winfrey. Clearly the Siegel Center had been baffled by the letter that came with the check, but had, at the very least, honored the donor's request that the kids get the money for their programs. Though still not on speaking terms with Pete or Bridget, I attended the event so I could give a full and detailed report to the donor that evening. Naïvely optimistic people irritated Mr. D, so he opted to stay home and watch old *Cagney & Lacey* episodes now that he owned the complete series on DVD. His attraction to Tyne Daly is one of the great mysteries of the universe.

Principal Burke was there, taking credit for Wakefield High School's support of the Special Olympics, even gave the opening address to kick off the games. To hear him talk, you'd think he was a regular Nelson Mandela.

Coverage of the Special Olympics event had even made the front page of the local newspaper with a quote from Burke in the article about how thrilled he was to support the work of the Siegel Center. Buried on page eighteen of the same edition of the paper was a story about the bust of local drug dealer Robert Elliott. Before reading it in the paper, I had never known Skinhead Rob's last name. In addition to possession of several hundred hits of Ecstasy, he had been brought up on federal charges for trafficking in forged identification.

The police had secured a warrant for Rob's basement lair with information from a reliable source. For his sister's sake, it was probably a good thing that he was being held in a federal prison without bail to await trial.

The Booster Club was selling drinks and snacks for the Siegel Center's event, the money they raised designated to support the second annual Special Olympics event the following year. I went for a hot dog and a Coke in the break between track-and-field events and came face-to-face with Pete, who was taking orders at the Booster Club booth.

Pete's eyes narrowed and the half of his face that worked correctly twisted into a scowl. "What do you want?" he asked.

"Just a dog and a Coke," I said. "That is, assuming the dogs are kosher."

"Why are you even here?" he asked.

"For someone who's not talking to me, you sure have a lot to say," I observed. "I just want something to eat and I'll be on my way."

"You hurt Bridget. A lot. But she's such a saint, she doesn't even hate you," Pete said with disgust. "So you know what? I hate you enough for both of us."

"Look," I said, "there's nothing I can do to make it right. If there was, I'd do it, but there's not."

"You're a liar," he said quickly. "You don't care about anyone's feelings but your own."

I wasn't going to argue. "Are you going to give me a hot dog or what?" I asked.

"I want you to say you miss having me around and you want us to be friends again."

"Oh, yeah," I said with an ironic frown of agreement, "because I miss having someone around who pukes in my car and constantly talks about stupid sci-fi books."

"I knew it," he said with a snap of his fingers. "If it was a lie, you'd be willing to say it but since it's the truth, you can't. You do miss having me around."

"*Pffft*."

"Admit it. I'm your best friend," he said smugly. "If you admit it, just once, I'll forgive you for being a heartless, amoral asswipe and be your friend again."

I took a minute to mull it over, then asked, "And if I admit it, will you also give me a hot dog?"

"Maybe," he said as he crossed his arms over his chest.

I glanced back over my shoulder at the line of people watching our exchange, with interest or impatience depending on their worldview.

"Fine," I said. "I'll admit it, but only because I'm starving."

"No," he said with a shake of his head. "I want you to say it. Say I'm your best friend."

We eyed each other coldly for a long minute before I relented. I really was hungry. "Okay. You're my best friend."

"And you miss having me around."

"And I miss having you around," I mimicked.

His face spread into his signature lopsided smile and he triumphantly handed me a soggy hot dog wrapped in tinfoil. "That'll be three dollars," he said, then barked to the next person in line to give him their order, dismissing me without another glance.

During the second half of the games Cynthia, aka Flipper Girl, sat beside me in the bleachers. She wasn't allowed to do most of the events, because her heart condition prevented her from participating in the more strenuous activities. She held my hand with her non-flipper arm and sometimes rested her head against my shoulder as we watched the spectacle together. I sang her James Taylor's "Something in the Way She Moves" because it made us both feel better, and I wished I had my guitar with me to do it justice.

At the end of the day there was an awards ceremony, during which everyone was given a medal for being awesomely unique. Bridget was there, hugging each of the kids as they walked off the stage, a big smile on her face, her eyes shimmering with tears. Watching her brought a smile to my face too, even if I had to experience her joy from a distance. I left before I had the chance to talk to her. Ken was out of the picture now, but it didn't matter anymore. Bridget was out of my reach.

THIRTY-NINE

IT WAS GOOD TO HOLD HER IN MY ARMS AGAIN.

B.B. King had named his guitar Lucille, after a woman he saw two men fighting over in a bar once. I had never named my guitar. There was no woman who was her equal. At least, there never had been before. Maybe a lifetime from now, I would start calling my guitar Bridget, but I doubted it.

My right arm rested comfortably on the curve of the guitar's body, like resting your arm on the curve of a girl's waist while you lie in bed. Natural.

The inmates at Sunrise Assisted Living liked it when I played the older music, like the gypsy tunes of Django Reinhardt or the ballads of Jim Croce. It was the point at which I connected with them. Good music never stops being good, no matter how old it is.

"It's so nice that your grandson comes to play," one of the old ladies was saying to Mr. Dunkelman, loud enough that I could hear. They said everything loud enough that everyone in the room could hear, had forgotten that when you're young you can hear everything and read small print.

"Yeah, he's a dumb-ass, but he's an okay kid," Mr. Dunkelman said, his arms crossed over his belly as he sat back in his wheelchair, waiting for me to play. "Jesus, hurry up, would you?" he said to me. "*Dancing with the Stars* is on in forty-five minutes."

"If you keep talking, I'm not sure how I'm supposed to start playing, *Gramps*," I said to him as he rolled his eyes heavenward.

I gave one last tug on the tuning pegs and caressed the strings to test their responsiveness. The calluses on my left hand were still fresh, the skin around them red and raw. I had let the nails on my right hand grow a little long, like the bluegrass players who used their nails to pick out a tune instead of relying on a piece of plastic.

I spoke to the cluster of old people who sat around in straight-backed chairs waiting for me to play. "Ladies, I'll play a love song if you promise to control yourselves. This is a, uh—" I stopped to clear my throat, stalling. "—this is a song my dad used to play for my mom. It's by Herb Alpert, who was slicker than snot when it came to making the ladies swoon. I can't sing like he did, but at the very least it will be in tune. So, it's called 'This Guy's in Love with You.' It's one of my favorites."

As I was playing I caught movement out of the corner of my eye. Normally once the guitar and I were otherwise engaged I didn't notice much of anything around me, but when I was at Sunrise Assisted Living my senses were always heightened for the possibility of running into her.

Bridget.

She sat toward the back of the crowd, Dorothy beside her, lost in her own fabricated world. Dorothy and I had that in common.

I played a few of the old hippie tunes that were my dad's favorites. Played a few for the sake of beauty, Bob Dylan and James Taylor, including Cynthia's favorite, "Something in the Way She Moves." I wrapped up with a John Denver, "Rocky Mountain High," to a round of everyone clapping and singing along. It was the first time I had hit the high note on "fly" without my voice breaking since before puberty.

A few of them stopped to congratulate me on my playing, but soon they had all moved on to their eight o'clock TV commitment, *Dancing with the Stars.*

Bridget hung back, still in her seat at the back of the cluster of chairs once everyone else was gone.

"Hello, Jesse," she said, on her guard but polite as always.

"Hey," I said as I carefully set my guitar in its case and latched it. "It's good to see you," I said honestly.

"I didn't know you played guitar," she said. "You're really good. Amazing, actually."

"I haven't played much since my mom died."

"Was she a musician too?"

"No," I said with a shake of my head. "She was a muse."

"Right. Your dad. Pete told me he plays in a band."

"I'm sure my mom had plenty of better offers than the one she got from my dad. But he used to play for her. That's how he got her to fall in love with him."

"Better offers, how?" Bridget asked.

"Maybe from guys who could hold down a steady job instead of being a flaky musician. Maybe someone who could afford to take care of her."

"Oh, I don't know," Bridget said thoughtfully, her chin in her hand, elbow on her knee. "She probably enjoyed having someone to play for her more than she would have enjoyed having a lot of money. Money can't make you happy."

"I suppose," I said noncommittally as I slung my guitar case over my shoulder and turned to wave to Mr. Dunkelman before I left, but he was completely engrossed in his show and didn't notice me.

"I saw that you were at the Siegel Center event at school," she said as we started walking toward the exit together.

"Seemed like the kids had a good time," I said.

"They did," she agreed with a nod. "They had a great time. I'm glad you came to watch."

"I talked to Pete when I was there," I said.

"Oh?" she asked in a way that told me he had already repeated our conversation to her verbatim. "How did that go?"

I shrugged. "He gave me a hot dog and it wasn't laced with poison, so I guess that's progress."

"Yes. It's nice when your friends don't want to kill you,"

she said without any apparent irony. She thanked me as I held the door for her.

"So, I uh . . . I guess you're not seeing Ken anymore," I said, broaching the subject in a roundabout way.

"You guessed right," she said flatly. Bridget pulled up the collar of her coat and reached into her pocket for a pair of gloves.

There was a light snow falling. Christmastime was late for a first snow in Massachusetts. The tiny snowflakes would not survive their fall to earth, but they drifted onto Bridget's eyelids and turned her hair into a shimmering halo under the streetlamp.

"I never should have tricked you into going out with Ken," I said, wanting it off my chest. "You have every right to hate me, but I wanted to tell you—"

"Was that your idea?" she asked, cutting me off. "The fake cousin with Down syndrome?"

"Two months ago I probably would have used that line myself to get you to sleep with me," I said.

"But you've changed?" she asked skeptically.

"No," I answered quickly with an earnest shake of my head.

She paused, seeming to debate with herself what she should say next. I waited patiently until she said, "Look, I know you were the one who arranged for Theresa to win homecoming queen. I know you were the one who got it so Burke would let us use the school for the kids' Special Olympics event. Your friend, Joey, she told me everything. I even know that you got your grandfather to donate the money that paid for the whole event."

My grandfather. Maybe that was a confession to save for another time. I was already mentally composing the angry text I was going to send to Joey for meddling. What I said was, "Whatever. I don't want to talk about any of that. I just wanted to tell you . . ."

She raised her eyebrows expectantly but said nothing.

"Well . . . shit, I'm not good at this," I said, my eyes on the sky.

"Did you want to tell me you're sorry?" she asked helpfully after a long silence.

"Yeah," I said with a sigh. "Yeah, I guess that's it. I am . . . sorry."

"Is that it? Is that all you wanted to tell me?" Badgering the witness.

"Maybe not," I said. "But it's all I'm going to tell you right now."

"Okay," she said, and turned as if to move away.

"You want to go get a coffee or something?" I called after her. "If you don't want to, I would understand—"

"That would be nice," she said.

She stepped in closer to me, and there was a look in her eyes that I hadn't seen before. A look that was kind of nervous, but like she might just kiss me if I didn't say anything to ruin the moment. I picked up a lock of her hair and rubbed it between my fingers. "If you don't ask me for much, I could spend the rest of my life trying to deserve you," I said in almost a whisper.

We played the silent game again, my eyes locked on hers as her lips started to melt into a pucker.

This time I won. A first.

"I thought I told you," she said, and there was a smile in her voice, "I'm determined to like you even though you don't want me to."

"Like me enough for me to kiss you?" I asked. "That kind of like? Or like me the same way you like the kids at the Siegel Center? You know, want to volunteer your time to try and rehabilitate me?"

She laughed and shook her head but stopped abruptly when I lifted a hand to trace my finger down the line of her jaw, my eyes on her lips instead of meeting her gaze. Her lips were right there—full and soft and warm—and her breath was tickling my chin. She was just opening her mouth to say something when I put my lips on hers and kissed her the way I had wanted to kiss her since the first time I saw her playing kickball with those dopey kids. As I put my arms around her and pulled her close, Paul Mc-Cartney started crooning "Maybe I'm Amazed" in my head and somehow I knew that meant this was it. This is what love felt like.

I'd have to tell Carter the next time I saw him.

ACKNOWLEDGMENTS

I feel almost guilty having just my own name on the cover of this book. It actually wasn't even a very good manuscript until my editor, Sara Goodman, got her hands on it. Mad props for her incredible sense of good storytelling. And Eliani Torres did an amazing job of copyediting what I mistakenly thought was a pretty clean draft.

Many thanks to my wonderful agent, Barbara Poelle, who took exactly nine days to find a publishing house for this book. Over a holiday weekend, no less. Talk about your unbridled enthusiasm. I will forever have a mental image of you doing cartwheels in your office, Barbara.

There are a lot of people who deserve more thanks than I can express in a limited word count: my husband, Kevin, for giving me the gift of time to write and encouraging me to put my stories out into the world; my freeloading kids, for being amazing and funny and kind; my mom, Ba, for teaching me to love the written word and helping to raise my children so they don't turn out to be wild animals; my dad, David, and his brothers, for gifting me a highly developed sense of humor; my aunt, Elizabeth, for believing this was a publishable work even after reading just a crappy draft; Laura Curzi, for keeping me sane, or at least maintaining the public appearance of sanity, while also reading and commenting on hundreds of drafts of my manuscripts; Chris(tina) Sobran and Kimberly Teboho Bertocci Riley, for knowing all of my faults and loving me and my family unconditionally anyway; Paul Lusty, for being a mentor, friend, and poop confidant; my Lucky Bar peeps, for providing me with endless clever dialogue (Jonny Newkirk) and wacky character inspiration (Chris Chernes); my beautiful cousin, Denise, just because it will make her cry to see her name in print; our Boston family, the Curzi-McCabes, for taking us in and treating us like blood; the incredibly selfless and loving friends and family who have shown so much support and enthusiasm for my writing and this first published novel; Michelle Wolfson, for her encouragement and advice during the early stages of my publishing quest; Dana, for being the perfectly attentive bartender and giving me a comfortable place to write; and, last but not least, Greta, Shonda, and Toni, for keeping my head on straight and my butt in shape.